THE VERY Merry MURDER CLUB

I have always loved mysteries. Curious crimes, quirky suspicious characters, pieces of a puzzle. I love the twists and turns, red herrings and misdirection, the eventual reveal of who did it and why. Mysteries can be creepy, chilling, funny. The possibilities are endless.

What I love most about this collection of mysteries and why I'm so proud to be part of it is how fresh it feels. These thirteen voices have all brought something new in to the mix. The stories are unique, unexpected, slick, fast paced and fun. They will surprise and confound you, make you gasp and even laugh.

When I was a young reader, I realise now that couldn't see myself as the hero of a story because of a lack of diverse voices in the books I read. We all deserve stories that we can see ourselves in and it's so important to be able to see someone different to ourselves as the hero too. The power of that is something I believe in so much. I am delighted to present this anthology alongside Robin and Farshore and I hope it will inspire a new generation of mystery fans. You can be the hero of a story! We all can!

Serena Patel

You might think you know what's going to happen in a mystery story. There's a crime, there are suspects and clues, and then there's a detective who solves the case. They're all the same, right?

Wrong.

One of my favourite things about mysteries is the way every single writer takes those ingredients and comes up with something totally new. They're each as unique as their author's brain, with fiendish puzzles, terrifying settings and wonderful characters that only that person could have come up with.

I loved being part of the original Crime Club anthology, and reading the unforgettable stories that the authors in it created and now I'm delighted to say that this brand-new collection by thirteen new children's crime writers is just as clever, funny, varied and (most importantly) very, very mysterious. These stories will sweep you away on adventures to Italian ski slopes, the London Frost Fair, and even an apparently normal street (appearances can be deceptive). They'll boggle your brain (can you solve the riddles of the haunted grotto? Why do the dolphins need to be protected?), and they'll introduce you to characters you won't be able to forget: a cat-burglar mum! Detective twins! A mysterious woodland Beast and a dance troupe on a mission!

So welcome to this wintery wonderland of clever codes, perilous missions and daring detectives. There's something for everyone and I hope these brilliant mysteries will help inspire you to tell your own story. Maybe we'll even see it in the next Crime Club anthology!

First published in Great Britain 2021 by Farshore
An imprint of HarperCollins*Publishers*
1 London Bridge Street, London SE1 9GF

farshore.co.uk

HarperCollins*Publishers*
1st Floor, Watermarque Building, Ringsend Road
Dublin 4, Ireland

Text copyright © Farshore 2021
Illustration copyright © Harry Woodgate 2021
Images on pages 2, 3, 395 © Shutterstock 2021
The moral rights of the authors and illustrator have been asserted.

ISBN 978 0 7555 0368 1
Printed and bound in the UK using 100% renewable electricity at CPI Group (UK) Ltd
2

A CIP catalogue record for this title is available from the British Library.

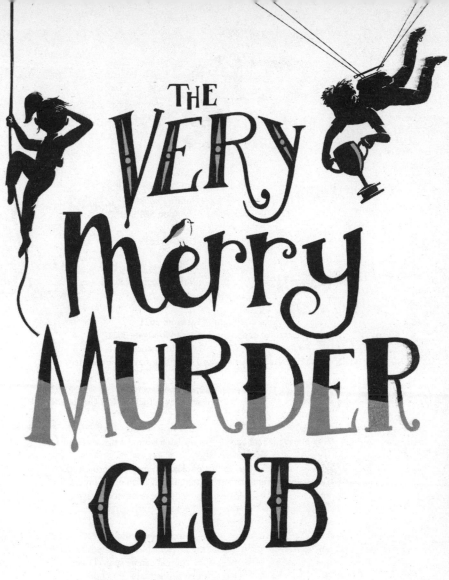

THE VERY Merry MURDER CLUB

EDITED BY
SERENA PATEL &
ROBIN STEVENS

CONTENTS
(WARNING, MAY CONTAIN FROSTY FOUL PLAY)

THE VERY MERRY MURDER CLUB

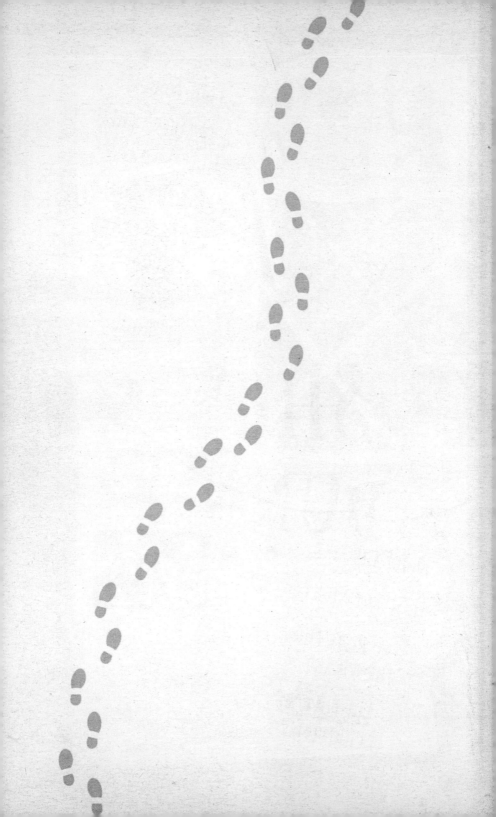

ELLE MCNICOLL

SHOE-DUNNIT

TOP SECRET

THE VERY MERRY MURDER CLUB

PROPERTY OF THE VERY MERRY MURDER CLUB

SHOE-DUNNIT

By Elle McNicoll

Ballerinas are extremely difficult to kill.

As someone who took a special interest in ballet, Briar knew this. She knew they were great athletes. She knew they put their bodies through the absolute extreme, in order to give an incredible performance. However, it was not just their fitness and strength that made them difficult to harm. It was also their nature. They were, in Briar's opinion, the most incredibly humble type of people. A competitive industry full of hardworking, sensitive and generous dancers.

Posy Lennox was not that kind of ballerina. She was, in that regard, exceptional.

Briar's parents owned the most in-demand inn in Aviemore and their eleven guests were currently snowed in while they were stuck in Inverness. Briar had managed

1

to avoid the high-maintenance, twenty-something former ballerina and her small but intense entourage. Their only run-in had been when Briar was waiting in the corridor upstairs to perform her housekeeping tasks. The party of three had all left Posy's room together: Posy, her mother Renee and Posy's publicist and manager Marianne Hobson. Posy and her mother had adjoining rooms and Marianne was next to them, whether she liked it or not. They passed Briar as she prepared to go in and clean.

'Strange little duck,' Renee had said quietly.

'Creepy, more like,' Posy snorted, not as quietly. 'I heard there's something weird about her.'

Marianne had given Briar an apologetic smile, patting her on the head as they all left.

Briar stood alone in the corridor and let the remarks fade away, like cigarette smoke. Briefly unpleasant, stinging her incredibly sensitive nostrils, but gone almost as soon as they had arrived.

Briar's nose was infamous. She could give her own hound a run for his money.

She made the beds in their rooms and avoided the urge to straighten their make-up bottles and organise their personal items.

The next run-in was later that evening, when Briar and Flute were setting up the dining room for dinner.

2

Posy stomped down the staircase and began to berate Jean-Claude at the front desk.

'Loud for such tiny feet,' Briar said to Flute, her basset hound, who was never far from her side. The little girl and the wrinkly dog watched the ballerina, now celebrity, as she launched into a tirade. It was true: her feet were absolutely tiny. Smaller than Briar's, even with twenty years between them.

'Do you know how many Insta followers I have?' Posy barked at the man behind the front desk. Briar gulped, exchanging a look with Flute. They both knew Jean-Claude's temper. Posy Lennox was perhaps about to meet her match.

'I don't care,' Jean-Claude said coolly. 'We have all been stuck here for days, listening to your tantrums, and I am sick of it! Tell your little followers, I do not care.'

'That's no way to speak to any customer, let alone me,' shouted Posy, filling her lungs with air and standing right up on the toes of her tiny feet. 'One word from me to my fans and this place will be tainted for the rest of its sad little life. Do you know who I am?'

'Sadly, I do,' Jean-Claude snapped back, pulling himself up to his full height. 'You're a has-been ballerina. Now get out of my reception area before I ring your neck. Post your little review. See what happens! *Je pourrais te tuer!*'

3

Briar knew Jean-Claude's threats were often empty but he was angrier than she had ever seen him. A rational person might have chosen to step away. But Posy Lennox was no rational person and her mother Renee looked every bit as enraged. The two stood side by side, like furious salt and pepper shakers, ready to take the man to task.

'Let's all just take a moment to breathe, shall we?'

Marianne the publicist appeared at the side of her client and her client's mother. Her face and voice serene, her eyes warm and understanding.

'He called me a has-been,' shrieked Posy. However, she did allow Marianne to steer her into the dining room. 'I want him sacked.'

'Oh, lovely,' Marianne said, picking up the little paper menu on their usual table. 'French onion soup. Just like old times, Pose. Might be as good as Matron's?'

Briar continued her task of placing water jugs on each table, taking care to look as though she had no interest in their conversation. But Briar's hearing was as refined as her nose, making eavesdropping not only easy, but sometimes completely unavoidable.

Martin Herriot, a travel writer for a broadsheet newspaper, sat just behind the three ladies. His piece on Highland hospitality would hopefully not be spoiled by the unexpected, extended stay. He made no effort to hide the fact that he was watching and listening to everything they did and said.

'When you let me manage you,' Renee spoke to her daughter in a tone of voice Briar imagined she had been using for about twenty years, 'we won't elect to stay in places like this. We can opt for more privacy.'

It was clear that this was a discussion they had had many times before.

'I've told you!' snarled Posy. 'I've *told* you, Mother, that you're not going to manage me. I can barely stand sharing a room with you, let alone working with you.'

Briar winced. Martin Herriot whistled quietly. The two old ladies who liked to play cards at dinner kept their eyes glued firmly to the aces and queens in their hands, but their lips were pursed tightly in disdain.

'Rude!' Jean-Claude shouted from the reception desk before storming into the kitchens.

'Posy, you're being awful,' Renee said, in a dangerously quiet tone.

When Briar's own mother chose a softly angry voice rather than a shouty one, Briar knew it was time to run. Posy typed furiously on her mobile phone, ignoring the weighted disapproval filling the room like mustard gas.

'Review posted!' she declared loudly, slamming her smartphone down on the table with a triumphant look.

'And I'll be speaking to your manager when it's finally possible to check out of this dump!' She threw a look of poison towards Briar and Flute. 'And there shouldn't be animals in the dining room.'

Briar looked out of the large bay window. She could see heaps of snow outside refusing to budge and still falling in defiant little flurries.

Little did Briar know that this was the last night Posy Lennox would spend at the inn.

Briar woke up at the witching hour.

It was instantly clear why. Her hearing, better than Flute's at that moment, had picked up arguing and shouting from above. Briar's room was on the ground floor. She knew which guest had their room directly above her. Those small feet were stomping around and Posy's angry words carried all the way downstairs.

Statements like 'rather die than continue working with you' were bandied about before Posy's mother shrieked so loudly Flute startled awake and almost fell off the edge of Briar's bed.

Briar slipped from under her covers and moved to her door, opening it ajar to listen.

'Something's going to happen,' she told Flute stoically.

6

Posy's mother could be heard yelling about 'ingratitude', before thumping footsteps alerted Briar to the fact that someone was stomping downstairs. It was Posy, wearing one of the inn's dressing gowns and a pair of slippers that were as snug on her tiny feet as ballet flats. She was bellowing into her mobile phone, complaining to whoever was on the other end of the line about being trapped and about wanting to push her mother down the stairs. She barked one final profanity at the front desk before storming out into the snow.

Briar watched her go.

'I need a better signal, I can't hear you. Hold on.'

It was the last thing Briar ever heard her say.

A few hours later, just as the sun started to make an appearance, Briar put Flute on the leash for his regular morning walk. She put on her coat and boots and set out into the cold. There had been no further snowfall or noise after last night's disturbance, and as Briar shut the inn door behind her, she noticed Posy's solitary footsteps were still fresh and clearly visible in the white blanket laid out before her.

'Careful, boy,' Briar said, steering Flute away from the lonely trail of prints. 'Something's up. Footprints going

out,' she murmured. 'None coming back.'

It was true. The footprints were as obvious as stains on a white carpet.

And there were none returning to the inn.

Briar set off towards the woodland, clutching Flute's lead and making sure not to step on Posy's tracks as she followed alongside them. If Posy Lennox was trapped in a gorge or suffering from hypothermia somewhere, the prints were Briar's best clue.

'Don't disturb a possible crime scene,' she said to Flute.

Flute made a grumbling sound.

'It could very well be a crime scene,' Briar retorted, tugging the stubborn hound along. 'I know you don't like the snow on your paws but she might be in trouble!'

Some assistant, Briar thought.

They headed further onward. When Flute started making suspicious snuffles, Briar knew they were close – though she was nervous about what lay ahead.

She was right to be.

As they neared the edge of the woods, Flute barked and Briar spotted her.

Posy Lennox. Face down in the snow.

A police officer tried to force a cup of tea and a shock

blanket into Briar's hands.

'Strange,' Briar said to Flute, bending down to wrap the foil blanket around the basset hound instead. 'I'm not in shock. I was pretty certain we were going to find what we found.'

Flute gave one small bark in consolation.

'Her phone was missing,' Briar mused thoughtfully, meeting Flute's quizzical gaze. 'Did you notice? She was on the phone when she stormed out and I didn't see it anywhere on her when I checked for a pulse.'

Posy's palm had been open, as if still clutching the mobile. Only Briar had found no trace of it.

Renee Lennox could be heard wailing in the dining room. Marianne, looking pale and drawn and shocked, was trying to calm her down. The front desk manager was hiding from the police in the small inn staffroom, muttering about Posy Lennox ruining everyone's Sunday.

'You were the last person to see her alive, Jean-Claude,' Briar said to the employee, matter-of-factly.

His face turned a strange puce colour. 'Maybe! But she stormed off into the snow late at night. I didn't follow her.'

No, Briar thought. That was certainly true. She had not seen or heard him follow Posy, and there were no other tracks in the snow. A quick glance down at Jean-Claude's feet confirmed they were at least a size twelve. A lack of prints in

10

the snow leading up to Posy's body was certainly puzzling.

Briar looked over at the police detective, who was trying to comfort Marianne and Renee. He had come on foot as the snow was still too heavy to drive through. The prints leading to the spot where Briar found Posy had been taped off.

'Do you think he'll notice the right things?' she asked Flute, her voice a doubtful whisper.

Flute gave her a look that said, *They never ask the right questions*. Briar nodded in agreement and turned back to Jean-Claude. The detective could spend this valuable time getting people teas and coffees. Briar was going to find out if foul play was involved.

If the detective was going to lurk around a snowed-in inn, he clearly did not believe Posy Lennox had collapsed from natural causes.

Therefore everyone at the inn was a suspect.

'So what do we know?' Briar said to Flute as they sat upstairs. 'Posy has a massive argument with Renee at three in the morning. She storms downstairs on her mobile phone, shouts at reception and then heads off into the snow. No sign of injury. Just rudeness.'

Flute's ears were draped across the carpet as he rested

11

his head on his front paws and stared up at Briar, listening.

'She heads off on her phone, trying to get a better signal. No other guests were signed out. There were only her footprints there a few hours later when you and I found the body.'

Flute sniffed.

'No blood on the body,' Briar added. 'No sign of a struggle. No sign of anyone else being there at all. Except the missing phone.'

'What are you muttering?'

Briar and Flute both startled as Renee Lennox appeared on the landing, clearly blurry-eyed and distraught. She was exiting her bedroom and eyeing Briar and Flute with irritation.

Briar said nothing. Hotel guests often believed Briar to be dim and she was perfectly happy with that. It would make her investigation much easier. Posy's mobile phone was missing, and it wasn't a leap to assume that the suspect had it.

'It doesn't make any sense,' Renee went on, leaning against the wall of the corridor and staring off into empty air. 'She's the healthiest person I know. She's always been that way; ballerinas have to be. She doesn't smoke or drink alcohol. No coffee, only tea. Why would she pass out? What happened?'

12

Briar quietly noted Renee's use of the present tense. She tried to fix her face into an expression that would look sympathetic. In truth, she *was* very sympathetic. Only, her way of showing sympathy was to uncover the murderer rather than offer boring platitudes. Although, Briar had to admit, Renee probably would not find a lot of comfort from a young girl and her dog.

'You and Posy fought last night.'

Renee jumped at the sound of Briar's voice, clearly surprised. 'Well. Yes. But mothers and daughters always fight, it's completely normal!'

'Why were you fighting?'

Briar had a mental notebook in her mind and an imaginary pencil was poised, ready to take notes.

'Posy doesn't want me managing her,' Renee said sniffily. 'She wants to keep working with Marianne without me "interfering", in her words. But I'm the one who really knows what she needs.'

A motive, certainly, no matter how distraught the woman seemed. Briar watched Renee slip downstairs, still crying. She glanced down at Flute. He growled ever so softly, just to let Briar know he too was not entirely convinced.

Briar knocked on the door adjacent to Renee's. 'Housekeeping?'

When no one replied, Briar opened the door and

13

stepped inside. It was Posy's room, still smelling of her expensive shampoo. Briar moved carefully about, making a show of straightening the bedspread and plumping the pillows while her eyes darted around the quiet space.

Flute stood on guard by the door.

'Nothing untoward,' Briar murmured. Then her eyes fell on the dressing table. There was an overflowing jewellery case, a few photographs and Post-it notes taped to the mirror and too many cosmetic bottles to count.

Briar moved closer to look at the photographs. They were a couple of years old, from Posy's days in the ballet. The photograph showed Posy backstage in what looked like a dressing room, wearing a beautiful white and silver costume. Loving ballet as she did, Briar knew it was Odette's costume from *Swan Lake*. Posy was beside the ballerina playing the black swan, and the two were standing on the absolute tips of their toes. On pointe.

Briar had attempted to stand on pointe before getting in the shower once. She almost broke her ankle. It was extremely difficult.

Another photograph showed Posy with a ballerina Briar remembered well: Louise Clarkson. Briar had seen her in *The Nutcracker*, and her talent had made the large theatre, full of smells and sounds and other people, completely worth it. Louise Clarkson had fallen down some stairs and injured her back so badly she had been forced to give up dancing.

She and Posy smiled out at Briar from the photograph.

Briar carefully returned the small picture and moved into Renee's adjoining room. She spotted a broken mug on the floor. She moved towards it, careful not to stand on the fragments, when she noticed something curious.

A large box of teabags stood next to the hotel kettle. It was not the brand Briar's parents provided in their guests' bedrooms.

Flute growled softly from his spot by the door. Briar glanced over, checking to see if someone was coming. But Flute's eyes were fixed on the dresser and the box of teabags. Briar trusted his instincts as much as her own. She carefully lifted the already opened lid of the box and picked up one of the large, unfamiliar bags.

Her nose did not pick up hints of jasmine or camomile. No sense of orange or lemon. In fact, the only real scent Briar's incredibly adept nose could pick up was a touch of garlic.

'Garlic tea?' she mused, a little dumbfounded.

Certainly not your typical blend. In fact, Briar's nostrils stung a little. She bristled at the pang of discomfort and took a step back.

'Something's up with the tea, Flute.'

15

She knew it might irritate the detective, but she quickly pocketed two of the teabags and then returned the box to its place.

'Come on,' she said to her basset hound. 'We need to start asking questions.'

Briar and Flute found Martin Herriot, the travel writer, and Marianne, the publicist, in the drawing room. Marianne was sniffing softly while emailing people on her laptop.

'I'm cancelling Posy's engagements,' she said when Briar appeared. 'This is . . . I just . . . I'll never get over this.'

Herriot patted the young woman on the shoulder, a little gingerly.

'Where's Mrs Lennox?' Briar asked.

'With the detective,' Marianne replied sadly. 'They're trying to work out how Posy fell ill.'

'Fell ill?' Briar asked.

'Unlikely that she lay down in the snow,' Herriot said to Briar, in that slow tone that adults enjoyed so much. 'She would have died from hypothermia. It will have been an aneurysm or something that killed the poor thing.'

He seemed a little too sure, Briar thought. An aneurysm was just a possibility. For that matter, so was spontaneous

16

combustion. But Briar knew in her heart that neither of those things had caused Posy's demise.

'Posy and her mother were fighting last night,' Briar said steadily. 'Before she went out.'

There was no question asked outright. Only implied. Briar preferred to make statements and then let people fill in the pauses themselves.

'They've been fighting for a while,' Marianne said regretfully, blowing her nose and wiping her eyes. 'As long as I've known them both, they've been volatile. But certainly, since becoming Posy's PR person, it's got worse. Renee . . . she likes things to go her way. If they don't, she'll act.'

Herriot's eyebrows shot up at the insinuation. Briar merely nodded. It seemed true enough, given everything she had witnessed between the two of them. But it wasn't evidence of foul play.

'What were the events leading up to Posy's argument with her mum?' Briar asked lightly.

'Oh . . .' Marianne placed her laptop to one side as she tried to remember. 'After dinner, she went to her room for her usual routine. Bath, skincare, meditation, et cetera.'

Briar winced. It was not the most convincing testament to the positive powers of meditation if Posy Lennox was one if its disciples.

'Then I think she would probably have gone to bed around one,' Marianne continued. 'Renee too. But Renee often snores and that really riles Posy up – she's a light sleeper. So they started to argue. Then Posy stormed off.'

Briar's mind was on the mobile phone. Still a missing link.

'I know this must all seem very frightening,' Marianne said gently, squeezing Briar's arm. 'But don't be scared. These tragic things happen.'

Briar nodded but then looked over at the detective, who had just entered the drawing room. 'But what if it wasn't an accident?'

The detective caught her words and glowered at her, wagging a finger. 'Now don't start that. You'll only upset yourself and other people.'

'There is no evidence that this was natural causes,' Briar said.

'There is only one set of tracks leading to the crime scene,' the detective retorted pointedly. 'Apart from yours and that dog. Unless you wish to confess something, it's impossible for someone to have followed her.'

'Maybe they put their own feet in Posy's tracks,' Herriot suggested.

No, Briar thought. Posy's feet were too tiny. The smallest at the inn. Nobody could have traced her steps without altering the prints.

Briar moved out of the drawing room and into the kitchen.

'Jean-Claude!'

The front desk manager was having his lunch. He grimaced when he saw Briar and Flute. 'Get that *chien* out of the kitchens.'

'Jean-Claude, what did you hear from upstairs last night?' Briar asked. 'Before Posy came back down?'

Jean-Claude made a grumbling sound, not unlike Flute. 'I was summoned at about two in the morning,' he said resentfully, 'to bring miss her precious warm milk for her tea.'

Briar stared. 'Milk for tea? At two in the morning?'

'To relax, she said. Not that it helped. They kept fighting, you must have heard it.'

'I did. Did you see her drink the tea?'

He frowned. 'I think so. Yes! She took a sip and told me the milk was too warm and that's when I left. I was so done with her.'

Briar was starting to feel a little sorry for Posy but she pushed on. 'And then you stayed at the front desk for the rest of the night, after that.'

He shook his head. 'No. About five minutes after she left the inn –'

19

'Who, Posy?'

'Yes. I was called upstairs again. Mrs Lennox had broken a mug and injured herself, so I had to help her put a plaster on her finger. Why the questions, Briar? You don't think I did anything, do you?'

While Briar was sure Jean-Claude was capable, she did not. But it was interesting to learn that he'd brought Posy milk for her strange-smelling tea and was then alone with Renee Lennox after Posy had left.

'Did you clear up the broken mug?' asked Briar, knowing the answer.

'No,' he replied. 'Mrs Lennox said she would do it. I came back down here.'

'Where there was no sign of anyone.'

'*Oui.*'

Briar nodded, making eye contact with Flute. 'Thank you, Jean-Claude. I'm off to do some research. We'll be serving tea as usual at three o'clock.'

She left, her authoritative words lingering behind her.

Briar checked in with her parents over the phone. They were still trapped in Inverness, blissfully unaware that a potential murder had taken place at the inn. Briar decided not to mention the fact. She then researched a few things on the computer before finally sneaking back upstairs to the guest rooms with Flute.

This time she was investigating a different room.

The incredibly neat and tidy bedroom was not in need of any real cleaning, but Briar mussed up the bedding just so she could have something to busy herself with if interrupted. It was only when Flute started to actively sniff and fuss around the bottom of the bedspread that she finally started investigating properly.

'What is it, Flute?'

Briar hunkered down on the carpet and lifted the bedspread. While most of the room was shipshape, the space under the bed was extremely cluttered. There was an open suitcase with clothing pouring out of it, a few paper coffee cups and some crumpled pieces of paper.

Then something curious. A pair of beautiful baby-pink pointe shoes. The shoes a ballerina wore in order to go right on to the tips of her toes, an excruciatingly painful yet beautiful form of dancing. The proper, professional kind that you would see onstage in Covent Garden. Briar lifted them carefully in order to examine them more closely. A size eight, or thereabouts, so they certainly had not belonged to Posy.

As Briar was feeling the very tips of the pointe shoes, something caught her eye. The owner of these shoes had tucked something inside one of them. Something very revealing.

Briar quickly put all of her new evidence in her bag of cleaning supplies.

'Come on, boy,' she said to Flute, her voice full of triumphant resolve. 'It's time to serve tea.'

Teatime in the dining room. Marianne and Renee Lennox sat together, looking exhausted. Herriot and the two bridge ladies were over by the window. The detective was by himself.

Briar rolled her trolley into the room and shut the door firmly behind her. Flute sat down like a large, hairy doorstop and glared at the guests.

Briar stopped the trolley. 'I know what happened to Posy Lennox.'

Her statement was met with a stunned silence. Renee Lennox made a small, sputtering sound and Herriot swore softly. The detective merely rolled his eyes and fixed Briar with a disdainful look.

'This isn't a game, young lady,' he said drily. 'A woman has lost her life. A tragic accident. The coroner will prove as much.'

Briar decided to ignore him. It wasn't his fault he was

22

woefully underqualified and out of his depth. Of course he thought this was a mere accident; he had only just arrived. Briar, however, had been observing every guest in the dining room for over a week. She knew their comings and goings and she knew that Posy's death was no accident.

'Posy Lennox was in perfect health yesterday,' Briar said calmly, addressing the whole room. 'Her lungs were breathing easily as she screamed at Jean-Claude. Her mind was sharp when she argued with her mother in front of everyone, right here in this room. And her fingers were working perfectly as she fired off a nasty review on her mobile phone.'

She would return to the phone later.

'How can you say that?' cried Renee.

Briar threw her a look. They were just facts.

'Last night, Posy went upstairs and spent a few hours unwinding. She had trouble sleeping and was still awake at two in the morning. That is when she called Jean-Claude up from the reception area, requesting some warm milk for her tea. Correct?'

She was looking at Renee when she said it. Mrs Lennox looked slightly affronted but she nodded. 'Yes.'

'And she drank that tea, Mrs Lennox?'

'Well, yes.'

'Exactly!'

23

Briar reached into her bag and withdrew the two teabags she had swiped from the bedroom. She held them up.

'These are not the brand used here at the inn,' she told the room cheerfully. 'My parents are very particular about Scottish breakfast tea. And this is nothing close. It was originally a herbal blend, but you can tell by the strange and rotten smell of garlic that there is something wrong with it.'

One of the elderly card-playing ladies gasped. 'What was wrong with it?'

Briar paused for dramatic effect and then answered, 'Poison.'

Marianne clapped her hands over her mouth and Renee stared in what looked like a mixture of confusion and rage. Herriot and the elderly ladies leaned forward, listening intently.

Briar continued. 'Posy drank the poisoned tea, none the wiser –'

'That rude man poisoned my daughter!' shrieked Renee, almost leaping to her feet in distress and alarm and pointing at Jean-Claude. 'I want him arrested!'

'There is absolutely no evidence she was killed, let alone poisoned!' the detective cried shrilly. 'This child has an overactive imagination.'

'No,' Briar said casually. 'I just see things. Anyway,

as I was saying . . . Posy drinks the tea at around two in the morning without knowing about the poison. She then starts fighting with Mrs Lennox, as their rooms are adjoined. The whole inn can hear them. It wakes me up.'

'Don't brush past the poisoning,' Renee interrupted sharply. 'If she was poisoned, Jean-Claude did it.'

'No,' sighed Briar, a little irritated. 'Don't you see? The *teabags* were poisoned, not the milk that Jean-Claude brought up.'

'How could the teabags be poisoned?' Marianne asked, sounding dazed. 'We brought them with us.'

Briar would get to that. 'Posy wakes the whole place up and then storms downstairs. She calls someone on the phone and, after a few choice words to Jean-Claude, she leaves the inn and heads out into the snow. Her tiny little feet are the only tracks and they don't show her coming back.'

Renee whimpered. Flute growled.

'Jean-Claude was seemingly the last person to see Posy alive,' Briar went on. 'But he was called upstairs once more to help Mrs Lennox with an injury after a mug was broken.'

Renee glanced down at her plastered finger.

'This left the front desk empty for around twenty minutes. Someone could easily have followed Posy

Lennox out of the inn at that time to check that their poisoning had gone as planned.'

'How?' Herriot asked, his face a crumpled mask of confusion. He was clearly playing the whole scene out in his head. 'There was only one set of tracks!'

'If we are going to entertain this ridiculous narrative,' the detective said, 'at least allow me to poke holes in it. Why would the killer follow Posy if they knew she had drunk the poison?'

Briar smiled triumphantly. 'Because Posy had something that this particular killer needed. Her mobile phone.'

'Oh, this is so exciting,' chirruped one of the bridge ladies. 'What next?'

'The killer followed Posy and, after checking that she had succumbed to the poison, grabbed her mobile phone. The killer was probably put out by Posy's midnight wanderings – they would have much rather snatched the phone from her room – but they improvised.'

'How?' the detective yelled hoarsely. 'The tracks!'

Briar took a deep breath. 'The killer was being blackmailed by Posy. All the evidence is inside the mobile phone.'

Briar reached into her pocket and drew out the pink smartphone she had found tucked inside the pointe shoe under the bed only a short while earlier.

'You see, Posy knew the killer in a former life,' Briar said. 'They were ballerinas together. The killer was always envious of Posy. They were envious of a mutual friend and colleague as well. The killer pushed that friend and colleague down the stairs in a now infamous fall that shattered that ballerina's career. Only Posy knew. And Posy was using this information to blackmail the killer so they would follow Posy's wishes.'

An icy silence followed this conclusion. Posy's publicist and manager made a small sound of disbelief, her blue eyes scanning Briar's face in complete horror.

'For god's sake,' Marianne said. 'What preposterous allegations. Come on. It's no secret that I was in the ballet with Posy, years ago. But the rest is all lies.'

'Not lies,' said Briar fiercely. 'You couldn't stand Posy. I know a mask when I see one, Marianne, and you always wore one around her. You were pretending. You were rivals and you couldn't stand that she was better than you. Louise Clarkson was better too. So when Posy found out what you had done to Louise, she blackmailed you. Threatened to ruin what reputation you had.'

Briar placed the mobile phone beside the two poisoned teabags and then drew out the photographs

27

she had taken from the bedroom.

'You had the teabags poisoned in advance and brought them with you. Last night was a fresh box, your first and only attempt. You succeeded. Posy drank from the poisoned tea and was dead mere hours later.'

'You can't prove they're poisoned,' Marianne said. 'Besides, how did I get the phone?'

'You walked inside Posy's footsteps, of course.'

'Are you mad?' cried Marianne, laughing shrilly. She gestured at her large feet. 'I wear a size eight. Posy wore a size three. You're joking.'

'This is the part where I almost admire you,' Briar said evenly. She drew out her final piece of evidence and placed it on the tea trolley.

The pointe shoes.

Marianne's face became very pale, while everyone else stared in surprise.

'Your feet are certainly bigger than Posy's,' Briar said quietly. 'But you can stand and walk on pointe. It wasn't far. You just needed to get to the body and retrieve the device. Which you did. By standing on the very tips of your toes, walking on pointe inside Posy's footprints. Probably the best performance you've ever given and no one was there to see it.'

Herriot chuckled and the detective made some strangled

28

noises of confusion, staring at Marianne and Briar.

'Well,' Briar amended. 'Not exactly "no one". My parents have CCTV.'

'What?' both Marianne and the detective said simultaneously.

'Oh yes. In the woods. It's disguised as an owl. Dad's idea, very clever. He has the files from it too. He'll access them when he gets back from Inverness.'

Renee glanced at her daughter's publicist, clearly disturbed by the obvious fear on Marianne's face. 'But this can't be true. Marianne? Tell her it's a mistake.'

'She's lying,' Marianne said, her voice raspy. 'For attention. She's not well, she's not right in the head.'

'Sorry,' Briar said plainly. 'I'm very right in the head. Want to know a fun fact about some autistic people, Marianne? We have incredibly heightened senses. I can hear and smell extremely well. Better than you. Better than anyone in this room.' She gestured to Flute. 'Possibly even better than him.'

Flute grunted in denial.

'So I can pick up the scent of poison in these teabags,' Briar went on, holding the teabags high. 'And I notice things other people don't bother to look at. Because no one knows better than me that there is always something deeper going on, underneath the surface.'

'You can't prove any of it,' Marianne hissed, a little desperately.

Briar forced herself to make eye contact with Marianne as she dropped both poisoned teabags into the boiling pot of water. She stirred, never breaking their stare.

'Here,' she finally said, pouring a generous cup of tea and holding it out to Marianne. 'Tea is served. Have some.'

Shocked, stunned silence.

Marianne stared at Briar. Briar stared right back.

'Careful,' Briar finally said, her voice a murmur. 'It's piping hot.'

There was a brief moment where Briar thought Marianne might either flip the table or dash the scalding hot tea out of her hand. Instead she gave a weak laugh and all the remnants of pretend shock disappeared from her face.

'I think it's safe to say that everyone in this building had a motive,' she said silkily. 'I was the only one who had an actual plan.'

'Oh my god,' breathed Renee.

'A murderer?' squeaked the detective. 'Here?'

'I'd love some tea!' said one of the bridge ladies.

'No, it's poisoned, Deborah,' scolded the other.

'Let's call some of your officers, detective,' Herriot said

sternly, eyeing Marianne. The publicist now wore a calm and serene expression, as if she was now free. 'We have a confession of sorts and you should have your CCTV soon.'

Briar hurried to the window and poured the tea out on to the snow. It sizzled and scorched as it hit the gentle white puffiness, leaving the poison out in the open for all to see.

'How did you know it was murder?'

Herriot asked the question, while he and Briar watched the detective place Marianne in the back of a police car. The snow had thawed a little so the police were now able to get in and out.

Briar spoke very matter-of-factly, leaning down to scratch her basset hound's ears. 'Because people like Posy Lennox, who are rude and obnoxious and unkind to people, tend to live a long time before natural causes get them. It could never have been an aneurysm or something like that. Marianne was right about one thing: everyone wanted to kill her. She was just the one brash enough to do it.'

Herriot laughed, bemused. 'You're an old soul, aren't you?'

'No, just autistic.'

'Well, you solved the case,' he said. 'DI Useless over there would never have found out. We all underestimated Marianne. And you, Briar.'

The serious little girl snapped Flute's lead on to his collar for a walk. She couldn't help reflecting on the strange day. It had definitely not been a normal Christmastime at the inn.

'It's all right,' she told Herriot, tugging her hound along behind her. 'I'm used to being underestimated.'

ROOPA FAROOKI

IT'S SNOW CRIME

TOP SECRET

PROPERTY OF THE VERY MERRY MURDER CLUB

IT'S SNOW CRIME

By Roopa Farooki

'Ho-ho-HO!'

Ali exploded from the back seat, throwing old chocolate wrappers in the air like confetti. Tulip jumped beside her. Nan-Nan hit the emergency brake and her Nan-mobile stalled. She turned and skewered both Ali and Tulip with a look of steel.

'She did it,' the twins said together, pointing to each other.

Tulip bristled with the unfairness of this and said even more forcefully, 'No, SHE really did it!' – the same time as Ali said the same thing.

'Stop that!' they said together.

'No, YOU stop it!'

Nan-Nan rolled her eyes and waved airily at the beeping traffic moving around her. Some drivers even

35

wound down their windows to complain at her. She just beamed at them and gestured towards her wheelchair sticker.

'Bet you feel bad about yourself now,' she told the hecklers. 'Road raging at an adorable old lady with a wheelchair.'

She put the car back into gear and moved off, commenting in the rear-view mirror, 'Driving without legs is easy. Driving with you two in the back? *That's* the dangerous bit.'

'It wasn't me,' complained Tulip – just as Ali said the same thing a split second later: '. . . wasn't me.'

Nan-Nan shook her head. 'I keep telling you two not to talk in creepy twin unison. It weirds out the normals.' As she pulled up at their school, she added casually, 'Pop quiz! What's Father Christmas's favourite Minecraft tool?'

'Hoe-hoe-HOE!' yelled Ali competitively. She realised she'd given herself away a moment later, but then grinned. 'Yeah, so it was me yelling just then. Christmas prank. Totally worth it.'

'We all knew it was you,' said Nan-Nan. 'Why are you being so annoyingly perky? I prefer you when you're ignoring us for your own sinister reasons.'

'Duh! Cos it's almost the holidays!' whooped Ali. 'Mum's getting three days off from the hospital. She's not working Christmas, so we get to do festive stuff. Stockings! Chocolate! Crackers! We're gonna be so stuffed with merriness we're gonna be sick!'

'Ali's a bit excited,' Tulip apologised. 'And has really got her ding-dong-merrily-on-high hopes up. Which means it's definitely not going to end well.'

'Ugh, you're such a downer,' complained Ali. 'Gloom and Boomer. Can't believe I have to share Christmas with you.'

'You don't,' said Tulip, trying not to look smug. 'I'm volunteering at the Festive Grotto with Zac. It's set up outside the kids' ward at the hospital.' Zac and his brother Jay were the other twins in their class. Zac was the nicer one, and was always annoyingly volunteering for things.

'Aargh! I can't believe you're dumping me for Christmas,' said Ali. 'Zac's the worst. Probably has elbow-ache from all of his halo-polishing.'

'*Christmas* is the worst,' corrected Nan-Nan. 'You're just brainwashed by the internet into thinking it's fun. It's basically a national day of family arguments and sugar-loading.'

'Grinchy much?' said Tulip, interrupting Nan-Nan before she could give them her whole anti-Christmas speech. 'Poor grumpy old Nan-Nan. If you had a lawn, you'd be yelling at kids to get off it.'

37

'Of course I would,' said Nan-Nan. 'I'm an active agent in a covert super-spy ring. I haven't found half the traps I buried, in case my international enemies catch up with me. Some of them are pretty sharp. The traps, obvs. Not my enemies.'

'Yeah, enemies are real noobs,' agreed Ali.

'Thanks for the lift, Nan-Nan,' said Tulip, looking pointedly at Ali. 'We were meant to walk, but it's cold, and *someone* left her coat at school.'

'I didn't forget it,' said Ali, offended. 'I left it in a locker with itching powder in the pockets, to frame and shame someone on *my* enemies list . . .'

'That sounds like a fascinating back story that I have no need to know,' said Nan-Nan. She nodded outside and rolled down the window, stretching out her hands to catch the first flakes of snow. 'Made it just in time. Wouldn't want you to be caught in this.'

'Snow's hardly even weather,' pointed out Tulip. 'It pretty much dissolves on contact.'

'It does on this wet little island,' agreed Nan-Nan. 'In Greenland I could build whole igloo forts and cosy hobbit holes out of the ice.'

'Don't you mean Iceland?' said Ali.

'Nope,' said Nan-Nan. 'Iceland is green, and Greenland is icy. They did that on purpose to confuse people.' She

38

nodded towards their class teacher Mr Ofu at the gates, and waved them in. 'Off you go. Spit spot! I'll collect you if it's still snowing.'

The last day of school was just busy work, which did nothing to calm Ali down. They made twisty wreaths with ivy stripped from the brick walls at the back of the playground and then watched a holiday movie with winsome singing and CGI animals.

'Shame Zac and Jay aren't here for this,' commented Tulip, bouncing along to the film's high-energy soundtrack.

'Where are the losers, anyway?' complained Ali, as though she'd only just noticed they were absent. Tulip had seen her looking disappointed as she pulled her itching-powder-loaded coat back out of Jay's locker. 'It's irresponsible not to be here. Everyone knows they usually bring the end-of-term cookies.'

'Yeah,' said Tulip. 'The teachers are crazy disappointed. No homemade cookies, no handmade gift boxes.'

'Suppose their parents gave them the day off,' said Ali. 'They're not big on religious-themed activities. Their mum wouldn't even let them play *Tomb Raider* at Easter.'

'They're not allowed any games,' pointed out Tulip.

'And I'm not sure tomb raiding is really in the spirit of Easter.'

'Nah, that's chocolate,' agreed Ali.

At the end of the film, Mr Ofu rolled up the blinds and blinked at the sea of blinding white light outside. In two hours, the snow flurry had become a thick blanket several centimetres deep, covering everything in blurry, fluffy wonder.

'OMG, it REALLY snowed!' yelled Ali. 'Proper Greenland igloo-fort-hobbit-hole snow! Ho-ho-ho!'

'No-no-no! How am I going to get my car out in that!' said Mr Ofu. 'My boyfriend just made us waffles.' He showed them the Insta photos he'd been scrolling through during the film credits.

'Aw!' said Tulip. 'He made breakfast for teatime? That's like the most merry thing ever.'

They were packing up their things when the school announcement system screeched into life. It was Mrs Khan, trying hard to sound curt and official.

'Could Nurse Han please report to the school hall? The younger classes tried to do a conga in the snow and we have some unfortunate ice-related injuries.'

'Lol, the Year Threes are cray-cray,' said Ali. 'Why didn't *we* do a conga line?'

The speaker system started up again. Mrs Khan

40

sounded even more stressed.

'I've been informed that Nurse Han is already on holiday, as she has apparently posted a "Merry Christmas from the Beach" postcard on her Facebook page. Honestly, she could at least PRETEND it was a family emergency. So, if any teacher, or students, any two students, possibly TWIN students, can help out . . .'

Mr Ofu grinned and opened the door. 'Tulip, Ali, I think that's Mrs Khan putting out the bat signal. Do you wanna go to the hall?'

'Finally,' squealed Tulip. 'We're wanted for our cool medical know-how and not just for our great one-liners.'

'Speak for yourself,' said Ali, but she was grinning. She fist-bumped Tulip, pulling back with wavy fingers. 'Let's go sort out the Year Threes. Dumb cray-cray baes.'

In the hall, there was a long line of Year Three students with scrapes and bruises, and jagged fingernails, and ice-burn injuries.

'So a conga in the snow is a bit more dangerous than it sounds,' said Tulip sympathetically, wiping antiseptic along a cut knee and adding a plaster.

'This is SOOOO dull,' complained Ali. 'No one's even got a bone sticking out. At least Mum gets to poke about in brains like a zombie.'

'Mum's operation yesterday took six hours,' Tulip

41

pointed out, efficiently slapping an ice pack over a swollen arm. 'You've been here five minutes and you've already had enough?'

'Yeah, brains are way more boring,' agreed Ali. 'At least, yours would be.'

Tulip opened her mouth to retort, but Ali switched on a festive mixtape from her phone and she was drowned out by jingling bells.

Tulip and Ali finally patched up the last injured student.

'Good work, girls,' said Mr Ofu, who had no idea whether it was good or not, as he was squeamish about injuries and got wobbly just being in the hall on vaccination days. 'You'd better wait here for your grown-up to get home. The snow's really deep out there.'

Tulip and Ali got their stuff and waited around. Soon they were the last kids in school. Mr Ofu had disappeared for his waffles. Mrs Khan was pacing around impatiently, telling off Nurse Han on WhatsApp. But Nan-Nan still hadn't turned up. Tulip finally called her.

'Where are you, Nan-Nan? We're kind of stuck here.'

'I'm stuck too,' Nan-Nan complained. 'At the hospital. Couldn't call. I'm literally all tied up. Can you get here by yourselves?'

'What, like ski there?' said Tulip doubtfully. 'Isn't that a bit dangerous?'

'Of course it is, sweetie,' said Nan-Nan. 'You've met me, right?'

She hung up and didn't answer when Tulip called back. Tulip didn't bother leaving a message. She knew Nan-Nan never listened to them.

'What's going on?' said Ali, pulling out her earbuds. 'When's the old lady picking us up?'

'She said she's *literally* tied up,' said Tulip. 'You don't think she actually meant it?'

'Aargh!' said Ali. 'That's so Nan-Nan. She couldn't even wait for school to end before getting sucked back into some stupid super-spy scheme. We were promised a holiday! There's meant to be a proper takeaway tonight!'

'Yeah,' agreed Tulip. 'Nan-Nan wants us to go straight home, spit spot. But I think we should go to the hospital, find Mum and *tell* on Nan-Nan.' This wasn't exactly what Nan-Nan had said, but Tulip knew that Ali was more likely to want to do the opposite of what she was told.

'No WAY am I going home,' said Ali, on cue. 'Hospital? I'm on it!' She grabbed a pair of rackets from the sports hall and tied them to her feet with some balloon string left over from a Year Four Christmas party.

'Snow shoes?' said Tulip. 'Great idea. You're soooo

43

clever, Ali.' Snow shoes were a lot safer than skis. She tried not to look too pleased with herself. Everything was going to plan.

They left school and stamped towards the tube station on their DIY snowshoes. Their black witch cat, a stray who had adopted them, jumped off the wall at the end of their street, and followed them.

'Go home, Witchy, you'll get lost,' fussed Tulip.

'We tried to lose her last time, remember?' said Ali. 'Dumb furball always finds her way back.' She opened up her PE kit, and Witch jumped in. 'What?' she said defensively when Tulip looked at her. 'It's cold out. And I'll just burn the kit if she pees. I'm growing out of it anyway.'

When they got off at the tube stop near the hospital, Tulip was expecting Nan-Nan to be there, waiting for them. She wasn't. The snow was even deeper in this bit of town. Cars were getting stuck on the main road. There was no way the Nan-mobile or Nan-Nan's wheelchair could have made it here.

Tulip looked around wildly. 'Nan-Nan said she was stuck. Do you think she's stranded?'

But as she started tramping up the street towards the

44

bus stop, Ali realised something worse. No cars could get out. Which meant no cars could go in.

'Nooo,' she said. 'Mum might get stuck in the hospital. What if the other docs can't come in to take over her shift?'

The twins looked at each other in horror.

'Christmas will have to be cancelled!'

They heard beeping, and a cheerful ice-cream van jingle, and a friendly voice calling out to them: 'My queens! Are you stranded in the snowy world of wonder?'

It was their friend Momo, a social work student and part-time cabbie. He beamed, his super-white teeth competing with the snow. His neatly shaved head was topped with a Christmas pudding bobble hat.

'Ugh, put those teeth away, it's bright enough already,' complained Ali. 'I'm gonna report you for brushing with plutonium. It can't be legal.'

'Please do not,' said Momo, looking slightly alarmed. 'The accusation would appear most unseemly on my ongoing residency application.' He gestured towards the van. 'I believe that you require supervised transport? As buses to the hospital are not running, your Nan-Nan has just booked me to take you there. Via the supplies entrance. For unknown reasons.'

'That's nice of Nan-Nan,' said Tulip, climbing into the

ice-cream van. 'Are you an ice-cream guy now? Where's the cab?'

'After the last incident,' said Momo, who'd been attacked by the twins' evil nemesis, Evelyn Sprotland, 'I decided ice cream was safer. And the van is most inexpensive in the winter months.'

'And most delicious,' agreed Tulip, pushing a button, grabbing a cone and making herself a swirly 99 Flake. 'Add this to Nan-Nan's tab, please.'

'That's really annoying of Nan-Nan,' complained Ali. 'She doesn't have time to talk to us, but enough time to complete Momo's customer safety PDF on his booking app.' She showed it to Ali on her phone.

Momo's van made it down the road to the hospital better than Nan-Nan's Nan-mobile would have done. He had cunningly customised it with a couple of traffic cones on the front, acting like scoops to push away the snow.

'You sure *snow* how to get around,' sniggered Tulip.

Ali groaned. 'I'll pay you to throw her out right now,' she whispered to Momo.

'And that's *snow* joke,' added Tulip relentlessly.

As Momo pulled up slowly at the supplies entrance. Ali leaped out and ran inside.

'Mum!' she shrieked into the building. 'Tulip's torturing me with snow puns!'

46

'Sorry, I'd better go after her,' said Tulip, giving Momo a hug and leaping out of the ice-cream van too. 'Could you watch Witch for us! Thanks!'

'Wait, my queens,' called Momo. 'I am meant to accompany you! Your Nan-Nan is wrapped up!'

'You mean tied up?' said Tulip.

'She definitely said wrapped up,' said Momo.

Tulip ran inside after Ali, leaving Momo struggling to park the van.

Inside, the hospital wasn't as Christmassy as usual. Tulip was sure there were fewer bits of tinsel and fairy lights around than there had been last week.

'Do you think Nan-Nan's been Grinching and taking down the fun stuff?' asked Ali, messaging their mum. 'C'mon, Mum said to find her in the Festive Grotto. Maybe she's volunteering there too, like you and Zac. Must be catching.'

When they got to Paediatrics, the Festive Grotto was a ransacked disaster. Santa's chair was overturned, the fairy lights had been ripped down, and scraps of wrapping paper and torn tinsel littered the fake snow floor.

'My babies,' squealed Mum. She ran towards the twins and rolled them up in a big cuddle. 'What are you doing here?'

'Your irresponsible mother forgot to pick us up,' sniffed Ali. 'You need to tell her off, Mum.'

'She told us she was tied up. Or wrapped up,' added Tulip, snuggling up to Mum. 'What's happened here? Have the toddlers on the ward gone rogue and smashed up the place?'

'Not all toddlers are like you two,' commented Mum. She sighed. 'The grotto was really lovely until a little while ago. Now all the decorations are gone, the donated presents are gone and Santa has disappeared!'

'You had a Santa?' said Ali.

'The staff take it in turns,' said Mum. 'But it looks like whoever it was on the last shift has run off with the presents.'

'Someone's stolen Christmas presents from the sick kids?' said Ali. 'AND during a snowstorm, so we can't even replace them? That's a real jerk move.'

'Add up the clues,' said Tulip. 'If we can't get presents in, they can't get presents out. So the Santa Stealer must still be here.'

'Double Detectives are on the case!' said Ali, looking way too excited. 'Ho-ho-ho!'

'Is she still doing that?' said Mum, looking at Tulip sympathetically. 'Well, I'm glad you munchkins have got a project to keep you busy. I've got a patient to see on the ward: a lovely little boy with an annoying little lump in his brain that I have to sort out.'

'Poor thing. You mean you're reviewing him for an operation?' asked Tulip, glancing at Ali. Mum's neurosurgery operations took hours.

'Ugh, a brain lump! How long is that gonna take you?' asked Ali. Mum looked at her. Ali shrugged and added, 'Or something less self-centred?'

'Sorry, munchkin,' said Mum, kissing Ali's head. 'It'll take as long as it takes. My colleagues can't come to the hospital to take over from me. We're snowed in.'

'It's snow joke,' repeated Tulip sadly. 'Snow problem,' and Mum kissed her too. Then her bleeper went off and she apologetically ran into the ward to answer it.

'So that's another holiday wrecked,' said Ali, slumping in the demolished grotto among all the torn gift wrap and the squashed and broken decorations. 'Hey, there's floor chocolate!'

'Don't eat floor chocolate,' said Tulip. 'Let's find Nan-Nan and tell her we've got to track down some Sinister Present-Stealing Santa.'

'They're probably working together,' grumped Ali. 'Nan-Nan's just a stumble away from working for the dark side.'

Tulip tried to pull Ali up, but ended up falling into

the smooshed grotto herself. Then she caught a flash of red at the end of the corridor. A red robe, a big tummy, a white fluffy beard and a white wig crammed under a red hat, with a jingle bell tinkling jauntily at the end.

The Santa pushed open the double doors, but stopped short on seeing the twins in the smashed grotto.

'Hey, you!' yelled Ali. 'Sinister Santa!' And she leaped up and ran towards him.

The Santa stepped back fearfully and dashed away.

'Get back here, you present-stealer!' Ali shouted.

'Well, running away does make him seem guilty,' said Tulip, getting up to chase Ali chasing Santa.

The Santa wasn't that big at all under the robes and padding, and had pretty quick legs. But Ali managed to catch him at the café, sliding down the banister and cutting off his exit, then ruthlessly knocking a huge potted plant over him.

'Gotcha,' she yelled. She jumped on his chest, and triumphantly picked up a Flake from the floor beside him. 'Floor chocolate!' she said. 'Just like you left at the grotto.'

'Wha—?' Santa started to say, but then Tulip arrived and saw the shocked faces of everyone in the café staring at Ali, sitting on Santa. They all looked pretty appalled

50

that a ten-year-old would want to tackle a sweet old Santa to the ground.

'I think you guys need a bit of context,' Tulip said apologetically to the people in the café.

'Yeah, why aren't they giving me a round of applause?' complained Ali. 'I caught the bad guy.'

There was a slow handclap on the other side of the potted plant.

'Wow, Ali,' said Jay. 'I thought your Nan-Nan was the one who was anti-Christmas. This is a new ho-ho-LOW from you.'

'Are you all right, sir?' said Zac, giving his hand to help the Santa up. 'Get off, Ali, it's not funny. You're so gonna be on the naughty list.'

'I am NOT on the naughty list,' said Ali.

'Of course not, my queen,' said the Santa, standing up. It was Momo, winking at her from above the beard. He gave Ali and Tulip some Flakes from his robes, obviously taken from his ice-cream van.

'I hope you enjoyed our interactive theatrical holiday performance,' Momo said to the café, making a deep bow. Tulip bowed too. Ali shrugged and joined in. 'Come find me in the Festive Grotto outside the Sunshine Ward for treats, and my energetic, most excellent elves will give you some festive goodwill.'

Zac and Jay took Momo's Santa sack and handed out the chocolate to the children in the café. Everyone gave them a cheer.

'So I don't think the Santa who stole all the presents was Momo,' said Tulip, once they were outside the café.

'Well, duh,' said Ali, looking crossly at Momo. 'What are you doing in costume?'

'Your mother messaged me to volunteer, as the hospital Santa was most regrettably missing,' said Momo. 'I have the outfit in the ice-cream van, for festive emergencies, as I am a people person who enjoys spreading goodwill.'

'Why did you run away?' asked Ali.

'You are most terrifying,' explained Momo, reasonably enough. 'And it seemed you had already destroyed the grotto in some sort of anti-Santa protest. I was most fearful for my costume.'

'It wasn't us. We found it like that,' explained Tulip.

Momo nodded sagely. 'Ah. Then I shall tidy it up,' he said decisively. 'The children need their grotto.'

'And we'll find the evil Santa and the stolen presents,' agreed Ali.

'Do you need a hand?' asked Jay. 'We've got nothing to do for a while. Mum's in the chemo chair and Dad's sitting with her.' Jay and Zac's mum had been having treatment for her cancer since the summer.

'Oh,' said Tulip. 'We were wondering why you weren't at school today.'

'It's Mum's last session for a while,' said Zac happily. 'It's gonna be the best Christmas ever. She even hand-loomed all our stockings.'

'That's nice,' said Tulip. 'Our mum has told us we're probably gonna have Christmas here. She's got emergency surgery planned and no cover.'

'Aw, that sucks,' said Jay.

'It really does!' agreed Ali.

Tulip caught Zac and Jay up on what had happened, while Ali wolfed down her Flake.

Zac frowned. 'So, one secretive sinister Santa has trashed the grotto and gone missing?' he said. 'And the presents have been stolen?'

'Yep,' said Ali. 'Thanks for the useless recap. I hate it when people recap.'

'*And* your Nan-Nan is gone,' said Jay.

This was actually news to Ali and Tulip.

'Um, yeah, I suppose she has,' said Tulip. 'Didn't really think about Nan-Nan being gone.'

'How could you NOT think about that?' said Zac. 'We keep telling you to work on your powers of observation.'

'And we keep ignoring everything you say, so this is really on you,' said Ali.

'To be honest, Nan-Nan is always heading off mysteriously,' said Tulip. 'We don't really notice it any more. She's just so Nan-Nan all the time.'

'She won't be interested in this mystery anyway,' said Ali. 'Nan-Nan is anti-Christmas. There's probably a long and sad story from her past that we don't need to hear.'

'So your missing Nan-Nan, who hates Christmas, disappears in a hospital, where the grotto gets mysteriously trashed and all the presents get stolen, along with the tinsel and fairy lights?' said Jay. 'Am I the only one hearing this?'

'Hey, you don't get to accuse our Nan-Nan of random crimes,' said Tulip. 'That's Ali's job.'

'Ho-ho-ho!' yelled a voice behind her.

'Stop it, Ali,' complained Tulip. 'That's getting older than Nan-Nan's leather jacket.' She turned round and saw Ali pointing outside the café.

'Wasn't me,' said Ali, unnecessarily, as suddenly a sea of Santa Claus-types came pouring into the hospital, wearing curly wigs in different colours.

'Do you think Mum messaged every spare Santa in town?' asked Tulip in wonder.

The Santas were spreading around the hospital,

yelling 'Ho-ho-ho!', ringing bells and carrying sacks of small goodies and Christmas crackers.

'It's so magical,' said Zac, his eyes wide. 'The Santas have saved Christmas!'

'How are we meant to find *bad* Santa now?' said Tulip. 'They can just hide in the crowd. There must be eight Santas at least.'

'Two each,' said Ali. 'I like those odds.'

'Let's go,' said Jay to Zac.

They chased after a Santa in a gold curly wig, walking with another in a weave of rippling black curls.

'Ooh, so sorry,' said Zac, pulling off the two Santas' beards while he stumbled accidentally on purpose.

'We've got you, young man,' said the Santas in strident female voices, catching Zac kindly.

'Oh well, you don't seem like the bad guys,' said Jay, looking at the sweet old ladies in the costumes.

'Take exception to that, kid,' said the Santa in the black wig, putting her beard back on. 'We can be as bad as we want.' She winked. 'There's something going down in this hospital. We got called out.'

'You're part of Nan-Nan's SWAT team,' said Ali, running up. 'Agent Golda and Agent Ebony! Why did Nan-Nan call you here?'

The SWAT team, AKA the Senior Water Aerobics

56

Training Team, were Nan-Nan's elite all-female spy team. Tulip and Ali were honorary agents for covert operations.

'She said she was tied up,' said Agent Golda.

'Or wrapped up,' added Agent Ebony.

'Nan-Nan's in trouble,' Tulip said, slapping her forehead. 'That's not just a phrase! We've heard it too many times.'

'Are all these other Santas on the SWAT team?' asked Zac, looking around.

'Seven of us are. But I don't know who that one is,' said Agent Ebony, pointing to a tall skinny Santa. 'None of us have a plain white wig. Too blasé. We like our wigs to have a proper colour pop.'

'After that Santa,' screeched Tulip.

The skinny Santa, who had been meandering casually down the corridor, stepped into a lift just as the girls starting running towards the sliding doors. He gave a loud and deranged cackle of triumph. His brown eyes twinkled with menace behind the half-moon specs and face fur.

'Too late, evil twins! Guess what? Evil wins!' he crowed as the door locked shut and the lift moved upwards.

Tulip turned to Ali. 'Evil wins? Did you hear who that was?'

Jay and Zac joined them, breathless from running.

57

Zac sucked on his blue inhaler. 'Honestly, we don't know why you're even surprised any more,' he said.

'Mad dude in costume with a stupid hat and glasses?' Jay agreed. 'It's ALWAYS him.'

Tulip nodded. 'Not evil wins. But Evelyn!'

She and Ali shook their fists at the lift and said in furious unison: '*Evelyn Sprotland!*'

Evelyn Sprotland, who had tricked their mum for months with his poisoned creepy-sleepy chocolates, because he'd had an unrequited crush on her since they were fourteen. Evelyn Sprotland, who had jealously attacked Momo in his cab and cut the artery behind his knee. Evelyn Sprotland, with an utterly forgettable face, who always managed to escape in a sneaky disguise.

Momo came towards them, back in his own clothes and carrying Ali's gym bag. 'Some most gracious Santa ladies who know your Nan-Nan have relieved me at the grotto,' he said. 'And this ferocious feline was most mightily annoyed when she woke up in the back of my ice-cream van.'

'Ah, Witchy,' said Tulip, hugging the cat. 'Did you have a nice catnap?'

'Never mind that, dumb fluffball,' said Ali. 'Time to hunt a Sprotland!'

She grabbed Witch and pushed her nose towards

Sprotland's lift. Witch hissed, picking up the Sprotland stink. She had always hated him.

The lift came back down, doors opening, to show the empty Santa suit in a fat puddle on the floor.

'He's out of disguise,' said Jay. 'Now he could be anyone. That guy is so bland, he's basically invisible.'

'Not to a black witch cat,' said Tulip with pride, as Witchy ravaged the Santa costume. Picking up the scent and spitting out a mouthful of red fluff, the cat began streaking down the hospital corridor.

'Good Witchy!' yelled Ali, pointing the way. 'Go get that evil Mum-poisoning-Momo-stabbing-present-stealing freak!'

Everyone stared at her in horror, as it looked like she was pointing right at another one of the SWAT Santas, who was sweetly handing out candy canes.

'Something terrible must have happened to that little girl one Christmas,' whispered one of the café customers.

'Oh, honestly!' Ali rolled her eyes. 'You can't spit around here without hitting a hairy dude in costume.'

They chased after the black streaking shape of Witch as she ran right out of the hospital and into the snow.

'Dumb cat, he can't be out here!' shouted Ali.

But then they saw him, face down, with something around his legs. It was the missing tinsel. And the missing fairy lights from the hospital decorations, twinkling with triumph.

'Ouch,' he complained. 'The tiny icicle lights are really spiky!'

'Nan-Nan made a trap in the snow!' laughed Tulip, and she jumped on Sprotland and tied him up, fastening the fairy-lights cord and tinsel firmly with a couple of neat surgical knots. 'Not fairy lights but scary lights! Looks like you got a bad case of tinselitis!'

'We got you, Evelyn!' said Ali, pouring the itching powder out of her pockets over the sprawling villain. Witch scratched and clawed at him crossly. 'You got itchy with Witchy!'

'Girls!' yelled Nan-Nan.

Her voice was muffled. Tulip and Ali looked all around but couldn't see her.

'Dig by the handicapped space!' came the muffled voice again.

And then they ran and started digging, and found Nan-Nan sitting in a neat hole in the snow, wrapped up in gift wrap and tied up with present ribbon – except for a single hand which she must have wriggled free.

'OMG, he caught you and left you in a hole,' said Tulip in horror.

'Nonsense,' said Nan-Nan briskly. 'He might have

caught me and wrapped me up, but I made the ice hole as a practical shelter to keep me warm. Sprotland doesn't have a clue about how old ladies might succumb to hypothermia. It was most comfortable.'

'You're the worst, Ruby,' spat Evelyn towards Nan-Nan, coughing out snow.

'No, you're the worst,' said Ali. 'And my Nan-Nan could have got really sick, you jerk.' She was going to kick him, but Zac pulled her back.

'Why did you do it?' asked Zac mournfully. 'You destroyed the Christmas grotto and stole all the presents!'

'What, they were stolen?' howled Evelyn. 'Noooooo! I DONATED all those presents!'

'You ... *gave* the presents?' asked Jay, confused. 'Aren't you the bad guy?'

'I was the one who stole the presents,' said Nan-Nan proudly. 'I got a tip-off that a very suspicious donor had dropped a load of wrapped boxes off at the children's ward and was lurking around near your mum.'

'They were chocolate!' protested Evelyn.

'They were poison!' said Nan-Nan. 'I tested them. You filled them with your sleeping-sickness serum.'

'I was poisoning the children to save them later! I was going to save their mum's patients! I was going to be her hero!' squealed Evelyn, looking utterly deranged.

'Finally! She was going to be AMAZED by me.'

Mum came out of the hospital, still in her scrubs, munching on a piece of chocolate.

'Noooo, Mum!' said Ali, taking a running leap and swatting the chocolate out of her hand.

Mum looked sadly at the chocolate on the ground. 'That was from Momo,' she said.

'Oh, three-second rule,' said Ali, picking it up and dusting off the snow. Mum took it back.

'So, suddenly there are a lot of Santas in wigs around, spreading festive fun,' Mum said, munching happily. 'Thanks, Mamma,' she added to Nan-Nan. 'I knew you'd sort it out.' She looked curiously at Nan-Nan wrapped up in the ground. 'Are you doing a Houdini trick again? You've not done that since I was little.'

'My dearest! My snow angel!' Evelyn yelled piteously at Mum, wriggling towards her through the snow like a caterpillar. 'I did it for you!'

Mum glanced up from untying Nan-Nan. 'Evelyn?' she said, looking across at him. To be fair to Evelyn, she did look a bit amazed. 'What are you doing lying there wrapped up in fairy lights? That's a really silly way to impress me. You'll catch your death.'

'No worries, Mum. It'll be a lot warmer for him in prison,' said Ali as they heard distant sirens.

She and Tulip and Jay and Zac did a four-way fist-bump, and pulled back with wavy hands.

❄

Later, they were all sitting in the tidied-up grotto, with Momo's ice-cream machine pumping out treats for the patients and their visiting families.

'Ho-ho-ho!' said Ali as she handed over another swirly 99 Flake ice-cream cone.

'Aw,' said Mum, wheeling her brain-surgery patient out of the Paediatrics ward. 'Isn't it nice how Ali's got into the festive season? This young man and I are going for a trip to theatre. See you in six to eight hours.'

'We'll save you some Flakes,' Tulip said to the little boy, who gave her a big grin and a thumbs up.

'Oh well,' said Ali. 'No stockings, no crackers and no proper takeaway.'

'Gotta surprise for you,' said Nan-Nan with a grin. She waved her hand, and Momo appeared with a tray of steaming takeaway cartons and a big bag of Christmas crackers.

'Aw, Nan-Nan,' said Tulip, hugging her.

'A pleasure,' said Nan-Nan. 'I've had fun today. Grinched away poisoned presents, holed up in the snow, tinsel-trapped the bad guy. *Finally*, this is a Christmas I can get on board with.'

'And we brought the stockings,' said Zac. 'They were meant to be a present for you. Mum hand-loomed them, like we said, and Dad helped us fill them with all the unhealthy stuff you like.'

Jay shuddered, holding out the stocking like a bomb. 'It's all empty calories. There's not a single fruit bar with no added sugar, and no carob or anything. It's gross.'

'Aw,' said Ali, diving towards Jay with her hands outstretched and taking her stocking, pulling out the sweet treats. 'THIS is the true spirit of the festive season.'

'What, chocolate?' hazarded Tulip.

'Why am I suddenly super super itchy?' complained Jay, scratching madly under his clothes.

'Pranking Jay,' grinned Ali, hiding the itching powder back in her pockets.

ANNABELLE SAMI

THE
BEAST
OF
BEDLEYWOOD

TOP SECRET

THE VERY MERRY MURDER CLUB

PROPERTY OF THE VERY MERRY MURDER CLUB

THE BEAST OF BEDLEYWOOD

By Annabelle Sami

6.20 P.M. 30TH DECEMBER

Tamsin and Rumi Kamal were grounded. But it kind of wasn't their fault this time. If Harry Brigham hadn't ding-dong-ditched the house of their school's 'police liaison officer', everything would have been fine.

But instead, Tamsin and her older brother were escorted back home by PC Kingsley. He'd even put his uniform back on, despite being in the middle of his dinner. Tamsin felt a knot of worry form in her stomach as they made their way back to the huge tower block where they lived. She closed her eyes and prayed: *Please don't let Mum be home.*

'Why are you dragging *us* back and not Harry?' Rumi grumbled as they waited for the lift to their flat.

67

'Yeah, he got to go home on the bus!' protested Tamsin.

'Because this is the third time I've caught you two messing around this Christmas break,' PC Kingsley retorted. 'If Harry messes up again, I can assure you I'll drag him back to his parents' house too.'

Tamsin and Rumi rolled their eyes at each other. Yeah right.

Harry Brigham would get away with it because his parents were teachers at the school and PC Kingsley knew them. *Harry Brigham* lived in a big house on the nicest road in Bedley. Tamsin and Rumi lived on the eleventh floor of the largest high-rise block of flats in the area. That's why PC Kingsley was bringing them home and not *Harry Brigham*.

The rickety lift arrived and they all stepped in, standing in uncomfortable silence. PC Kingsley was a wide man with a permanently red face. There wasn't much room for Tamsin and Rumi who, though they were only eleven and twelve, were already five foot nine. Everyone always thought they were twins, thanks to their matching thick black hair, golden eyes and dark brown skin.

The lift trundled up all eleven floors and creaked to a halt. The siblings reluctantly stepped out, followed by the police constable who was watching them closely. Tamsin immediately smelled the aroma of onion and

68

garlic sizzling in a pan and groaned. That only meant one thing – their mum was home.

'The one time she isn't working at the hospital,' Rumi groaned.

PC Kingsley knocked on the door of their flat. Three sharp knocks.

'Hello?'

Tamsin watched their mum's face as she opened the door. It went from surprised, to confused, to *volcanic levels of angry*. Her thick black hair was scraped back into a bun and she was in her nurse's uniform with a stained apron tied over the top. Tamsin felt like her mum was always either at work or getting ready to go there.

'Good evening, I'm PC Kingsley. Now I'm afraid I caught your kids misbehaving today ...' He launched into a lengthy account of Tamsin and Rumi's bad behaviour over the past two weeks of the Christmas break. Tamsin thought this was overkill – they hadn't broken any laws! They'd only skateboarded where they weren't meant to ... And Rumi did try and do parkour *inside* the library ... but they hadn't damaged anything!

Once the PC had finished and their mum apologised for the hundredth time, she shut the door with a click, turning around extremely slowly.

'How many times do I have to tell you kids to behave

yourselves?' she boomed, her eyes icy cold. 'You're grounded, both of you! I don't even know how long for. Just go to your room!'

'But, Mum, it's New Year's Eve tomorrow, we were gonna watch the fireworks with the gang,' Rumi protested, his eyes wide and pleading.

'Do I look like I care?' Mum responded.

Tamsin and Rumi shook their heads sadly.

'Exactly, now go to your room.' She turned on her heel and stormed back into the kitchen, muttering angrily as she went.

6.30 P.M. 30TH DECEMBER

'We've messed up big time, Tam,' Rumi sighed, lying on his bed. 'I can't believe PC Kingsley showed us up in front of Mum.'

'Well, it was our fault,' Tamsin said, staring at the ceiling. They shared a room with two single beds on either side, and a balcony at the far wall. Tamsin liked her bedroom, but it was small. That's why they hung around outside. 'I guess we shouldn't have skateboarded outside Sainsbury's either.'

'But where can we skateboard then? They've closed up the skate park. It's not our fault there's nothing to do around here.' Rumi sat up in frustration. 'And Mum's at work all day so we have to make our own fun.'

Tamsin went over to the balcony, staring out into the darkness. It was only 6.30 p.m. but the sky got pitch-black at this time of year. Rumi came and joined her, sitting on one of the garden chairs they'd placed there. The best thing about being eleven storeys up was the view. They could see all the way out across Bedley and even into the larger city beyond. Just behind their building was a small bit of woodland that the locals had managed to save from being tarmacked over. It was only the size of a park, but they'd turned it into a nature reserve with paths to walk through and a central clearing. The locals called it Bedleywood.

Tamsin looked down into the tiny woodland. A black shadow swooped in front of her face and dropped down into the dark trees below.

'Bat!' she said, holding on to the balcony side and looking down into the trees.

'I don't see a bat,' Rumi complained, squinting.

'There!' Tamsin pointed, spotting another shadow dart across her view. 'Next to that man . . . What's he doing?'

From up high like this, Tamsin and Rumi could see the figure of a man, making his way towards the small, circular clearing in the middle of the woods. A few eager neighbours were already setting off fireworks a day early

and if it wasn't for the extra light they provided, he would have been hidden.

'Whatever he's doing, he's doing it in the dark, in the woods. So, it's probably illegal,' Rumi said knowingly.

'How do you know that?' Tamsin challenged him.

'Well, I am one year older than you, Tam. That makes me both older *and* wiser.'

Tamsin scoffed. 'You're still only twelve!'

'OK then, genius, what do you think he's doing? *Bat watching*?' Rumi whacked her arm.

Tamsin watched the man intently, following his path through the dense canopy.

'He's heading to the fairy tree,' she said, pointing to the clearing where the large, twisted shadow of a tree loomed.

'Don't call it that,' Rumi scoffed. 'We're not babies any more. It's a yew tree.'

Tamsin, Rumi and their friends had played by the old yew tree as kids. It was wide and tall, with a trunk that looked like lots of small, thin trees merged into one. They twisted, creating gaps and crevices that the kids decided fairies lived in.

'Fairy tree . . . next you'll tell me that man's the Beast of Bedleywood!' Rumi laughed.

'Shut it, Rumi,' Tamsin sniped. 'I know the Beast isn't real.' Her eyes followed the man, who was now in the clearing by the yew tree.

The council had put up notices in their block a few weeks ago. The old yew tree was being torn down because of 'safety concerns'. Someone at the council had apparently only just realised that yew trees were poisonous. So the council put up a big metal fence around the tree and a couple of diggers had been parked there for a week now.

'I don't see why they have to get rid of it,' Tamsin said quietly, still watching the man who was circling the metal fence.

'Yeah. Just put a sign up or something. "Poisonous, do not munch on bark",' Rumi chuckled. 'Mum said it's the first step to them building more houses on the woodland.'

The small figure of the man hopped over the metal fence and slung a backpack off his shoulders.

Tamsin's eyes went wide. 'He's definitely not a worker, right?'

The man moved closer to one of the diggers and crouched down on the floor, but it was impossible to see what he was doing. They were too far away.

Suddenly, their bedroom door was flung open.

'Right. I'm off to work. It's my last night shift.' Their mum had miraculously changed from her pyjamas into her nurse's uniform in the space of ten minutes.

74

'OK, Mum. Have a good shift,' Tamsin called from the balcony.

'Dinner is on the stove.' Their mum paused, taking a few steps into the room to look closer at Tamsin and Rumi. 'And I don't need to tell you that if you leave this room, I will hang you from the washing line outside, right?'

From the blazing look in her eye, Tamsin knew her mum wasn't joking.

'We know, Mum,' Rumi replied. 'And we're sorry.'

She stared them down for another few seconds before she left the bedroom. They heard the front door slam a few seconds later.

'Mum is the scariest person I've ever met,' Rumi gulped.

'Tell me about it,' Tamsin sighed. 'Wait, the man!'

She whirled back around to look into the clearing but the man had gone.

'Now we'll never know what he was up to . . .' she sighed, deflated.

'Unless we went down and looked,' Rumi said quietly.

Tamsin whacked him. 'You heard Mum!'

Rumi held his arms up defensively, walking back into their room. 'I know, I know. I'm just saying, you're the one who loves the fairy tree.'

Tamsin followed him in, shutting the balcony doors behind her. '*Yew tree.* I don't love it. I just think it's sad they're demolishing it. And I want to know what that man was doing.'

But Rumi had already gone into the kitchen to find the food their mum had cooked. With a rumble of her stomach, Tamsin decided to do the same.

7.30 P.M. 30TH DECEMBER

They both ate dinner in silence, mostly playing on their phones. But even endless scrolling on social media couldn't get Tamsin's mind off the man and the yew tree.

'OK, so . . . say I dropped something off the balcony,' Tamsin started. 'We'd have to go and get it right? And we wouldn't be sneaking out. We'd just be going to get the thing.'

Rumi looked up from his phone and smiled. 'I see . . . and what exactly have you dropped off the balcony?'

Tamsin got up from the table and rushed into their room with Rumi following. She grabbed the old blue blanket from her bed and headed out on to the balcony. With one swish, she dropped the blanket over the side. It drifted down on the breeze and into the woods below.

'Oh no, my blanket!' Tamsin pulled a shocked face.

'Don't worry, little sister, I will come with you and protect you as you retrieve your blanket,' Rumi said in a rehearsed, robotic manner.

Tamsin knew what they were doing was wrong, but she also knew there was no way she was going to sleep that night without investigating the yew tree. Even as her mind mulled it over, her body was putting on a big coat, grabbing a torch and her keys.

Before she knew it, they were out the door.

8.15 P.M. 30TH DECEMBER

It was really dark now and the air was biting cold. Tamsin felt it pinch her cheeks as soon as they left the side entrance of their tower block and walked around to the back of the building. The woods started almost immediately behind the flats, beyond the car park.

Silently, the siblings walked towards the path that cut into the thick of the trees. Tamsin walked beside Rumi, shining the torch ahead. As soon as they entered the woods, the noise of the city was muffled by the trees, and the quiet dark engulfed them.

'Maybe this was a bad idea,' Tamsin said in a low voice.

77

'Are you afraid the Beast is going to jump out and grab you?' Rumi grabbed Tamsin and shook her.

'No!' she countered, shaking him off. 'Let's just check out the tree, get my blanket and head inside.'

They trudged on through the small woods, heading for the clearing.

'The Beast of Bedleywood is a hideous creature, with sharp teeth and huge claws . . .' Rumi recited in a dramatic voice. 'It guards the fairy tree, and anyone who dares go near it will hear its terrifying *screech* before –'

'Stop it, Rumi!'

Rumi laughed loudly, his breath coming out as mist in the freezing air.

They reached the clearing and headed to the metal fences.

'And how exactly are we supposed to get over?' Rumi complained.

'We're tall. What, can't you jump?' Tamsin smirked. She hopped and caught on to the railing, swinging herself over in a swift movement.

As Rumi struggled his way over the fence, Tamsin started looking around on the ground by the diggers. What was the man doing here, this late at night? He'd definitely been getting something out of his backpack, but everything around the digger just looked like rubbish.

78

'Empty crisp packets . . . ew, a mouldy banana!' Tamsin complained. 'People need to take better care of the woods.'

'Yeah. But one man's trash is another man's treasure,' said Rumi, holding up a red bead bracelet covered in mud. He tried to force it on her wrist.

'Ugh, stop it, Rumi!' Tamsin pushed him away and walked around to the other side of the digger. Something caught her eye. A red-and-yellow label, torn around the edges and discarded on the floor by the large wheel. She turned the torchlight on it and read:

Danger: Fire or projection hazard
Keep away from heat
Explo—

'It's a warning label! I wonder what it's from?' Tamsin's mind whirred with the possibilities. 'It's definitely a clue. I bet that last word says explosion.'

'Or . . . it's a piece of rubbish like everything else on the ground here,' Rumi scoffed. He opened up a sandwich bag and got out a mini sausage roll, munching loudly. Tamsin knew he'd come along purely out of boredom, rather than wanting to figure out what the man was doing. But now she'd found this scrap of paper, something seemed fishy to her. She just *knew* it.

All of a sudden, there was a rustle of leaves and a twig snapped somewhere in the bushes.

Tamsin and Rumi froze, sausage roll held in mid-air.

'What –'

'Shh,' Tamsin instructed, listening intently. Her breath had quickened. Was someone watching them?

A low snarl emitted from the bushes, followed by a rumbling growl. From the light of her torch, Tamsin could see Rumi's eyes wide with fear.

Someone wasn't watching them. Some*thing* was.

Tamsin turned off her torch and motioned to Rumi to follow her. Quietly, *slowly*, they picked their way over to the fence. The growling was moving through the bushes now, crunching twigs and leaves underfoot.

'We need to hop the fence again,' Tamsin whispered. 'As soon as we're over, run as fast as you can back home.'

'What about the blanket?' Rumi whispered to her, looking over his shoulder in the direction of the snarling.

'We'll get it tomorrow. Now come on.'

Once they were both perched on top of the fence, Rumi counted down in whispers.

'One . . . two . . . three. Go!'

They jumped down and ran as hard as they could. Tamsin heard the clang of metal followed by the strangest noise ever. It was like a howl mixed with a baby's wail or an ambulance siren. Whatever it was, it struck fear right in her heart and she and Rumi ran all the way back to their block of flats without looking back.

8 A.M. 31ST DECEMBER

New Year's Eve. After a restless night's sleep, Tamsin was eating cereal on the sofa when Rumi walked in.

'Rumi,' Tamsin began. 'What was that last night?'

They hadn't spoken a word after getting back from the woods. But before she went to bed, Tamsin safely tucked the label she'd found away in her backpack, certain that it meant something.

'A fox,' Rumi said quickly, not looking at Tamsin. 'Probably a mum guarding her babies.'

'It was *not* a fox,' Tamsin said, banging her cereal bowl down on the table. 'We've heard foxes before. That was like a ... like a ...'

'A Beast?' Rumi looked at her intently. 'Let me get this right – not only do you think you're uncovering some kind of mystery with the man at the yew tree, now you think the Beast is real too? You're more immature than I thought, little sis.'

81

Rumi sauntered out of the room, chuckling to himself. Tamsin felt the anger rising in her stomach. She knew Rumi was pretending not to be scared. But that *wasn't* a fox. And that label wasn't just rubbish either. But what could she do? She was grounded on New Year's Eve, and there was no way she was leaving the flat with her mum around.

1.30 P.M. 31ST DECEMBER

It was well after 1 p.m. by the time their mum appeared in the doorway, hair plaited and shiny with coconut oil, shopping bags at the ready.

'You're both coming with me to the market this afternoon. It's the first New Year's Eve I'm not working for a while so we're going to have a *nice family dinner*. Together.'

The market was surprisingly busy for New Year's Eve, with shoppers braving the frosty air to stock up on groceries before the long weekend. Tamsin's mum headed straight for the fruit and veg stall and started picking up tomatoes, checking their skins as she went.

The market was always noisy with men yelling about fresh fish, bargain bananas and SAUSAGESSSSS at all times. But today it was even louder. There was a group of around ten people standing behind a table handing out leaflets to passers-by. A banner was hung from the table that stated 'Save the Yew Tree!'.

'Look, Tam. You wanna join your mates and save the fairy tree?' Rumi giggled, pointing at the group.

Tamsin rolled her eyes and ignored him, scanning the crowd. PC Kingsley was there too, standing imposingly next to a man in a fancy suit. Fancy Suit Man was having an argument with one of the protestors – a blonde guy wearing a tie-dye shirt and ripped jeans.

'You should've listened to our demands, Councillor Reed!' the blonde guy spat. 'You don't care about the public.'

Tamsin narrowed her eyes. So, Fancy Suit Man was a councillor.

'I can assure you, Dylan, that we care *very much* about the public,' Councillor Reed replied, patting his forehead with a handkerchief. 'But the yew tree is unsafe and toxic to children!'

'LIES!' a young man who was standing on a box shouted through a megaphone. He had blonde hair too, like Dylan, which he'd tried to twist into locs, and was wearing a beige kurta. He'd even wrapped red prayer beads around his wrist.

'Doesn't he realise those are two very different looks?' Rumi snorted, looking in the man's direction.

'And cultures. Neither of which he comes from.' It always annoyed Tamsin and her mum when people wore Indian clothes for fashion, without knowing where they came from.

The young man started yelling through the megaphone again. 'All Councillor Reed cares about is money! He is killing the earth!'

The man jumped down from the box and approached Councillor Reed angrily. PC Kingsley stepped forward too, coming face to face with Megaphone Guy. It looked like something was about to kick off.

Dylan, who appeared to be the leader of the group, quickly intervened, pulling back the young man with the megaphone. 'All right, Guy, that's enough.'

'Sorry, Dylan. You know how passionate I get,' Guy replied, looking at Dylan wide-eyed. 'I'd do anything for you – and the cause, of course.'

'I know.' Dylan patted Guy's shoulder. 'Just go hand out some leaflets, please.'

Guy saluted at Dylan before grabbing a pile of leaflets and aggressively handing them out.

Councillor Reed cleared his throat. 'I'm sorry, but the yew tree will be torn down tomorrow morning. That is final.'

'The yew tree is over a thousand years old! How could you?' Dylan shouted.

84

'Yeah, how could you?' Guy chipped in, looking to Dylan for approval.

But Councillor Reed was already walking away, followed closely by PC Kingsley.

Tamsin felt herself starting to walk towards the protestors, eager to ask them some questions. This Dylan guy was their leader and he didn't seem pleased about the tree being torn down. Could he have been who they saw sneaking around the tree in the dark?

'Stop right there.' Tamsin heard her mum's voice behind her and she instantly whirled around. 'I don't want you going anywhere near that group. You're already in enough trouble as it is.'

Then she grabbed Tamsin and Rumi by the arm and led them to the fishmonger's.

'Wait here and *do not move*,' she said, before joining the long queue inside the shop. Tamsin and Rumi hung to the side of the door, sulking.

'What are you two doing? Hanging out with your *mum*?' sneered a voice that grated on Tamsin's nerves.

Harry Brigham.

He waltzed up to them with another boy from Rumi's class in tow. They were both wearing huge puffa jackets with the hoods done up around their faces.

'We're grounded, thanks to *you*.' Rumi crossed his

arms over his chest.

'Just leave us alone, Harry. We don't want to speak to you.' Tamsin copied her brother, crossing her arms and giving her sternest expression.

Harry tutted at them. 'Come on, I thought we were mates! Anyway, I thought you might wanna see what we're doing tonight.'

Harry unzipped his puffa and flashed a black-and-gold package at them. Tamsin's eyes grew wide.

'Fireworks? What are you thinking, Harry, that's dangerous.' Rumi tried to grab the fireworks but Harry pulled away.

'We're just gonna have fun,' Harry smirked, looking at his friend who nodded in agreement.

But Tamsin had spotted something else. A warning label on the firework packet in red and yellow, just like the one she'd picked up near the yew tree. Anger grew inside her and she rushed towards Harry.

'I know what you've done, I saw you!' she raged, unsure of why she was so angry.

'Whoa!' Harry looked genuinely concerned and zipped his puffa back up tightly.

'We used to play by that tree together as kids, all of us! Now you want to blow it up for a laugh?' Tamsin put her hands on Harry's puffa and shook him.

86

'I – I don't know what you're on about,' Harry stammered, holding his hands up.

'Tamsin Kamal, what on earth are you doing?'

Tamsin froze. Her mum had caught her, again. She dropped her hands to her side and Harry and his friend promptly ran away. Tamsin turned to see her mum, bag of fish in hand and face like thunder. This was not good.

'Is Harry the one who played pranks on the policeman's house?' Mum asked, her face serious.

Tamsin and Rumi both nodded silently.

'Then I didn't see that. But don't you *dare* let me catch you acting out in public again.'

She marched off ahead, leaving Tamsin and Rumi staring at each other in astonishment. They kept well behind her the whole walk home.

11.50 P.M. 31ST DECEMBER

Sitting on the folding chairs on their balcony, Tamsin and Rumi gazed at the night sky. Soon it would be filled with hundreds of colourful explosions stretching all the way to the horizon. They'd had their *'nice family dinner'* at 8 p.m. and now Mum was watching the New Year's Eve concert on TV.

'Do you really think it was Harry Brigham messing about with fireworks down by the yew tree?' Rumi said, looking straight ahead.

'Maybe . . . I mean the fireworks he was carrying had the same warning label as the one I found by the digger.'

'But Harry only does bad stuff so he can brag about it. That's why he came to show off to us at the market.'

Tamsin sighed. Rumi was right. It just didn't make sense for Harry to be the mystery man in the woods. Her anger at him getting them in trouble with PC Kingsley had clouded her judgement earlier.

'Five minutes until the fireworks!' Mum shouted from the other room.

Tamsin got up and rummaged through her backpack to find the label. She looked at it hard, wishing some clue would jump out at her.

'You still kept that, huh?' Rumi said as Tamsin came back out on to the balcony, label in hand.

'Ten . . . nine . . . eight . . . seven . . . six . . .' Mum started counting from the other room.

'Well, guess what? I still kept *this* –' Rumi pulled out a red beaded bracelet from his hoodie pocket.

Tamsin inhaled sharply.

'Let me see that!' she cried, grabbing the bracelet. It wasn't wooden after all, but a mala prayer bracelet made of red seeds. Just like the one she had seen earlier on –

'Happy New Year!' Mum burst into their room, her hands in the air.

Outside, a cacophony of booms and bangs lit the night sky in multicoloured sparkles.

'Happy New Year, Mum,' Rumi said, giving her a hug.

'Happy New Year,' Tamsin murmured, staring at the beads in her hand.

Mum pulled Tamsin into the hug too, before rushing back into the living room to hear her favourite singer crooning 'Auld Lang Syne'.

As soon as she'd left, Tamsin turned to Rumi.

'I know who the man in the woods was!' she whispered, careful not to let her mum overhear. 'It was Guy.'

'Which guy?' Rumi asked, confused.

'No. *Guy*. The guy from the protest group who was desperate to impress the leader, Dylan.' Tamsin shook the beads in her hand. 'He was wearing some of these; he probably has hundreds of them. Don't you remember what he said to Dylan. "I'd do anything for you." Maybe Guy's planted explosives on the site in protest.'

'OK, stop saying guy.' Rumi rubbed his face with his hands. 'So what do you want to do? Tell PC Kingsley, who already hates us? Oh, or tell Mum that we snuck out the house when we were grounded?'

Tamsin's shoulders drooped. Rumi was right. There was nothing she could do without getting them into trouble. But what if explosives had been planted somewhere near the yew tree? It was being demolished tomorrow morning! They could be triggered and hurt someone.

'What can we do, Rumi?' Tamsin asked in a small voice.

Rumi shrugged and yawned. 'Nothing. Go to sleep and hope nothing bad happens tomorrow.'

The fireworks were dying down outside and the cold breeze was blowing into their room from the open balcony doors. Tamsin shivered and shut them, resolving to go to bed and put it out of her mind. But as the doors closed she was sure she heard the sound of a faint howl in the distance.

6 A.M. IST JANUARY

Tamsin had awful dreams all night. Of snarling beasts with huge paws and sharp claws chasing her through a forest filled with vines. Finally, she woke up, having made a decision. She walked over to Rumi's bed and shook him awake.

'We have to tell Mum,' she said firmly.

Rumi blinked open his eyes. 'What? Why?'

'Because . . . it's the right thing to do. And even though it means admitting we snuck out, we could be saving someone's life!' Tamsin waited patiently, staring at her brother until finally he gave in.

'Ugh, fine. But you have to tell Mum it was all your idea and that I just went to protect you.'

'Deal.' Tamsin stood up to go but Rumi caught her arm.

'Maybe wait an hour or so. You don't want her to be sleepy *and* angry.' He shuddered at the thought.

7.05 A.M. 1ST JANUARY

Tamsin crept into Mum's room, a hot cup of coffee in hand. As soon as Rumi shut the door behind them, Mum shot up in bed.

'What? What's wrong?' she garbled, half asleep.

'Uh, nothing, Mum. Well, something. But first, have some coffee.'

As Tamsin told the story of the mystery man and the potential Beast, Mum's face again went through a curious range of emotions: confused, furious, shocked and, finally, concerned. When she'd finished speaking, Tamsin wasn't sure how Mum was going to respond, but she braced herself.

Mum took three big glugs of coffee and banged the mug down on the bedside table. Then she swung her legs out of bed and stood up, searching for clothes in her wardrobe.

'Firstly, I am absolutely furious with you both,and you are grounded for an extra week,' she said, strangely calm. 'Secondly, Rumi, how dare you let your sister head into danger like that?'

'But I –' Rumi protested, falling silent as Mum raised her hand.

'And Tamsin, throwing your blanket out of the window? Ridiculous! Now, both of you, go and get some clothes on. Quickly.'

Tamsin and Rumi stood looking at Mum, shocked.

'Where are we going?' Tamsin said quietly.

Mum sighed dramatically. 'To stop the workmen from getting blown up!'

7.20 A.M. 1ST JANUARY

Tamsin and Rumi walked quickly down the small path that led into the woods, following Mum, who paced ahead.

'To the right, Mum. In the clearing,' Tamsin called.

Her stomach was fizzing uneasily with nerves and she knew Rumi felt the same. He'd been chewing his nails the whole ride down in the lift.

In the clearing, about six workmen in hard hats and high-vis vests were gathered inside the metal fences. The protest group surrounded them, shouting slogans as police prevented them from scaling the fence. PC Kingsley and Councillor Reed were among the group, giving statements to two news reporters who had come to cover the commotion.

Tamsin searched the protest group and spotted Guy, standing close to Dylan, still wearing his mala beads. Good, she thought, holding the bracelet they'd found as evidence in her pocket. I can compare them to prove my case.

Mum approached PC Kingsley and Councillor Reed, her head held high. 'Excuse me, but I believe there is a significant hazard that needs your attention. My children found an explosives label at this site and believe they could be planted somewhere around here in protest.'

PC Kingsley stopped his press interview to look at the label Mum was holding in her hand. Then he glanced up at Tamsin and Rumi.

'Not you two again.' He rolled his eyes.

That really got Mum's attention. 'My children may not

93

be the best-behaved kids in the world, but they don't lie. They found this label here and I think with all the upset around this tree being torn down, it's worth investigating. Don't you?'

PC Kingsley looked down at Mum, who was about a foot shorter than he was. She glared back up at him, not backing down.

He called over to Tamsin. 'All right then. Where did you find this label?'

'Over there.' Tamsin pointed. 'By the digger.'

PC Kingsley fought through the small crowd of protestors and whispered something to one of the workmen through the fence. Tamsin watched as the workman wandered over to the digger, gave it a once-over and then, finally, dropped to his hands and knees, and looked underneath the vehicle. All of a sudden he shot up, white-faced, and called out: 'There's something here! It looks like a plastic bottle filled with powder! Right next to the engine.'

'A bomb?' exclaimed another workman.

At this, the crowd fell silent.

'Right, everyone vacate to the edge of the clearing, now,' PC Kingsley instructed.

The three other police officers pushed everyone back, reporting the incident through their walkie-talkies.

As PC Kingsley inspected the underside of the digger himself, Tamsin kept her eye on Guy, who had gone bright red and was talking in hushed tones with Dylan. She noticed he was slowly backing away from the group, obscuring himself in the trees behind. He was trying to escape! It was now or never . . .

'HEY! Stop him!' she shouted, pointing at Guy. '*He* planted the explosives. He's trying to get away!'

Guy froze and Tamsin thought he might give up but in a split second he had bolted, running into the thick of the woods. Two of the policemen gave chase and Tamsin tried to run too, but Rumi held her back.

'They'll catch him, Tam, leave it.'

PC Kingsley approached Tamsin and she felt Mum grip her hand tightly.

'And how exactly do you know he's guilty?' the policeman huffed, looking at her dubiously. Dylan, the leader of the protestors, had come over too, shock all over his face.

'Well, apart from the fact that he's just run away . . .' Tamsin started but Mum squeezed her hand tight. 'I found this at the crime scene when we found the label. It's the same as the one that Guy wears. I'm sure you could find his DNA on it . . . or something. Plus we heard him at the rally saying "I'd do anything" *for you.*' Tamsin looked at

Dylan pointedly. 'You didn't know he was planning this?'

Dylan shook his head quickly. 'I only preach peaceful protest.'

Just then a commotion from the crowd revealed Guy, in handcuffs, being brought back by the two officers. He was panting and crying at the same time. When he saw Dylan looking at him, he suddenly cried out –

'I did it for us! For the tree! Deeds not words!'

'Shut up, Guy,' Dylan yelled, his eyes bulging out of his head.

So much for peaceful, Tamsin thought.

PC Kingsley turned to leave as the police were calling for everyone to evacuate the area, but Mum cleared her throat.

'PC Kingsley? Aren't you going to thank my children?' she asked.

The policeman turned, half laughing. 'Why on earth would I do that?'

'They did the right thing. They came forward and solved a case for you.'

PC Kingsley said nothing for a while. Then he turned and muttered, 'Stay out of trouble,' before walking away.

Mum bit her lip and turned to Tamsin and Rumi. 'Well done, kids. But you're still grounded.'

As they walked the path through the woods back to

96

their block of flats, Tamsin felt lighter. Everything was out in the open now. She also felt absolutely exhausted. But something caught her eye. A flash of white in the bushes to the left. Followed by a crunch of leaves and a weird low wail. The hairs on her arms stood on end.

'What was that?' Rumi said, munching on something. Only *he* would bring a sausage roll out with him for an emergency intervention.

The wail came again, though this time it sounded more like a howl. Tamsin's skin crawled.

'It's the Beast of Bedleywood,' she cried. 'It's real!'

The flash of white came crashing out of the bushes, leaping in front of them to reveal –

'A husky!' their mum exclaimed.

The dog stood in front of them, Tamsin's old blanket held in its mouth, before running up to Rumi and sitting in front of him.

'The Beast of Bedleywood carries a blankie!' Rumi wiped tears from his eyes as he laughed out loud.

'He must have smelled your sausage roll before as well! He's hungry.' Tamsin couldn't help but laugh too, from tiredness, confusion and nerves. Everything was just too strange and it was still only 8 a.m. on New Year's Day.

'It looks abandoned,' Mum said, examining the husky's fur. 'Poor thing. We should take it to the vet.'

Mum was full of surprises today it seemed. She picked up Tamsin's old blanket and wrapped it around the husky's torso.

'Mum . . . if we take it to the vet and it doesn't have an owner . . .' Tamsin ventured.

'Can we keep it?' the siblings said together.

Mum straightened up and dusted off her trousers. 'You know what . . . maybe a responsibility is exactly what you two need. I know I'm not around much and at least he would keep you occupied.' She stroked the dog's head and he licked her hand. 'He reminds me of the dog we had when I was little . . . OK, *if* he doesn't have an owner, you can keep him. But he'll be *your* responsibility.'

Tamsin and Rumi cheered, which made the dog howl loudly again.

'Why do huskies sound so *beastly*?' Tamsin asked as they continued their walk down the lane.

'I don't know,' her brother said, feeding the dog bits of sausage roll to get him to follow them. 'But that would be a good name. Beast!'

Mum chuckled as she walked ahead. 'Beast. I like that.'

7TH JANUARY
BEDLEYLIFE.BLOG.UK POSTED AT 3.30 P.M.

The New Year brought a host of surprises for two young Bedley residents this year. Not only did they stop the detonation of a homemade bomb using firework explosives, they also solved the mystery of the Beast of Bedleywood.

The bomb was placed in protest at the demolition of the old yew tree and was planned to be ignited by the heat of the digger engine once switched on.

Yesterday, Councillor Reed issued a statement that the yew tree *will not* be torn down stating his 'concern over a lack of green spaces for local residents'. Though many claim it was instead the work of the Save the Yew Tree pressure group that got the councillor to back down.

As for the so-called Beast of Bedleywood, it was in fact a stray husky dog who has retired to protect the eleventh floor of the nearby tower block with the two teenage heroes.

And they say nothing happens around here.

Read a full account of these events in the blogposts above!

Happy New Year!

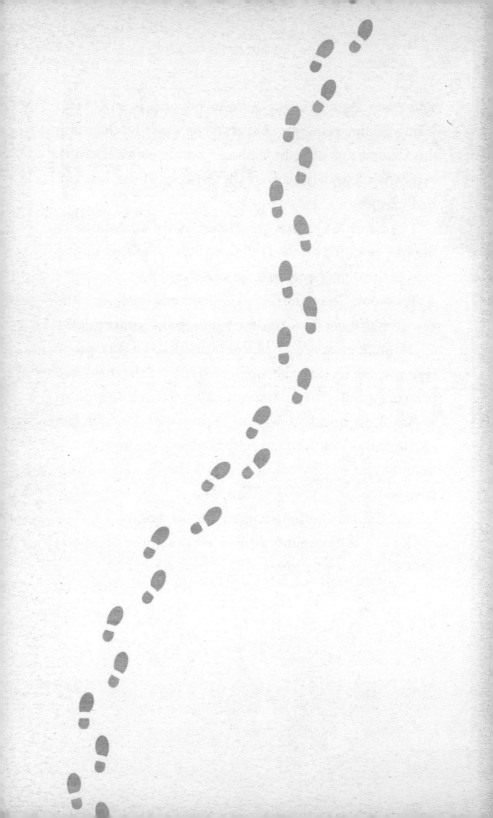

ABIOLA BELLO

THE CHRISTMAS HEIST

TOP SECRET

THE VERY MERRY MURDER CLUB

PROPERTY OF THE VERY MERRY MURDER CLUB

THE CHRISTMAS HEIST

By Abiola Bello

THE STEAL

Twelve-year-old Roe smiled at the audience who were on their feet applauding. Roe was breathing hard and sweating but she felt so alive when she was dancing onstage with Masquerade dance group. Her parents were waving manically as they recorded the performance for her elderly grandparents. All the dance group's hard work and rehearsing after school had been worth it.

The Masquerade crew walked off the stage, congratulating each other, when Roe heard someone say, 'Wow, you were rubbish.'

It was Sabrina Martez, from Pledge dance group. Sabrina, alongside her dance crew, looked Masquerade up and down like they were a bad smell. Pledge had won the Drop That

Beat competition two years in a row but today they had stumbled during their routine. Thankfully Masquerade had been flawless and Roe knew that this was their year.

'Ignore her,' Roe's twin Roman said.

'Loved your trip onstage,' Roe sang and Sabrina glared at her.

Masquerade's choreographer Jada, a budding music producer who'd just celebrated her eighteenth birthday, beckoned them over to the side of the stage, where the judges were making their final decision.

'And the winner is ... MASQUERADE!'

Masquerade jumped up and down, hugging each other. Jada beckoned them to follow her on to the stage to receive their trophy. The bright lights made Jada's brown skin glow.

The stage manager suddenly ran onstage and whispered something to Randy J, the presenter. Roe didn't miss the way Randy J's mouth dropped open as he eyed Masquerade before turning his back on them, hiding the trophy from view.

'What's happening?' Maria, a petite olive-skinned girl asked.

Jada smiled. 'I'm sure it's fine.'

But it wasn't.

Randy J, who had just been smiling at them, now looked uncomfortable. He held the mic to his lips and said, 'I'm

104

sorry to tell you, ladies and gentlemen, but Masquerade have been disqualified.'

Roe shook her head, convinced she had misheard.

'What?' Jada cried.

'No!' Roman yelled.

Even the audience jumped to their feet shouting. And that's when Roe realised that Masquerade were definitely out of the competition.

'Please excuse us, I need to speak to Masquerade offstage.' Randy J gestured at the dance crew to follow him.

Roe followed in a daze, with the rest of her teammates dragging their heels behind her. They were joined by Ada Adams, the creator of the show, and Ayo Bakare, Pledge's choreographer.

'Ayo, what are you doing here?' Jada asked but Ayo didn't respond.

Ada took off her glasses and massaged her forehead. 'I'm sorry, Jada, but we have to take all allegations seriously.'

'Allegations?' Jada gasped, her hazel eyes wide. 'I don't understand.'

Ayo spoke now. 'You deliberately ruined our music because you knew we would win *again*. There was a track added so my crew messed up. That's your fault. Masquerade don't deserve to win. We do.'

'That's completely untrue!' Jada never raised her voice,

105

which was one of the reasons why Roe loved learning from her. 'Ada, Ayo asked me to change one of the soundtracks that I made for them. I also created four other crews' sets. Ayo signed it off so I don't know what version that was, but it wasn't mine.'

Ayo scoffed. 'You're lying. I didn't sign off anything and I asked you to email it to the technician.'

'But I wanted to double-check! So I sent it back to your email, then you signed it off and said *you* would send it in.'

'No, I didn't,' Ayo responded.

'YES, YOU DID!' Jada roared and everyone jumped. Jada shook her head as if realising where she was. She turned to Roe and the Masquerade crew. 'I'm sorry for yelling, guys. Can you go back to the dressing room while I sort this out, please?'

Roe didn't want to leave. Nothing was making sense. But the presenter shooed them to go.

'I don't get it,' Roe whispered to Roman as they trudged back to the dressing room. 'Jada's the most honest person ever. There's no way she messed up the soundtrack. Why would Ayo say that?'

'I know, right? It doesn't make sense,' Roman said, brushing back his black locs from his face.

After a tense wait for Roe and the crew, Jada came back

to the dressing room not too long after with tears in her eyes. 'I'm sorry, guys, but they believe Pledge and have given them our trophy.'

Everyone began to shout over each other. This was finally their year to win and Pledge had ruined it.

August, an Italian-Jamaican girl with waist-length curly hair said, 'They're going to love rubbing it in our faces at the Christmas Showcase next week.'

Finally the crew sank into shocked silence.

Roe tied her long locs into a bun as she stood up. 'I'll be back.'

Roman went to go with her but Roe shook her head. Her heart was pounding. She could only imagine how confused her parents were. There was no way she could show the video to her grandparents now. She wanted to scream at how unfair it was and cry because of how hard they had worked. She left the room and leaned on the door, breathing hard.

She was going to find out the truth.

THE PLAN

Roe and Roman's parents tried to cheer them up on the way home and reassured them that they'd still had an amazing performance. But Roe could barely respond. She ate her dinner in silence. When their parents finally left Roe and Roman alone in the kitchen, Roe said, 'We have to get that trophy back.'

'How? It's not like we can just walk into Pledge's dressing room and take it back,' Roman said as he ate a cookie from the counter.

Roe paused, a smile spreading across her face as an idea formed. 'You genius! That's exactly what we're going to do.'

Roman chocked on his biscuit. 'I was actually joking, Monroe!'

Roman only called her by her full name when he was annoyed with her. But Roe wasn't listening. She was already formulating a plan.

The next day, Roe had sent an emergency text to the rest of the crew and they all gathered in Roe and Roman's living room. Their mother loved to bake and had left them a plate of gingerbread men to eat, which the crew had almost devoured in one go.

'What's the big emergency? I've got homework to finish,' blonde-haired Justin asked. He was the tallest of the group and his long skinny legs stretched out in front of him.

Roe stood up. 'Pledge stole our trophy yesterday and it's just not adding up. Jada has done soundtracks for years and never messes up. There's no way she would ruin our chances of winning.'

'I agree,' August said, playing with her curls. 'But how can we prove it?'

'At the next show, we sneak into their dressing room while they're performing and take our trophy back,' Roe said.

'Err, no we don't,' Roman said. He ate another gingerbread biscuit and Roe wanted to throw the plate at him.

'It was your idea!' Roe argued.

'And I said I was joking!'

'Why would they have the trophy with them?' Maria asked.

'Do you remember when Pledge won Drop that Beat last year?' Roe said, pacing back and forth around the room. 'Every show after that, they brought that trophy just to show off and take pictures for social media. I'm hoping they'll do the same thing.'

'But it's not like we can then show it off and tell everyone we have the trophy back,' Maria said.

'It's the principle!' Roe said. 'It's ours.'

Quiet, red-haired David was in deep thought. 'We

would need another trophy,' he said.

'David!' Maria squealed. 'You can't be serious.'

'Maybe we can order a cheap replica online?' Justin suggested.

Roe sighed. 'I've already looked. But first we need to figure out how to buy it.'

'I've got some Christmas money from my nonna. We can use that,' August offered.

The whole crew stared at her and August blushed.

'Roman, say something!' Maria jumped to her feet, red in the face. 'We will get in so much trouble and won't be able to dance ever again.'

Roman shrugged. 'Only if we get caught.'

Roe caught his eye and he winked at her. She grinned. Her brother always came through in the end.

'Have you all lost your minds? There is still no proof that the music wasn't messed up. It's not like we have Jada's lap–' Maria stopped abruptly.

'The laptop!' Roe said and Maria put her head in her hands. 'We need to look through it to find the emails between her and Ayo.'

'Gingerbread man?' Roman asked, offering the plate to Maria. She only tutted in response.

110

THE EVIDENCE

Roe went into rehearsals the next day with a new energy – despite Maria still insisting that it was a terrible idea.

'Hey, guys,' Jada said, sadly. 'I know last weekend didn't go the way we planned, but we've still got one last show before Christmas so let's smash it.'

Roe cheered with everyone else as she glanced at the laptop that was hooked up to the speakers.

'OK, spread out. Let's run the set,' Jada said.

They got into partners. Roe was opposite David. They were a great match as they were a similar height.

The winner of Drop That Beat would get to perform their winning set at the Christmas Showcase, while everyone else had to perform a Christmas-themed dance. Thankfully, as back-up in case they lost, Jada had taught Masquerade a Christmas dance based around a Christmas masquerade ball, as that was the crew name. She'd even got her seamstress mum to create ball gowns and suits for them that *looked* hard to dance in but were actually really spacious. Halfway through the dance, they would take the outfits off so they could backflip safely in tracksuits.

Jada handed them each a mask. Roe stroked her pink one, which had fake jewels that sparkled as they caught the light. It looked amazing against her dark brown skin.

'Let's practise with the masks on,' suggested Jada.

Roe caught herself in the mirror. The mask covered most of her face. It was perfect. Jada pressed play and they went through the routine. The waltz part was fine because David was leading, but then it turned into hip-hop and the beats got faster, while the dance involved floor work and multiple flips. It became hard for Roe to see through her mask, and she stumbled as she landed her backflip. Once they were done, they were all breathless and Jada was clapping.

'It looks great,' Jada promised with a smile. 'I know the masks will take a while to get used to. Let's run it again.'

Jada walked to her laptop. But before she had a chance to press play, August shouted, 'Oh no!'

She had spilled her water bottle over the floor.

'OK, no one move. Let me grab some tissues,' Jada said, hurrying out of the room.

'Quick,' August hissed.

Roe hurried to the laptop and minimised iTunes. Then she clicked on Google Mail. Thankfully Jada's email was automatically saved on her laptop.

'Anything?' Roman asked appearing beside her.

'One sec.' Roe typed in AYO and a page of emails came up. She quickly read each one but there was nothing there.

112

'Maybe she deleted them,' Roman said, glancing at the door. 'Check the bin.'

Roe clicked on the trash can, where there were loads of soundtracks with familiar dance crew names.

Roman tapped on the screen. 'There,' he said excitedly.

Roe saw a file labelled *Pledge: Drop That Beat*. She emailed it to herself before sending it back to trash.

'Quick, she's coming,' Maria called from the door.

Roe quickly logged out and maximised iTunes. She ran back to her position just as Jada came into the room.

'Right, let's clean this mess up.'

Roe sighed, relieved. Jada hadn't suspected a thing.

THE TECH GUY

As soon as rehearsal was done, the Masquerade crew stood around the corner from the studio so Jada wouldn't see them hovering. They were supposed to go straight home as soon as dance was over, but even though it was freezing, Roe wanted them to listen to the soundtrack she'd just emailed herself.

She pressed play on her phone. By the end it was clear that it was the exact same soundtrack Pledge had used at the show.

Roe felt a wave of frustration. 'Jada said this wasn't the version signed off, but this is the only Pledge, Drop That Beat soundtrack that I could find.'

'If Jada is innocent, how can we prove it?' Justin asked.

Everyone fell silent. August's reindeer Christmas jumper kept lighting up every few seconds, distracting them.

'Sorry,' August said, quickly zipping up her jacket. 'Now what?'

'What if we just hear the music?' Roman said slowly.

Roe rolled her eyes. Honestly! 'We just did,' she replied, even slower.

Roman glared at her. 'I meant, what if we hear the version sent in for the comp?'

Roe frowned. Sometimes this twin telepathy worked, but right now she had no clue what Roman was getting at.

Roman now looked eager. 'Haven't you noticed that the organisers for the Drop That Beat competition and the Christmas Showcase always use the same tech guy? The one with the big arms and cool tattoos.'

'So?' Roe said. Roman flicked her on the head. 'Ow!'

'He'll have a laptop that will have everyone's music –' Roman said.

'Oh! Because Jada said Ayo agreed to send in the soundtrack. So we can compare this version with what

Ayo emailed in!' Roe finished off.

Roman high-fived her. 'Took you a minute, didn't it?' he teased and Roe stuck her tongue out at him.

'OK, so how are we going to get into the tech guy's laptop without getting caught?' David asked with his hands under his armpits, in an attempt to keep them warm.

'We'll have to do it during the Christmas Showcase tech run, because we'll be stuck in our dressing room once the show starts,' Maria reminded them.

August put her arm around Maria. 'Finally, she's joined the heist!'

Maria shrugged August off. 'I haven't! I'm just pointing out all the flaws in your ridiculous plan.'

'Wait, I've got it,' Roe said and everyone looked at her. 'We can get back our trophy *and* prove that Jada is innocent. But it's going to take all of us working together.' She stared at Maria. 'Even you. Are you in or out?'

Maria went bright red with all eyes on her. She eventually huffed, 'Fine!'

They huddled up and listened as Roe broke down the plan.

THE TROPHY

It was the last rehearsal before the show. The set looked amazing, the masks were manageable and Roe landed all of her flips. Once they had finished, Roe and her friends gathered around the corner of the studio and August took out the fake gold trophy. Roe held up the cheap knock-off and grinned.

David used a magnifying glass to look over it. 'It looks . . . perfect,' he finally announced.

'I told you.' August smiled smugly.

'Luckily it's not engraved with their names,' Roe said. 'OK. The only way we'll get away with this is if we have an alibi. So remember, we have to switch the trophies during our dance.'

'Let's work out where there are breaks in the music,' Justin suggested. 'Then we can work out who will do the switch.'

Roman played their Christmas Showcase soundtrack through his phone. 'Oh, here's a good opportunity,' he said in excitement. 'This is when the voiceover comes on. The lights will go down and we change. Is everyone in the routine after this?'

Everyone nodded apart from Roe.

'I'm not,' she said.

'Are you fine with doing the switch?' Roman asked.

Roe nodded. She was more than fine; she was excited. Pledge were going to get a taste of their own medicine.

THE HEIST

It was the day of the Christmas Dance Showcase and Masquerade arrived at the theatre. It was decorated with tinsel and a six-foot-tall Christmas tree stood in the corner. The stage had pretty fairy lights draped above it.

As soon as Roe sat down, Pledge walked in. Ayo was waving at everyone, carrying a black sports bag with a white P on the front. Roe spotted a gleam of gold in Ayo's bag. The trophy! She looked at the rest of her friends and saw they had spotted it too. Jada huffed when she noticed it. Justin silently got up and left the auditorium. The plan was in motion.

'Here you go.'

Jada handed out the running order. Roe grinned when she saw it. It was just what she thought would happen. As the winners of the previous competition, Pledge were ending the show and Masquerade were on just before them.

'Can I listen to the soundtrack?' Maria asked and Jada

117

handed over her phone.

'Where's Justin?' Jada asked looking around.

'Toilet,' they all said.

One of the runners tapped Jada. It was time for tech – their technical rehearsal.

'Maria, are you done practising with the music?' Jada asked with her hand out. 'I need my phone.'

'One sec,' Maria called with her back to Jada.

Roe's phone pinged with a message from Jada's phone with Masquerade's updated soundtrack. Roe nodded at Maria and watched as she turned off the phone before showing Jada.

'Your battery died,' Maria said with a shrug.

Jada groaned. 'You're joking! I need my phone for tech. It's got our music on it . . .'

'I've got the music,' said Roe, jumping up. 'Remember? You sent it to me.'

Jada frowned. 'I did?'

'Yeah, and I'll take it to the tech booth. I'll be quick,' Roe said.

'Can I go to the toilet?' Roman asked.

Jada sighed loudly. 'Be quick, please! And why isn't Justin back?'

'I'll get him,' Roman said.

Roe and Roman ran out of the auditorium together.

Then Roman followed Roe to the stairs that led to the technician's booth.

'I can probably distract him for a few minutes but make sure to take out the aux lead *before* you play the music,' Roman warned. 'Or everyone will hear you playing Pledge's soundtrack.'

Roe stopped mid-walk, suddenly nervous. 'How will I know which lead to take out?'

Roman waved his hand. 'It's easy. It should say "aux" on it.'

'Got it!'

They reached the top of the stairs. At the end of the corridor they could see Justin talking to the tech guy. If anyone could talk about music and gadgets, it was Justin. The tech guy's back was to them, so Roe was able to sneak easily into his booth. Roman stood guard ready to distract the tech guy once he made his way back.

Apart from the light from the laptop, the technician's booth was dim so it didn't distract from the lighting onstage. Roe walked carefully across the wires on the floor. The soundtracks were lined up in a playlist on the laptop. Most choreographers emailed their music in prior, but Jada preferred to use her phone, ever since one of the shows had said Masquerade's email file was corrupted and they almost hadn't been able to perform.

Roe could see Pledge's set at the bottom of the playlist labelled *Pledge: Drop That Beat 2*.

Roe noted the time of the soundtrack. It was the same length as the one she'd emailed herself from Jada's laptop. She typed in *Drop That Beat competition* into the tech guy's emails.

'Oh hi, I'm lost . . .'

Roman's voice sounded like he was walking away from her. That meant he was trying to stop the tech guy from coming into the booth! Time was running out.

Attached was *Pledge: Drop That Beat* soundtrack, but this version was longer at three minutes and fifteen seconds. Jada's version was three minutes and *five* seconds – a ten second difference.

Had Pledge sent in the wrong soundtrack for Drop That Beat? Drop That Beat didn't allow crews to do a tech run so maybe that's why Pledge didn't realise it was the wrong version?

Roe squinted at the name signed at the bottom of the email – and gasped.

It wasn't Ayo or Jada that had sent in the music. It was Sabrina!

Roe wanted to hear the soundtrack for herself and record the longer version on her phone. But there were so many colourful wires tangled up and she couldn't find

120

the aux lead! Her hands started sweating.

That was it! A picture to show that Sabrina had been the one to email the doctored music and the clear time difference in the soundtracks! Roe could show it to the organisers and clear Jada's name. She quickly took out her phone – which slipped, crashing noisily to the floor.

'What was that?' the tech guy asked outside the booth.

'What was what?' Roman said in a high-pitched voice that only happened when he was nervous.

Roe snatched up her phone and took the pictures of Sabrina's email and the time difference on the tracks. But because her hands were shaking, they came out blurry.

'Come on, come on . . . ' she muttered to herself.

She tried again. This time the pictures were clear as day. She emailed them to Roman.

'Listen, kid, I've got to go – what are you doing?'

Roe jumped. The tech guy was standing in the door of the booth, staring at her, with Roman nervously behind him.

'Oh, hi! We need to play Masquerade's soundtrack from my phone, please,' Roe said, smiling sweetly.

The technician grunted. He pulled out the aux lead from the pile of wires and handed it to Roe to plug it in her phone.

'Close call,' Roman whispered in Roe's ear. His phone pinged and he peered at it. 'Got your email.'

They ran down the steps and stood on the stage in

position for tech.

'All OK?' Jada asked.

'Perfect,' Roe said, and her friends let out a sigh of relief.

'Roe, when you come back onstage you need to be on the opposite side, so now you have to run around the back of the stage and change,' Jada explained.

'Oh, OK,' Said Roe. But inside she was panicking. The plan was to run to the dressing room, which was just off the stage, and swap the trophies. But now running around the stage was going to take up their precious time.

'Practise it when we run it with the music,' Jada instructed. 'OK, now, Justin . . .'

'Now what?' Roman asked Roe.

Roe threw her hands in the air. 'I have no clue!'

The soundtrack played and they ran through the dance with the lighting. Running around the back of the stage took too long – there was no way Roe could run to the dressing room and be back on stage in time. Pledge were waiting in the wings for their turn to tech, and Ayo was there holding the black bag with the trophy.

And Roe had another great idea.

'What if Ayo stays out in the foyer?' Maria asked.

The Masquerade crew were seated in the dressing room.

122

The show had sold out, so unless Ayo had bought a ticket for the show, he would have to watch it on the TV in the foyer, or from the wings if there was space. Jada had bought a ticket.

'I'm not sure,' Roe said truthfully. 'But I *think* Ayo's watching from the wings. If he still has that bag with the trophy in it, I can swap the trophies then.'

'We just need to make sure Ayo is definitely there before we perform,' Roman said.

'If he's in the foyer the whole time we can kiss goodbye to getting our trophy back.'

Roe swallowed. She prayed that their plan would work.

They got dressed for their performance. Roe kept dropping her mask, Roman stepped on Maria's dress almost tearing it, August nervously bit her nails. Jada noticed.

'Come on, guys, it's the last dance of the year,' Jada said. 'Make sure you have FUN!'

But Masquerade's nerves weren't about the dance. They were about not getting their trophy back and clearing Jada's name.

Jada left them to go sit in the audience. Masquerade were in the wings. They were on next, followed by Pledge with the finale. David gave Roe a thumbs up from the opposite side of the stage. That meant that the fake trophy was by the stage in a bag. But then Justin appeared next to David, shaking his head.

'Ayo,' he mouthed.

Roe's heart dropped. That meant Ayo wasn't in the wings. Their whole plan depended on him being there, not out watching in the foyer!

The group before Masquerade had just started their performance. Everyone's dance was between three to four minutes long. If she ran . . .

'I'll be right back,' Roe said to August, who was next to her.

'Roe!' August called but – Roe was already running.

Dancers were walking through the corridor towards the stage. They watched Roe, amused as she ran past in her puffy pink Masquerade ball gown.

The foyer was noisy and packed with choreographers who didn't have a ticket. Roe scanned the crowd and spotted Ayo with a drink and the black bag with a white P on the front.

'Excuse me,' Roe said as she attempted to squeeze through in her big dress. She almost froze when she spotted Jada heading into the auditorium, holding a drink. If Jada saw her, she would question her on why she wasn't in the wings and Roe wouldn't have a clue what to say. Roe quickly walked to Ayo and tapped him on the arm.

'Hello?' Ayo said uncertainly.

Roe opened her mouth. Nothing came out. She hadn't planned this at all.

Ayo frowned at her. 'Are you OK?'

Roe said the first thing that came into her head. 'Sabrina's looking for you. She's in the wings.'

'Is she all right?' Ayo said in concern.

Roe shook her head. *Come on, come on!*

Ayo downed his drink and placed it on the table next to him. Roe turned back towards the stage. She looked over her shoulder to see Ayo was following her with the bag. Grinning, Roe broke into a run. She got back to the wings, breathless – and just in time. The previous dance group on stage was bowing.

'You had me losing my mind!' August said. 'Is he here?'

Across the stage, Ayo had just appeared in the wings. He placed his bag on top of another black bag, on a chair tucked just behind the curtains, before heading towards Sabrina. Roe watched as Sabrina shook her head at whatever Ayo said. He couldn't leave now – he couldn't!

She saw Ayo look at the stage. He didn't move. Roe felt dizzy with relief. He was going to watch the show.

The lights went down as the previous group came offstage and Masquerade walked on. Roe took a deep breath. They were so close!

The lights came up and the music started. Roe and David began the waltz, with Roe following David's basic box step. A hip-hop beat interrupted the classical music and the audience roared with delight as Masquerade began to dance the energetic choreography.

The lights faded to black and the voiceover filled the auditorium. Seizing her chance, Roe sprinted off the stage. Her mask made it challenging to see anything in the dim light, but thankfully everyone was in the wings by the front of the stage, so she didn't bump into anyone.

Roe felt around for David's bag in the dark and pulled out the fake gold trophy. The chair with Ayo's bag was in front of her, but she felt too conspicuous in her pink sparkly dress to approach it. Instead of changing at the back of the stage as planned, she pulled off her dress and threw down her mask. Now she was in all black, and completely blended in. She hurried to Ayo's bag and zipped it open . . . but it was empty!

No!

Thirty seconds left. The lights came back onstage and Masquerade began to dance. They were now dressed in all black, their costumes left on the side of the stage.

With the lights back on, Roe noticed this black bag didn't have the white P on it but there was another black bag on the floor by the side of the chair – it must have fallen off.

126

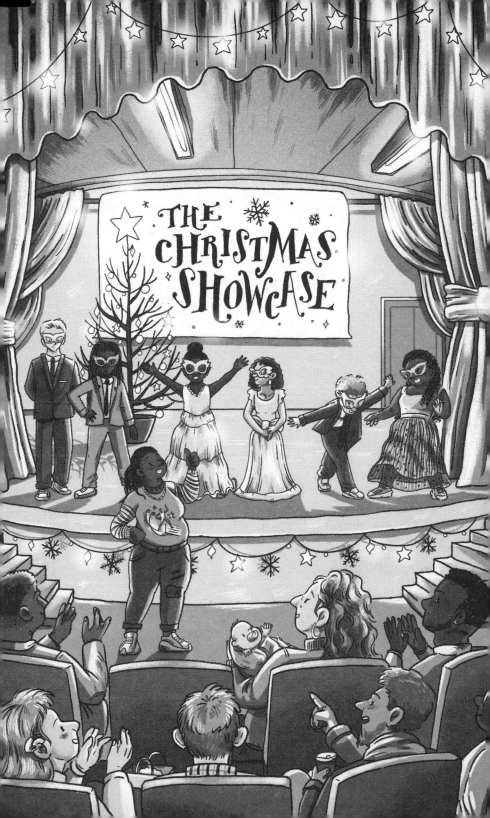

THE CHRISTMAS SHOWCASE

She quickly looked to her right, to see Pledge hypnotised by Masquerade's dancing. No one was paying attention to her. She opened the bag and there it was. *Their* gold trophy!

Roe quickly made the swap and held the real trophy close to her. Then she grabbed her pink dress and mask, and ran around the stage, tucked the trophy into the dress, flung everything down next to the other ballroom costumes and backflipped on to the stage . . . just in time for her cue.

Roman caught her eye. She winked at him.

They had done it!

Masquerade ended with their breakdance routine and they took a bow to a roar of applause before hurrying off the stage. They grabbed their clothes, masks and the trophy (hidden in Roe's dress) and went to the dressing room.

'Look at it!' Roe whooped. She held up the trophy and it glistened under the lights.

'I can't believe this actually worked.' Maria hugged her. 'Well done, Roe!'

'Quick! Hide it in Jada's bag before she comes,' Justin said.

Jada was heading to the airport straight after the show to stay with her dad for Christmas, and her suitcase was in Masquerade's dressing room. Roe tucked the trophy inside, underneath a beach towel. Roe wished she could see Jada's face when she saw the trophy!

As soon as they had changed back into their normal clothes, they waited for Jada. At last, their choreographer came into the dressing room with a massive smile on her face.

'That was brilliant, guys!' she exclaimed.

'We have something to show you,' Roe said stepping forward. 'We knew you didn't mess up their music and we found proof – Roman?'

Roman took out his phone. Jada peered at it.

'Sabrina signed it off and sent in the wrong music and Ayo blamed *me*?' Jada's eyes hardened. 'Oh, I'm emailing this to the organisers.'

Someone knocked on the door and Jada opened it. Ayo was on the other side of it with his fist poised as if he was just about to knock again, holding the black bag with the fake trophy inside it.

'Be cool,' Roe muttered to her friends from the side of her mouth.

'Ayo,' Jada said frostily.

Ayo grinned. 'Oh, I just wanted to say no hard feelings for the music and stuff.'

'I'm sure that will be resolved sooner than you think,' Jada said.

Ayo narrowed his eyes. 'What do you mean by that?'

Jada shrugged.

'Oh,' Ayo added. 'One of your dancers said Sabrina asked for me, but she didn't.'

'That was me,' Roe said, putting up her hand. 'Sorry, I must have misheard.'

Before Ayo could respond, Jada said, 'I have a plane to catch. Come on, guys.'

Masquerade grabbed their stuff and followed their choreographer and her suitcase out of the dressing room. Roe eyed Ayo's black bag and looked at Ayo, who was staring at her.

'Merry Christmas,' Roe said.

THE DAY AFTER

Colourful lights flashed and Christmas music blared from the speakers. Roe, Roman, David, August, Justin and Maria stumbled out of the bumper cars, laughing. Every year they came to the Christmas fair with their parents, who were currently sitting by the outdoor heaters.

'Chips, stat!' Justin said.

'I'm starving,' August said, clutching her stomach to emphasise her point.

Roe couldn't wait to eat cheesy chips smothered in

ketchup. The thought of it made her stomach grumble loudly.

'Chip stand!' she said, pointing in front of her.

The crew ran towards the stand, pushing each other, trying to get into the line first.

Roe breathlessly ordered a portion for her and Roman to share. Once everyone had their food, they walked around the fair to try and find the next ride to go on. Roe kept bumping into strangers as she walked with her head down eating the chips, occasionally hitting Roman's hand away so she could have more.

Everyone was in the Christmas spirit. Roe and Roman were even wearing the same Christmas jumper.

Roman suddenly nudged Roe. She looked up from her food.

Sabrina from Pledge was storming over.

Drop That Beat had issued a public apology on their social media to Masquerade and declared them winners. Sabrina confessed that she had accidently sent in the wrong version of Pledge's soundtrack and she didn't realise until the music was played at the competition. As an extra sorry, Drop That Beat were going to gift them a new trophy engraved with their name.

Roe grinned, showing all of her teeth as Sabrina zoomed in on her.

'Monroe!' Sabrina snarled. 'I know it was you! You gave us a fake trophy and I can tell by that stupid smile on your face that I'm right.'

Roe grinned harder. 'I'm just happy to see you, Sabs.'

'You're a big fat liar!' Sabrina screeched.

'Whoa, calm down.' Roman stepped forward. 'Why would you think we replaced your trophy?'

'Because we had to give the trophy back, only to find it was a cheap knock-off,' hissed Sabrina. 'The organisers accused us of replacing it so we could keep the original. Now they want us to pay towards your new one! We had the trophy during the show. I swear you took it . . .'

Roe laughed. 'We were dancing so how could we have done it?'

'Don't you owe us an apology?' August asked, with her hands on her hips. 'This is all your fault.'

'I didn't mean to send the wrong soundtrack. Jada created our soundtrack but Ayo wanted to remove a track. When she sent it over, I was already on Pledge's emails and downloaded it. I thought I sent the right version over for Drop That Beat. The soundtrack we used at the Christmas Showcase was the correct one,' Sabrina explained.

'Still waiting on that apology!' August said.

Sabrina went bright red before she turned on her heel

132

and left. Once she was out of sight everyone burst out laughing apart from Maria.

'Do you think she saw us?' she asked, biting her lip.

'No way, we were flawless.' Roe popped a chip into her mouth. 'I told you it would work.'

'That explains why you couldn't find Jada's soundtrack in her email. It wasn't under Ayo. It was under Pledge,' Roman said.

Justin scoffed. 'I bet she sent the wrong version on purpose 'cause she knew it was our time to win.'

All of their phones buzzed at the same time. Roe reached for hers first and held it up so that they all could see.

Jada had sent a group message with a picture of her on the beach holding the trophy. The message said:

I don't even know how this happened but look what I found! Now we'll have two trophies. This is the best Christmas gift ever x

PATRICE LAWRENCE

COOL FOR CATS

TOP SECRET

THE VERY MERRY MURDER CLUB

PROPERTY OF THE VERY MERRY MURDER CLUB

COOL FOR CATS

By Patrice Lawrence

My aunty's cat is called The Hammer. It's bothering Ulric so bad. Sometimes my baby brother's like a fox that's found a Chicken Spot wing that's still got more meat than bone. He's holding on tight to this and he ain't gonna let go.

'*The* Hammer,' he says.

'Yeah.'

'Like a cat Avenger.'

'What?'

He pushes back his beanie like he's giving his brain extra room to think. 'If it's got a "the" it's special. Like *The* Hulk.'

'Black Panther hasn't got a "the". Nor Green Lantern.'

'They're two words. And they don't begin with an "h".'

'Sometimes Avengers just call him Hulk,' I say. 'Maybe

the cat's The Hammer because he's got a long face.'

'And a handle?'

We look at each other and laugh. Our breath puffs out like alien poison. We're on our way to feed a cat we've never met before. The Hammer is Aunty Maria's cat but she isn't a blood aunty. Mum met her outside the posh Whole Foods on Church Street. They saw the price of the organic mangoes at the same time and made the same sound. They ended up having a conversation about how many mango trees they could buy in Trinidad or Guyana for the price of that one Alphonso.

It's supposed to be Mum who's doing the cat feeding, while Aunty Maria spends Christmas with her parents in Trinidad. But Mum's got lessons to plan over the holidays. She's a teaching assistant at Ulric's school, but when my grandma died last year she was all stressed out about wasting her life. She wants to train to be a real teacher so she's been doing loads of extra work.

Our older sister Melody's taken over cat duty while Mum's working, but it was nearly midday and she hadn't left her room. Me and Ulric didn't want The Hammer to starve so I swiped Aunty Maria's keys from the shelf over the radiator in the hallway and told Mum that me and Ulric would take care of it.

And, I'm gonna be truthful here, Melody says that

138

Aunty Maria's house is a bit weird. So of course me and Ulric want to see it.

Aunty Maria lives about a twenty-minute walk away. It's easy for Mum because it's between our flat and Ulric's school. He usually has to wait outside while Mum dashes the cat food into the bowl. He reckons it's like Mr Magorium's Wonder Emporium inside, full of magical toys. I think that Aunty Maria didn't have time for a proper tidy and feels too much shame to let anyone go inside, apart from Mum. (Mum knows that Melody wouldn't notice any mess. She says that Melody's legs bend at special angles so she can step over all the clothes on her bedroom floor.)

We cut round the back of the charity shop and through the small alleyway between Guys camping shop and God's Help hairdresser's. The alleyway doesn't smell good. It's like whoever passes through can't bear to carry their rubbish a few metres to put it in the bin. Or wait until they reach a proper toilet to pee. I hold my breath until we come out the other end.

And that's when the wind hits me. Me and Mum watched Simone Biles win her golds in the Rio de Janeiro Olympics. Mum had asked, 'Evie, don't you wish you could do that?' Nah. I don't. My body won't move that way, but this wind disagrees. It's pushing for a backbend.

I grab the wall. Ulric staggers into me. I catch him.

'Is it always like this?' I ask him.

'Yeah. Mum says it's a wind tunnel.'

'I believe her.'

'A wind tunnel is when there's a building with a square edge and . . .'

'Let's go feed The Hammer.'

I push away from the wall, taking my little brother with me. We turn into the street where Aunty Maria lives. It's not really a street, more a back road where people stash their wheelie bins and abandon their bruk-up bikes. There are fences on either side with gates. I feel a bit jealous that the folks here have got back gardens. Me and Ulric and Melody all got to play in our local park. It was all right, especially when they bougied up the playground. But imagine having your own garden . . .

Ulric tries to push open the back gate. I'm kinda surprised. I thought it would be bolted from the inside. He says the bolt's busted so it's just wedged to make it look locked. We need both our shoulders and after one big push we tumble through. If I was Simon Biles I would have added mid-air splits and a side flip.

Ulric points. 'Mum didn't leave it like that.'

Aunty Maria's back door is open. Not wide open, but you can see it's not shut. It's like when you slam a door

140

so hard it bounces open again. (Melody was into that for a while when Mum grounded her every time a teacher phoned up to complain about her big eyelashes or bronzer. Then I think she got bored of being angry. She's only shouted at me twice over the Christmas holidays.)

Ulric trots towards the open door. It's a wooden door with a glass panel in the top half. There's a curtain drawn across it. There's curtains across the two small windows either side too.

Melody keeps telling me I've got middle-child syndrome. I looked it up on Wikipedia and they don't reckon it's a real thing. But Melody says you can't believe everything you read on the internet. It's real. And I'm it. Apparently, I'm jealous of Ulric because he's taken my place as the youngest and furious with Melody for getting privileges that I don't. How *can* I be jealous of Ulric if right now I'm running after him?

'Wait!' I yell.

He turns around.

'I'm the oldest one here!' I puff. 'I should go first.'

'It's only the utility room,' Ulric says.

'What does that do?'

'It's for the washing machine and stuff.'

'The washing machine's got its own room?' I didn't even have my own room until last summer when we finally got moved to a new flat.

'Look!' Ulric's crouched by the step up to the door. 'It's glitter!'

'Maybe the washing machine had a party,' I say.

Ulric flares his nose at me, pushes past and walks right in. But –

There could be a knife-wielding murderer hiding round the corner.

There could be a booby trap with a tripwire and explosives.

There could be a dead body that's booby-trapped because it was the murderer.

'Ulric!'

His face reappears around the door. 'Man, you gotta see this.'

I walk into the house. The utility room opens into a kitchen-dining-room-den thing. It's kinda weird that there's a separate room for laundry but not for cooking. I can't see a TV, but there's a projector on the table facing a blank wall. No laptop, though. Then I see it. So you remember when I said that Aunty Maria doesn't want no visitors apart from Mum because she might have gone light on the tidying? Well, maybe I was speaking truth.

I can't see no floor neither. It's covered in pizza boxes and Coke cans. I tread on a foil bag that tells me it used to

142

have dough balls inside. The way my foot squelches, it's still partly occupied. I almost make a joke about hungry party washing machines, but it wouldn't be funny. This kind of mess isn't funny any time. I know, because Mum used to clean up people's houses before she was a TA. She got called in after parties and she'd go into detail about the nasty stuff she found. She hated doing it but she could fit the hours around our school.

I only met Aunty Maria a couple of times, but she didn't look like the type of person who lives off Domino's. Ulric picks up a box. There's a slice still left inside it. I know he's supposed to be growing, but the boy's already had breakfast.

'Ulric! Don't even think of it!'

'I'm not! You know I don't like ham and pineapple! But don't you see?'

I see Aunty's turning her front room into a Domino's waste heap.

'It's not mouldy,' Ulric says.

'Maybe Aunty tells them to hold the mould.'

'No! It means it wasn't hers. It's from after she went on holiday.'

'Folks broke in and ordered pizza?'

Ulric replaces the box gently on the floor. 'They must have.'

There's hard knocks on the front door. We both stand there. More knocks.

'Could be the cat,' I say. 'Maybe that's how he got his name.'

Ulric sighs. 'Cats can't make fists, Evie. Are you gonna open it?'

'I better.'

Are you gonna use your posh voice?'

'I don't have a posh voice.'

Ulric sniggers. I plod upstairs. Aunty Maria lives in one of those weird houses where the back's a different level from the front. The stairs are painted bright white and I can't see no dust or stains. There's coat hooks in a line on the hallway wall with one coat on each hook, no lumpy bundle of jackets and hoodies like our place. Beneath it is a shelf full of shoes. I spot some high-top Converse. A blue pair and a sparkly pair. Maybe that's where the glitter on her steps comes from.

The doorbell rings with more hard knocking. I try and open the front door. It doesn't budge.

'You have to unlock it,' Ulric says.

'I know.'

'You didn't, because you tried to –'

I take the keys out of my pocket. Ulric watches as it takes me three attempts to find the right one. Finally!

144

Success! The woman on the doorstep looks Somali. She's got eyeliner wings so perfect they could be printed on by computer. Once I took one of Melody's eyeliners from her mega make-up bag and had a go on my own face. I ended up looking like I had four eyebrows and two of them were under my eye. The woman's lipstick is dark blue, like she's been exploring Melody's make-up too.

The woman stares at us. 'Is Maria back?'

'I'm afraid not.' Posh voice! I really do have a posh door-voice! 'Aunty Maria won't be back from Trinidad until Friday.'

'Trinidad?' The woman raises her eyebrows. 'She borrowed my puffer jacket. My sister climbed a mountain in that.' She shrugs. 'And who are you?'

'I'm Evangeline. Ulric and I are here to feed The Hammer. Our mum usually does it, but she's working.'

The woman nods. 'I've seen her. I live there.' She points to a house across the road. 'I'm just checking things are OK. Especially after the police came last night.'

'The police?'

Me and Ulric say it together.

'The noise.' The woman shakes her head slowly. 'Maria isn't a party girl. She never has been. So last night . . . loud music, fast food delivered . . . Someone called the police.'

Someone. You can't live in our family without knowing

a guilty look when you see one.

'What happened when the police came?' I ask.

'Nothing. I reckon whoever was here made a quick escape out the back. Is there anything taken?'

'I don't know,' I say. 'They did leave a mess, though. My brother and I are about to commence cleaning.'

Commence cleaning. Ulric sniggers again.

'Well, don't the use vacuum cleaner. The poor cat hates loud noises. That's why I . . . er . . . someone called the police. Have you seen The Hammer today?'

Ulric and I look at each other. Um. Not yet.

'Well, you better check he's OK. It would break Maria's heart to lose another one.'

'We will,' I say. 'Thank you.' I close the door.

'I hope they didn't scare The Hammer away,' Ulric says.

'Shall we check upstairs?'

Ulric and me head up. We have a quick look in the bathroom halfway, then right at the top it's the bedrooms, two looking over the front and another one at the back. I try the handle of one of the front bedrooms. A part of me wishes it was locked. Entering without permission feels rude. Melody has me well-trained.

The door opens easily and I stare in from the hallway. The room's the same size as Ulric's, with a work desk, a

146

bookshelf, a map of an island on the wall and windmills. Windmills? There's a big basket full of the kids' plastic windmills you get in the pound shop. The shelves are loaded with models of the other kind of windmills, the ones that used to make flour. They're all sizes and made out of different stuff – wooden ones, plastic ones and even one that's a big glass bulb with blades inside it. I want to go and take a closer look but my way's blocked by a giant electric fan. It's the type they have in underground stations so staff don't have to clear too many fainted people off the escalators.

'Maybe Aunty Maria's the Avenger,' I say. 'Not The Hammer. And this is where she does her genetic modifying.'

Of course I'm kinda joking, but what if the other room is full-on Tony Stark, with glass cases full of flying suits and alien weaponry? I squint at the books. They're all about science. The only name I recognise is William Kamkwamba. He's an inventor from Malawi. We did an assembly about him in primary school.

'The Hammer definitely isn't in here,' I say.

I close the door and Ulric tries the next one.

'Locked,' he says.

I'm still holding the keys in my hand.

Ulric points at them. 'Hey! Look, Evie!'

147

I examine my hand and the keys closely. There are spots of silver glitter. We nod knowingly at each other.

'And ham and pineapple pizza,' he says.

So that's that mystery solved. Now we've just got to find The Hammer. I unlock the second door and Ulric pushes down on the handle.

'Man,' we say together. We didn't see this coming. And I don't mean a flying Iron Man suit hitting us in the face neither.

There are two metal clothes rails. No suits, flying ones or otherwise. The rails are jammed full of summer clothes, dresses and skirts and shorts. The shoe rail is packed with sandals and sliders. It's The Chamber of Clothes You're Gonna Take On Holiday to Trinidad, but Aunty Maria's locked them up like they've committed a crime.

Ulric's shuffling through the dresses, lifting up the hems and looking underneath.

'Ulric? That's a bit weird.'

'The Hammer could be in here somewhere. Maybe he misses Aunty Maria.'

'Cats don't have no loyalty,' I say. 'Let's try the last room.'

I lock the door again in case any of those shorts are planning an escape.

I try the handle of the back bedroom. A part of me

148

wishes it was locked too because this can only be Aunty Maria's room. The door opens – a bed, wardrobes, shelves, nothing unusual. There's a painting above her bed of a cat. It's a bit like the cheesy ones you get in charity shops.

Ulric makes sucky noises that he swears cats can understand. If The Hammer *can* understand, he's holding back on the meows.

'I'll check under the bed,' Ulric says.

I should stop him because that just seems rude. But it would be even ruder if Aunty Maria found a The Hammer skeleton beneath her mattress. Ulric takes my phone and shines the torch below. He stands up again and shakes his head.

Now I'm getting bubbles in my stomach. What if The Hammer really has disappeared? It's not our fault, but it feels like it is if we're the ones who discover it. Ulric's already marching back downstairs. I catch up with him by the front door.

'Are we gonna ask the neighbours to check their sheds?' I ask him.

'What about in here?'

It's the first-floor front room. (Or the ground-floor front room if you come in the front.)

I open the door just a tiny bit and a comet made of fur and whiskers shoots out and blasts down the stairs.

We follow her, calling her name, which makes it sound like we're actually threatening her. She stops in the utility room, sits down and looks up at us. She's a mega-furry black cat with whiskers as long as her body and eyes that could be green or blue.

Ulric reaches out his hand to her. When she doesn't scratch it to shreds, he picks her up and buries his face in her fur. 'She must be hungry.'

'Well, she's sorted if she likes pizza.'

'Very funny.'

There's a tray on the floor next to the tumble dryer with an empty cat food dish and a massive bowl of water. I go and rinse out the food bowl. When I come back, Ulric is holding a box of salmon cat biscuits in one hand and a small electric fan in the other.

'Does The Hammer prefer her breakfast extra cool?' I ask.

'It's just weird that the fan is with the cat food,' he says.

I think if Ulric and I were in a shipwreck and ended up stranded on a desert island and weren't rescued until ten years later, we still wouldn't have enough time to agree about what's weird and what isn't. A fan in the same cupboard as cat food? In our flat everything's crammed together. We don't have the space to be choosy.

Ulric pours biscuits into the bowl. He has that look

150

on his face, the fox-with-a-meaty-chicken-wing look. He stomps past me, up the stairs.

'Hang on!' I yell after him. 'We have to clear up!'

Stomp. Stomp. Stomp. Stop.

I sigh and run up and join him by the front door. He's staring into the room where we found The Hammer. I can't see nothing much. The curtains are drawn. I turn on the light and see a cat on a bicycle. It's wearing a yellow jersey and blue lycra shorts and a silver helmet that slopes back so the wind slides along it. It's crouched forward, its claws grasping the handle bars. It's not on its own. There are many more racer cats on bicycles behind it.

The picture has pride of place over the fireplace.

Ulric says, 'Peloton.'

I nod. (Mum learned the word when she was obsessed with the cycle racing in the 2012 London Olympics. Now she uses it even when it's just two old blokes on their bikes waiting for the traffic lights to change to green.) It's not the only catty thing in the room. There are *only* catty things in the room. It's like the Cat Kingdom from the film *The Cat Returns* is leaking into Aunty Maria's world. There are cat statues and a lamp with a tabby cat base and cushions shaped like cat faces with 3D whiskers lying over the sofa. And there are lots more freaky paintings. A cat paraglider. A cat dangling in mid-air on a parachute.

A cat blowing a . . .

'It's a euphonium,' Ulric says as my brain forms the words 'giant trumpety-tromboney thing'.

And there are framed photos too, all different sizes on the wall opposite the window.

'It's the same cat,' I say. 'In all the pictures.'

I reckon that most days I couldn't pick out one tabby cat from another, but even I can see that all these cats have the same very long whiskers and one dark grey paw. And suddenly I'm thinking of Mum in the months after Grandma died. We'd come home from school and see albums stacked up on the kitchen table full of photos from when Mum was a kid. She'd try and hide them when we came in. I heard her tell Dad that nothing could fill the hole Grandma left in her heart.

I say, 'Do you think it's the cat Aunty Maria had before The Hammer?'

'Yeah.'

Ulric and me leave, making sure we close the door quietly behind us. I glance at him. His chicken-wing look has set solid.

'Don't you want to know?' Ulric says.

'Know what?'

Of course there are many things I do want to know, but most of them are – well, I'm not gonna be asking my

152

little brother.

'About the windmills and the cat pictures,' he says. 'And the locked-up clothes.'

I kind of do, but I don't. I'm curious, yeah, but I don't want to dip my nose into Aunty Maria's secrets.

'I just need to check the garden,' Ulric says.

'For what?'

But he's gone again. By the time I've made it out the back, Ulric's in the middle of the grass doing a slow spin.

'Come on, Evie! You do it too,' he calls.

'No!'

'Please!'

If there really is a middle-child syndrome, what it actually means is that you're expected to please everyone.

'You have to, Evie. Then tell me what you see.'

I sigh. I suppose it's gonna stop my toes from freezing together. I go and stand next to him. I spin. Slowly. So what do I see? A fence. A gate. A big wooden box for compost. Flower beds with no flowers. Leaves and twigs. Washing-line posts. A fence. A gate . . . Ulric goes and peers into the compost box. I stop spinning.

'I don't know what Aunty's gonna grow with this stuff,' he says.

I go and look in the box then step back quickly. If anything's gonna assemble into an Iron Man suit with

154

a glove to grab my throat, it's right there. Aunty Maria seems to be composting a heap of metal stuff. Maybe some of them are car parts, though I wouldn't recognise a car part if it drove across my foot. There are whisk-looking things and metal paddles and motors and cogs. It's all pretty rusty.

'Aunty Maria's an alien,' I say. 'And she's building a ship to take her back to the Horseshoe Galaxy.'

Ulric shakes his head. He must have already given that serious consideration. 'Did you notice anything else in the garden?'

'Grass. And plants.'

'That's because it's a garden, Evie. See over there?'

I check where he's pointing. There's a tiny wooden marker below a bush, so easy to miss. We go over and take a better look. A tiny windmill is tangled in some plants just beneath it. I let Ulric crouch down for a better look. He's closer to the ground anyway.

'It says "The Plunger. Lost on 25TH July, 2019. Sorry, I let you down".'

I know folks can get fond of household equipment, but do they normally give them a funeral? And man, how do you let a plunger down? It's *supposed* to go down. Then up again. Then down. Then . . .

Ulric taps my shoulder. 'I think I get it now,' he says.

155

'Understand what?'

I had those words in my head. My mouth was open ready for the 'u', but that sound didn't come out of my mouth. That voice was Mum's. And just that second, the back gate bursts open followed very quickly by Mum and Melody. Melody looks like she's ready to bury me and Ulric right there under the bush next to The Plunger. To be honest, Mum doesn't look much different.

'What took you so long?' Mum shouts. 'I was so worried about you!'

'We were . . .' I look to Ulric for inspiration. He's still staring at The Plunger's grave.

Melody taps Mum's shoulder. 'Now we know they're safe, you can all go home.' She glares at me and Ulric. 'I can stay here and make sure the cat's all right.'

'I fed her,' Ulric grins. 'She's OK. But you'll probably need to clear up all that pizza stuff, Melody.'

Silence. Even the wind tunnel's holding its breath.

Then Mum sweeps past us towards the carpet of Domino's. Melody kind of hovers behind. We hear Mum swear loudly. Even from outside.

'Melody Jacklean Ramsey! Get here right now!'

The full name summons. That's phone confiscation *and* grounding. Melody throws a stink eye at us. Man, it wasn't us in there stuffing our faces with disgusting pineapple pizza, was it? She should have cleared up!

Me and Ulric follow at a safe distance. We don't want to miss this.

Mum's holding the dough-ball bag. 'What the hell happened here?'

Close up, I can still see a glitter stripe through Mel's eyebrow. What happened here was that my sister and her mates decided to meet up in Aunty Maria's empty house. Make-up was involved. Melody says nothing. Mum stacks empty pizza boxes.

'Get me a bin bag, Ulric! They're by the washing machine.'

He scuttles past me to the utility room.

'Did you bring your friends here, Melody?'

Mum says it like she will not accept 'no' as an answer. A thought streaks through Melody's head. (I shared a room with her long enough to work out her expressions, even when they move so quickly they leave smoke.) It's a thought about lying to Mum. It explodes silently in some safe part of Melody's head because she says: 'Sort of.'

Mum stands tall with her hands on her hips. 'Sort of? Who was it?'

Melody's cheek twitches. 'Kamasi.'

'Jordan's brother?'

'Yeah.'

If that was it, Mum would have relaxed. Kamasi's older but he's sensible. He's been looking out for his younger brothers and sisters for years because their parents aren't very good at it. But Melody's cheek was still twitching. There was more.

'And Michael.'

Oh. That's Kamasi's best friend. He's fifteen and rides one of those motorised scooters. No helmet. No hi-vis. No manners, according to Mum.

'Anyone else?' Mum asks.

'And Joy.' Melody's cheek relaxes. Joy was born in the hospital bed next to Melody. They have always been friends.

'So what happened?' Mum sweeps her arm towards the pizza boxes. 'Apart from this.'

Melody's cheek starts again.

'Melody?' That's not just a grounding voice. That's grounding until the *Friends* grandkids' reunion gets made.

Melody swallows. Then she takes out her phone. She fiddles with it and passes it to Mum.

'We promised not to show anyone,' she says quietly.

Mum stares at the screen. Melody watches her. Neither of them say anything. Then Ulric barges back past with the bin bags. He grabs the phone out of Mum's hand.

'Ulric!' Melody screams, snatching the phone back.

158

Ulric looks from Melody to Mum and back at Melody.

'Man!' he says. 'Did you do that?'

Melody can't quite hide her smile. She nods.

'You have to show Evie!'

She sighs then hands the phone back to Ulric who brings it to me. I scroll through the pictures, then stare at Melody. She gives me a little smile. I grin back. I can definitely see what happened. Kamasi and Michael sat there and let Melody do make-up on them. Not just lip liner and brow shapes, but Kamasi's been turned into Kamaji from *Spirited Away*. She's done face-contouring so Kamasi's head looks pointy, painted in Kamaji's sticky-out glasses-things and even added extra beard. Michael is Ryuk, the god of death from *Death Note* and my favourite character ever. She's done Joy as Harley Quinn with added glitter.

'I never knew you could do that, Melody!'

'Because you never asked.'

OK. Attitude Melody has returned. Especially when Mum reaches out to take Melody's phone from me and slips it in her pocket.

'Mum!'

'You're very talented, Melody. But still very grounded. If you get some lightning under you and speed up the cleaning, I may knock off some time.'

159

Melody snatches the roll of bin bags from Ulric and rips one off.

'Mum?'

I stare at Ulric. I wiggle my eyebrows at Ulric. I mouth 'no!' at Ulric, because when he says 'Mum' in that tone, whatever comes next is gonna have someone explode with embarrassment. He ignores me.

'Mum?'

'Yes, Ulric.'

Mum's too busy shoving dead Domino's into bags to notice the tone.

'Is Aunty Maria building a cat-cooling machine?'

Melody laughs out loud. Mum doesn't. My eyebrows go up and stay up.

'She had a cat called The Plunger, right?'

Oh! Now that makes sense. Sort of. The Hammer and The Plunger. Maybe she was starting a cat wrestling league. Though you don't normally bury wrestlers in your garden.

Mum nods. 'Yes. He died a few years ago.'

'On the hottest day of the year,' Ulric says.

The 25th of July! I remember it now! School had only just broke up for summer but Mum wouldn't let us out. She said that even Factor 50 plus our natural melanin wasn't protection for rays like that.

160

Mum nods again. 'Maria and some friends went for a picnic by the swimming ponds in Hampstead Heath. She stayed longer than she meant to. The poor cat couldn't come in for shade because the cat flap was set for outgoing only.'

Mum turns away from us and crumples up the last of the napkins. Melody holds open the bag and she drops them in.

'She hasn't really gone to Trinidad,' Ulric says.

'She told me she was going to Trinidad,' Mum says quietly. 'I wasn't going to question her. It's none of my business.'

'We went upstairs . . .' Ulric says.

'To look for The Hammer,' I add quickly. Mum's nearly cross face relaxes.

'There's a map in her study,' Ulric says. 'It's not Trinidad. It's the wrong shape.'

'It's Shetland,' Melody says.

We all look at her. Melody isn't known in our family for recognising islands.

She shrugs. 'I was looking for the cat too. I was a bit creeped out by all those windmills, though.'

'Did you see her books?' I say. 'There's one by William Kamkwamba.' And as I'm saying that, everything starts clicking into place. 'He built a wind turbine for his family

161

out of old car parts.'

Mum's looking really confused now.

'And all Aunty Maria's summer clothes are locked in another room,' Ulric says.

'And then there's the cat on the bike,' I say.

'Stop!' Mum throws up her hands like she's Doctor Strange conjuring a portal. Suddenly I do want to fall through a hole and be somewhere else because Mum's right. This isn't any of our business.

Mum's hands drop to her sides. 'I didn't know what to do with myself when my mum died.' Me and Melody glance at each other. Mum had been much more shouty, but sometimes she'd clamp on her headphones, listen to music and ignore us all. 'It's especially hard because you didn't really know her. She was so far away.'

I realise that me, Ulric and Melody have moved closer to Mum.

'I didn't want to talk about it,' Mum says. 'Mostly because I didn't want to deal with anybody else's reaction. And it's just so hard to think about, knowing that someone you loved is just – well – gone. So imagine I'm feeling like that because my mother's died, but what if it's a pet?'

'A pet mum?' Ulric asks.

I cuff him – gently – on the back. Mum laughs out loud though and wraps her arm around him. She kisses the

162

top of his head.

'People don't always take it seriously when pets die,' Mum says. 'Maria was so upset about The Plunger, especially as she thought it was her fault. Now she's very protective of The Hammer, but she's a bit embarrassed about it too.'

'That cat's proper furry,' Melody says. 'She could easily overheat.'

Me and Ulric nod.

'Not everyone's as understanding as you three.' Mum smiles. 'I suppose it was easier to say that she was off to visit her family in Trinidad than . . .' Mum scratches her head. 'Shetland? Why Shetland?'

I take out my phone and check. 'It's one of the windiest places in Britain.'

Ulric nods like he's driving the fact hard into his memory.

'And it's all for you,' Mum says.

I look round. The Hammer's padded into the room. It's hard to work out if her furry face is happy, but I know her stomach's full and she can walk across the floor without her claws sticking to a stuffed crust. She wraps herself around Ulric's feet. He picks her up and she purrs so hard I'm surprised Ulric isn't vibrating too. We all huddle together, just for a few seconds, then Mum pulls away.

163

'Unless you've been secretly inventing a clearing-up machine, Melody, then you better go and find the dustpan and brush.'

Melody nods, but me, her and Ulric swap a look.

'So which one of us is most like Grandma?' I ask.

Mum smiles, a real smile that makes her face glow.

'Well,' she says. 'Let me see . . .'

P.S. I actually do know why The Hammer is called The Hammer. It's because she was the biggest of the litter and likes to stomp across her brothers and sisters. Mum says we can't tell Ulric yet in case we shatter his innocence.

MAISIE CHAN

IT
TAKES
A THIEF
TO CATCH
A THIEF

TOP SECRET

PROPERTY OF THE VERY MERRY MURDER CLUB

IT TAKES A THIEF TO CATCH A THIEF

By Maisie Chan

I was looking forward to a normal Christmas this year, unlike last year, when my mum made me dress up as an elf and got Nanny So Kim to take me carol singing in the wealthiest neighbourhood in the city. Little did I know I was being used as a diversion. I probably should have been singing 'Ding-dong merrily on high . . . get a better security system!' That's because . . . and it's not easy to say this . . . my mum used to be the city's most infamous cat burglar. She was a thief called the White Rabbit, but she gave it all up for me.

We used to argue about it all the time because my friends weren't allowed to come over for play dates in case they found her sparkly stash. And I was always staying over at Nanny So Kim's place when mum was on the job, which was basically when she was stealing jewels from people she called 'the filthy rich'. I don't know how 'filthy' they really were. All I knew was that this Christmas I wanted us all to be together, instead of her being out on a job or in hiding from the police.

'Why can't you be more like Jade's mum?' I pleaded with her outside school a few months back. Mum had picked me up in her customised Mercedes Benz. Jade's mum was in her Volvo, the safest car you can buy, according to Jade. Mum glanced over at Jade's mum and snorted.

'Jade's mum! Are you having a laugh?' Mum said, flinging her long black hair over her shoulder. 'Jade's mum works as a community cop. That uniform would give me hives. Could you see me in that polyester nightmare?'

I shrugged my shoulders, because I couldn't. Mum was a bit glam, you see, and she had forty black designer catsuits that she wore for her jobs. You probably are wondering why she was called the White Rabbit then? Well, they're her favourite Chinese sweets. They're all milky and yummy. And not black like all of her outfits.

She'd told me, 'Alma, I love you. But I also love being the most infamous cat burglar in the city, it's all I've ever known. I love listening to the clicking of locks, the excitement and thrill of it all! And I'm the best at it. There's someone trying to muscle in on my turf but there's no way he's going to be better than me. How can I give that up?'

She plonked a golf ball-sized dollop of fancy caviar on to her Ryvita crackers and started munching on it. I made myself a peanut butter sandwich. Mum liked the finer things in life and was always moaning that I could buy whatever clothes and accessories I wanted instead of wearing dungarees all the time and having my nose in a book. But that's what I liked doing.

However, eventually Mum did give up her glamorous life of crime for me and told me she would definitely hand back her sparkly stash. What made her change her mind? Well, I'd told her – 'I don't want you to be in prison, you grew up not seeing your dad much because he was in and out of the clink, I don't want to be the same.'

She gave me the biggest hug and nodded. 'Well, if you put it like that,' she said, wiping a tear from her eye, 'I'll give it all up for you!'

A week later, Mum got a job as a locksmith (she had transferable skills), and she'd even helped out at the parent-council cake sale. Just between you and me, her lock-picking skills were more impressive than her baking skills. However, it was still great having her around more.

She'd only been on the straight and narrow for two months, but it was going well. But then everything changed on Christmas Eve and it was all the fault of Claude Van Twix (we'll come to him later).

Nanny So Kim and I had done some last-minute Christmas shopping and had arrived back at my flat just after lunchtime; it seemed eerily quiet. Mum was supposed to be home hanging tinsel from the ceilings, but none of that had been done. Usually, she'd have the latest tunes playing on the radio or be humming K-pop songs out of tune but when we opened the highly secure front door with our four keys, retina scan and fingerprint recognition – there wasn't a peep. It was too quiet.

'Maybe she went out to buy more food for tomorrow's Asian-fusion Christmas feast?' Nanny So Kim said. It sounded unlikely.

'Do you think she's back on the job?' I said. My throat suddenly felt dry. Was Mum back to her life of crime? I had that familiar sense of dread I used to get every Christmas Eve. Mum would be out all night (doing the opposite of Santa by taking stuff) stealing presents to give me for Christmas Day. Last year I got a diamond-encrusted baby rattle. What I really wanted was a set of new notebooks and some gel pens.

'No, she wouldn't, Alma; she's changed her ways,'

Nanny So Kim said, hugging me tight.

'They say once a thief, always a thief, don't they?' I said.

'Who the blooming heck are THEY anyway? People can change, trust me, I know.' Nanny So Kim looked at me and smiled. 'I'll go look in the bathroom. She might be having a soak. Or, knowing your mum, she might be constipated and need some plum juice and has gone out to buy more.' Nanny wandered off down the hall chuckling to herself.

I wasn't so sure. Something felt off. The hairs on the back of my neck were standing up. It was freezing in the flat even though I was wearing my navy duffle coat. A shiver went down my spine.

'Mum?' I called, putting down the bags on the sofa. I grabbed a roll of Christmas wrapping and held it up in the air like a baseball bat. Then I tiptoed towards Mum's bedroom. The balcony doors were open wide, the cold draught make the curtains flutter. I could see some of our potted evergreen plants had been knocked over. 'Mum, are you here?' Her bedroom was a mess – Mum was a neat demon so this was definitely not right. I looked around her purple and gold bedroom trying to figure out what was going on. Then I noticed, one of her stiletto heels was stabbed into the wall. There'd been a struggle. Maybe the police had worked out who she was? She must be in prison! This was the day I had been dreading all my life. I went into the hallway to find Nanny So Kim to tell her what I'd seen.

Then I heard a gasp.

Nanny So Kim poked her head around the bathroom door. She looked very pale.

'Alma, come quick, look at this message in the mirror before it disappears!'

The hot tap was still running, the bathroom was full of hot steam. I could hardly see a thing – I wafted away the white fog and stepped towards the mirror. Nanny So Kim turned off the tap and opened a window as the steam began to clear. And there it was. One word.

HELP!

The facts were: Mum was missing, she'd written a sign to us that said HELP and there had been a struggle. It meant only one thing. Someone had stolen my mum! They'd taken the White Rabbit!

I ran to the living-room telephone and flung the wrapping paper on to the sofa. 'We've got to call the police!' I urged. 'Mum's been cat burglar-napped!'

But as I picked up the phone, Nanny rushed over and gently took it off me and shook her head.

'Alma, your mum wouldn't want us to call the police. You know how much she dislikes Jade's mum, even though she's lovely. No, your mum would want us to deal with this. We have to think like a thief to catch a thief. We must be like her. We're going to steal her back!' Nanny So Kim looked almost excited. 'But first, I need a cuppa.'

'But where do we begin?' I exclaimed. Nanny So Kim and I weren't exactly cunning thieves. I was always daydreaming, and Nanny was too cuddly and forgetful. I put down the phone and sat on the sofa. Could we really get Mum back by ourselves? And who had taken her?

I racked my brain thinking about Mum – what would she do? What were her skills?

I always had my head in a book, not like Mum. She was observant, always looking around for the exits, or cameras. She would start by assessing the location. So I did that too. I looked around at anything that was different in our flat. The living room wasn't as untidy as Mum's bedroom.

So I went back to Mum's room to look for clues. Whoever it had been was taller than Mum because the Jimmy Choo shoe that poked out of the wall was quite high up – which meant she had aimed at someone tall. They had been looking for something because all the drawers were open. Then there had been some sort of struggle because the bed was a mess! Had the mum-napper been looking for Mum's sparkly stash not knowing that she'd given it back? But why take Mum if she didn't have anything valuable? None of it made sense.

Something near the bedside table caught my eye. I noticed a shiny gold thing with red foil writing – it was a Twix chocolate wrapper. I held it up. That was strange. Mum never let me eat in my bedroom and we never bought Twix bars.

'I checked the front door, it wasn't forced . . . so maybe she knew the kidnapper? Anything of interest in here?' she asked. She was holding her floral TO-DO LIST that she usually kept with her Polo mints and her knitting stuff in her bag. 'My memory isn't what it used to be. I'll take notes of anything we find,' she said.

'Mum doesn't eat these,' I said. Nanny So Kim took it and held it up. She frowned, then her eyes became wide like a French bulldog who'd seen a tasty treat.

'I know who it is!' Nanny So Kim said, writing in capital letters on the pad. It read: SUSPECT – CLAUDE VAN TWIX! 'It's him! He's the second-most famous cat burglar in the city after your mum! No one knows what he looks like. He's the one who's got her! The cheek!' Nanny So Kim looked like she would box this Claude Van Twix's ears for taking her daughter. 'He's fairly new to this area, and the word on the street is that he has a sweet tooth, hence his name.'

174

'That's so silly. A criminal who's named after a chocolate bar, really?' I said, sceptically.

Nanny So Kim cleared her throat. 'Ahem! Your mum named herself after the White Rabbit sweets, so it's not that silly, is it?' When she put it like that, I couldn't argue.

'He leaves the wrapper as his calling card,' Nanny So Kim said. She sniffed it and then held it up to the light. She wrote down the clue. 'One chocolate wrapper . . .' I thought it was daft to leave a calling card at a scene of the crime.

Claude Van Twix had ruined everything. And he'd littered too. That made me even more angry. I just wanted a regular Christmas and now Mum was gone and I wasn't going to get the family Christmas that I had wished for. I took a deep breath in. Then I saw a photo of me, Mum and Nanny So Kim on our holiday to Hong Kong's Disneyland. I missed Mum. Even though we were totally the opposite.

'Right, we ARE going to get Mum back and we WILL have a brilliant Christmas!' I stated. 'I'm not going to let some second-rate criminal ruin our Christmas!'

'That's the spirit, Alma!' Nanny So Kim said.

I put my hands on my hips and looked around some more. 'We know he didn't come through the front door because Mum's security system is pretty high-tech and we used our keys, so then he must have got in through Mum's balcony doors,' I said. They had been wide open which had lowered the temperature. We rushed to Mum's bedroom balcony.

'Look there!' I said. 'This potted plant has been kicked over and the soil's fallen out. Claude Van Twix must have stepped in it because look, here . . .' I pointed. 'He's left a shoe print! Quick Nanny, give me something to measure it with!'

Nanny So Kim rummaged around in her bag. I held up my hand, waiting for a ruler or tape measure.

'I've only got this,' said Nanny. In my hand I felt a tickly piece of rainbow-dyed wool.

'That will have to do,' I said. I used the wool to measure the footprint. It was long.

'Pass me some scissors,' I said.

Nanny passed me scissors from her bag. 'You've got a lot of stuff in there,' I added as I snipped the wool at the right spot.

'You never know when you might need something,' Nanny So Kim laughed.

I laid the wool next to my own foot. I was a size five. The thief had feet like a giant.

'My, my, my – what a big-footed thief we have,' Nanny So Kim said, impressed. 'I'd say from the size of this print . . . a size twelve? Or maybe a size thirteen. I know a shop in town where they sell shoes to men with extremely large feet. We should start there but we need to hurry up!'

'Something's bothering me, though,' I said. 'We're three storeys up. How on earth did he get up here?'

I looked over the side of the building and saw that the window-cleaning cage that used an electric pulley was at ground level. That must have been it. It was so simple.

'I think we need to try the shoe shop before it closes,' Nanny So Kim said. 'Let's disguise ourselves because it's one of those fancy stores for wealthy men with big feet. Let's go look in your mum's disguise closet.'

We found a couple of perfect outfits. I wore a black suit with a tie and stuck on a fake moustache and a bowler hat. And Nanny So Kim dressed as a delivery person with a motorbike helmet and a big square bag on her back.

'It's got my knitting in there in case I get bored on the way,' she said. 'And some egg tarts.'

We high-fived. We were ready to catch a thief.

We hopped on the bus back to town. Nanny So Kim got a few stares because her delivery bag was hitting people in the face as she passed down the bus aisle and she didn't have a bike. One guy said, 'Watch it mate!' and Nanny So Kim offered him one of her egg tarts which put a smile on his face. The moustache was making my upper lip itch a little.

The Christmas shoppers were still out in full force when we reached the centre of town. We ducked and dived through the crowds and reached the shoe shop that catered for big-footed men: **BIG SHOES EMPORIUM FOR GENTLEMEN.**

As I opened the shop door a golden bell above the door tinkled. I straightened my fake moustache which was slipping over my upper lip.

'Hullo,' I tried to say in a manly voice.

'Welcome Sir! Can I help you today?' said a man with a round face with freckles and horn-rimmed glasses. He was dressed in a navy-blue suit. He did have very large feet. Perhaps he was Claude Van Twix? I'd need to measure his feet to find out.

'Erm, no . . . no . . . just browsing.' I noticed the man looking at my black shoes which were Mum's. I'd stuffed them with socks in the toe area. He could obviously see that I didn't have extraordinarily large feet.

Nanny So Kim followed me inside.

'We didn't order a food delivery,' said the man, glaring at Nanny So Kim.

She went over to the side of the shop by the window and started to chatter on about how she couldn't take the egg tarts back. I began touching the huge shoes on display while keeping an eye on Nanny So Kim. Our plan

178

was that she would distract the man, whose name tag said HUBERT, with egg tarts while I tried to measure his feet with the rainbow wool.

Nanny So Kim offered him a shiny yellow tart. 'They're a gift from a friend of yours . . . let me look for the card.' She handed him the box and pretended to look for an imaginary card in the square delivery bag.

Hubert opened the white cardboard box. He noticed one was missing as there was a white cake wrapper in the bottom. Nanny had given it to the guy on the bus.

'Did you eat one of these?' he asked. I knelt on the floor beside him. Nanny So Kim shook her head and smiled at him.

'Me? Never . . . I'm a reliable delivery person. I would never eat a customer's delivery . . . but they're good, right?' she asked.

He took a bite from one and you could see his eyes close as they were so delicious. Flaky crumbs fell on my head. I managed to get the piece of wool alongside his feet. He had big feet all right, but not as long as the wool. He wasn't Claude Van Twix. I silently crawled away using my elbows. This must be what it was like for Mum when she had to crawl under laser beams. I smiled to myself – it was kinda fun.

'Ummmm, these are so good,' said Hubert. He looked at Nanny So Kim and held out his hand. 'Where's the card, I want to know who sent them.'

Nanny was a bit flustered. I quickly ran to the counter and wrote a card using some plain paper.

'Ah, you might be looking for this,' I said, handing the man a scrap of paper. He looked at it and was instantly flustered.

'Erm . . . Claude Van Twix . . . never 'eard of 'im.'

He was obviously lying and his accent changed. It went from really posh to like someone who worked on a market stall in the East End. 'I mean, I've never heard of this particular gentleman,' he quickly said in a fake posh voice.

Hubert wiped a bead of sweat that was slowly making its way down the side of his face. 'It's got really hot in here,' he said rushing over to the door and opening it. 'Anyway, you can go,' he said to Nanny So Kim.

She walked slowly in the direction of the door but was nodding her head towards the counter where an address book lay open. As he was holding the door open for her to leave. I rushed over to the book. Perhaps I would be able to find an address for Claude in there.

I flicked through the pages but couldn't see his name.

Hubert turned his head and watched in horror as my moustache fell off and stuck to the toes of my shoes. His face was aghast as he realised what was happening! He let go of the front door and began running over towards me.

180

He was about to grab me, when Nanny So Kim tripped him over with her foot and he fell into a shoe rack; the boat-like shoes fell all over the floor. She pounced and sat on top of him like a WWE wrestler. She got out her knitting wool from the delivery bag and wrapped it tightly around his wrists and legs. Then she took out a pair of long knitting needles.

I hurried through the rest of the pages of the logbook, but there was no mention of a Claude or any sort of address.

'You will talk! I know you know where Claude Van Twix lives!' Nanny So Kim said. I'd never seen her like that before! What was she going to do with those knitting needles? 'This is the only shoe shop that caters for large footed men in a hundred-mile radius.'

'You'll never find 'im!' Hubert blustered, red-faced. 'He's like a ghost!'

'Ha! So, you do you know him!' I said, rushing over. 'We need to find him now!'

'I'll get him to talk!' Nanny So Kim said with a look of determination on her face. She was enjoying herself; I could tell! She lifted the knitting needles.

Hubert lifted his chin. 'My clients work with me because I am a keeper of secrets. My lips are sealed tight like sandwich bags. You'll never make me talk!'

'Alma, take off his shoes and socks,' Nanny So Kim

said. 'It's T-time!'

'What's she doing?' said Hubert, terrified. 'I'm immune to torture, but don't hurt my face!'

I did as Nanny So Kim had asked and took off his shoes. The pong from his sweaty socks made me gag.

'Tell us where Claude Van Twix is, or your toes get it!' shouted Nanny So Kim. She held the knitting needles like chopsticks. I realised what she was going to do and couldn't help but smile.

'Never, you old crone!" Hubert declared.

Nanny So Kim began circling the tips of the knitting needles on Hubert's feet. Round and round and in figures of eight. At first he tried to keep in the laughs, his lips held tightly shut, but the tickles started getting more and more intense.

'Talk!' shouted Nanny So Kim.

'No . . . no . . . please make her stop . . . ha ha ha!' Hubert was thrashing around, trying not to laugh or spill the beans.

'Where is Claude Van Twix? Tell us!' I said. 'She can tickle you all day.'

Hubert let out a loud roar of laughter. His body squirmed and jerked on the floor. The agony was too much. Nanny So Kim increased her tickling.

'OK! ENOUGH! I can't take it any more, I'm going to

pee myself laughing! I will tell you where to find him!' Hubert said, tears streaming from his eyes. 'He lives above the pound shop on Fennel Street. It's a cover for his lavish lifestyle. But you'll never get in, he trusts no one.'

'See, I knew T-time would work!' said Nanny So Kim, satisfied. She stopped tickling him. 'Come on. Let's go.'

'What about me?' said Hubert. 'Aren't you going to untie me?'

'No,' I said. 'We'll call the shop next door when we get to Claude Van Twix's location. We don't want you warning him that we're coming.'

We left the shop and turned over the sign to read CLOSED. I held my hand up and Nanny So Kim gave me a high five. We made a cool team.

About thirty minutes later we arrived outside the pound shop. The door to the side of the shop was made of metal and had three locks.

'What would your mum do?' Nanny So Kim asked me.

'She'd pick the lock, of course,' I said. 'But neither of us know how to pick a lock.'

'Well . . . we can try. Here what about these?'

Nanny So Kim handed me a small crochet needle from her knitting bag and a bobby pin that she pulled out from her hair bun. I stuck them into the keyhole and jiggled them about. I didn't know what I was doing. It wasn't working.

'I see how she did it, but I can't do it. It's no use. I wish Mum were here to rescue herself!'

I stood up. I wasn't cut out to be a thief. We weren't going to get Mum back in time for Christmas. 'I think we should tell Jade's mum,' I said.

'Not yet. We can't give up so easily. She loves you and you love her – you're just like her, Alma, even though you don't think you are,' Nanny So Kim said.

I remembered how Mum had never wanted to give up being the infamous cat burglar. How she loved the excitement and listening to the sound of clicking locks . . . clicking locks . . . she listened to the locks!

'I know how to do it! Mum used to listen to the locks! We need a glass so I can hear what's going on inside!'

Nanny So Kim beamed and rushed over to a couple having a romantic dinner outside the bistro next door. She swiped a glass tumbler and rushed back with it. The couple sat open-mouthed and then shrugged their shoulders and went back to gawking at each other.

She handed me the glass and I put it against the metal door. I pushed my ear up to near the lock. I put the crochet needle and bobby pin back in and listened. I turned them this way and that. *Click. Click. Click.* And suddenly I felt it

184

move. The door opened! I had done it.

Nanny So Kim hugged me tight.

We tiptoed into the darkened stairwell. And at the top was a hallway and at the end a large oak door which was slightly ajar.

'So this is where the city's mastermind lives?' I whispered.

'This hallway isn't very fancy at all,' Nanny So Kim said. 'Second rate cat burglar!'

I felt butterflies in my belly. We were so close to getting Mum back from the evil Claude Van Twix.

Now we needed to find Mum and steal her back!

We tiptoed up along the darkened hallway. I held Nanny So Kim's hand, as I was feeling a bit scared. Perhaps I wasn't cut out for this cat burglar business, after all.

We snuck into the open door. Everything was covered in a warm gold and red wallpaper (just like Twix wrappers, this guy was obsessed!), works of art hung on the walls, even the air smelt expensive, and there was a gold box with hundreds of Twix bars in it on the coffee table. There was a grand piano in one corner of the living room and a painting over the fireplace with a sign that said, 'Do Not Touch The Monet!' This was definitely Claude Van Twix's apartment. When Hubert said the pound shop location was a front, he was right. We heard noises in one of the side rooms. There was a figure in black opening the wardrobe. Nanny So Kim got out her ball of wool, and I picked up a set of crystal apples that I could throw if need be. Claude Van Twix was gonna get it!

'Got ya!' Nanny So Kim said, grabbing the thief! She turned the person around; we'd finally caught . . .

'Mum?' I gasped. Mum looked at us both with a scowl.

'What are you two doing here?' she asked, obviously irritated. 'I'm on a job!'

Then she clamped her hand over her mouth.

'So you weren't kidnapped?' Nanny So Kim said, looking very cross. 'We've been worried all afternoon. We even tickled a poor man's feet for you. You owe us an explanation.'

'I admit I staged the kidnapping, wrote HELP on the mirror. I didn't want to tell you I'd –' But before she could finish what she was saying, we heard the front door opening. The whiff of chocolate filled the air. It was Claude Van Twix!

'Quick!' whispered Mum.

We all scrambled under Claude's golden bed like marines on our bellies. He entered the bedroom, took off his humongous shoes and flopped on the bed.

'Ahh, now who is the best cat burglar in town? I am!' he quipped to himself. 'The White Rabbit didn't know what

186

had hit her. I took her famous sparkly stash and now I am the best!' He chuckled to himself.

Nanny So Kim and I glared at Mum. She hadn't handed in her sparkly stash after all! I was fuming. I crawled out from underneath the bed and stood up tall.

'This is ridiculous! You are ridiculous!' I said to Claude Van Twix. Mum crawled out too, looking very sheepish. 'And you Mum, how could you? After you said you would give up your life of crime for me.'

Unaware he was interrupting a mother-daughter moment, Claude Van Twix exclaimed in awe, 'The White Rabbit, here in my flat? No one has ever found my hiding place before.'

Mum pointed her purple talons at him.

'I want my stuff back now!' she demanded.

Claude Van Twix smiled.

'You've looked everywhere haven't you and you still haven't found your jewels. You need to admit to me that I am the best cat burglar in town.'

Nanny So Kim slid out from under the bed and got out her knitting needles. Claude Van Twix put up his hands in surrender.

'I admit it. I couldn't find my stash here,' Mum told Claude, then she turned to me. 'And Alma, I'm sorry OK.'

'Shall I tickle him?' Nanny So Kim asked.

I moved forward to tell her to put down her needles and accidently tapped one of Claude's shoes. It felt heavy and hardly moved.

I lifted the shoe up. I looked at Claude's feet on the bed and got out my piece of wool to measure them. His feet were regular man-sized. So why were his shoes so big? I inspected the shoe further.

'I've got it! I know where he keeps the jewels,' I said. 'He keeps them in his size-thirteen shoes. Look!'

I grabbed one of Nanny So Kim's knitting needles and pried open one of the toes of Claude Van Twix's shoes. It sprang open like an oyster. Inside was a mountain of diamonds, rubies and emeralds. I scooped them out and handed them to Mum.

'My sparkly stash!' Mum said, delighted. She turned to Claude. 'And you, how dare you take my stuff! Why did you do it?'

Claude Van Twix smiled. 'When I heard you had retired, I thought it must be a sick joke. The White Rabbit is the best cat burglar ever! I needed to know for sure if it was true. So, I watched you for a while being a regular mum and working in your locksmith business. But then I saw you one day when I was cleaning your windows. You still had a stash of jewels. I had to be the best, and I could only be the best by stealing from the best,' he explained.

'You think I'm the best?' Mum said, obviously flattered. 'But I thought you wanted to take over as the best cat burglar in the city?'

'I did at first,' Claude Van Twix admitted. 'But then I saw how much you had. I don't mean the jewels. I mean the people around you. You have people who love you and want you to be on the straight and narrow. But I don't have that. So, I just wanted to be near someone who might understand me.' He blinked, embarrassed. 'I was actually hoping you would find me because I don't have any family. I just wanted to be like you and have what you have – a family.'

Nanny So Kim wiped her eyes. She felt sorry for the guy. She patted him on the shoulder. 'Enough of this silliness,' she said. 'You will come for Christmas dinner tomorrow. We've got enough food to feed a football team and we don't want anyone to feel lonely at Christmas.'

'And these are going back to their rightful owners,' I said, taking the jewels out of Mum's hands and putting them into Nanny So Kim's knitting bag. 'Both of you,' I said pointing at Claude and Mum, 'are going to change your ways. We will have a fantastic Christmas and your New Year's resolution is to go on the straight and narrow.'

Mum and Claude both nodded.

'Hi, my real name is Barry,' said the second most

famous cat burglar in the city.

'Pleased to meet you,' said Mum. 'My name's Charlotte, previously known as the White Rabbit.' She winked at me.

The next day was Christmas. Barry came over but used the front door instead of the window-cleaning cage.

We had traditional Christmas turkey with all the trimmings, but also added things that we loved to eat such as red bean desserts, green tea mochi and pak choi stir-fried with garlic instead of Brussels sprouts. Barry brought over a box of Christmas crackers and inside were fancy jewels instead of plastic toys. Mum and Barry got on pretty well – they understood each other. Barry told her how he'd been following in the footsteps of his dad, who was also a cat burglar. He and Mum had a lot in common.

We filled our faces with good food during our Asian-fusion Christmas feast and for a while we forgot anything had ever been wrong.

Finally, we sat down to watch a Christmas movie together. But there was a newsflash on the screen.

BREAKING NEWS!
We're sorry to interrupt your Christmas Day cheer, but the most extraordinary thing happened in the early hours of

190

the morning. While children everywhere were getting their presents from Santa, the Crown Jewels were stolen from the Tower of London.

Mum and Barry looked at each other, then at me, and shrugged their shoulders.

'It wasn't us!' Mum said. 'Cross my heart.'

Police are looking for a suspect who they have called THE CROCHET THIEF as they used a special crochet hook to get though the world leading security system.

We all looked at Nanny So Kim who was slurping on her green tea.

'What?' she said, looking innocent.

'Nanny!' I exclaimed.

DOMINIQUE VALENTE

THE FROSTWILDS

TOP SECRET

THE VERY MERRY MURDER CLUB

PROPERTY OF THE VERY MERRY MURDER CLUB

THE FROSTWILDS

By Dominique Valente

There was to be a hanging if it happened again. All the tribes of the Frostwilds had gathered in the heart of the vast frozen forest to listen to the Eldermistle's warning. Few dared to meet the burning coals that appeared to have replaced the elder's eyes, like a bear in ragged black fur.

'Someone broke Frostlaw and now the beast is stirring,' he said. 'When we find the offender, they will be punished.'

'Hear, hear!'

'The old ways are in place for a reason!'

As the wind began to howl, several people made the gelidsign by throwing an invisible trail of salt over their shoulders for protection.

Thirteen-year-old Frostine didn't. Her dark hair fell

195

across her face while she tried to readjust Godmor, her prosthetic leg. Part of it was stuck to the icy log she was on and the skin around her knee was pinching. The Eldermistle's eyes found hers and she stopped fidgeting, even though it hurt. She hastily made the sign, so he could move on.

When he did at last, she yanked her leg free and sighed in relief.

Her little sister, nine-year-old Iclyn, turned mischievous green eyes on her. 'Look at January Avery,' she whispered. 'Her guilty ears are practically giving her away.'

Frostine glanced at the cowering woman in front of her. The tips of January's ears were ruby red.

'Apparently, she gave Whit's hair a trim on a Tuesday,' Iclyn breathed.

Frostine spied Whit surreptitiously lifting a gnarled brown hand to cover the back of his shorn neck. She had to bite her lip to stop herself from grinning.

It wasn't supposed to be funny.

In the Frostwilds, superstitions were law, and breaking them came with consequences. The kind that cost people their lives. Everyone knew that breaking more than three in a year could rouse the Gelidbeast from beneath the frozen lake. The last time it had happened, forty years before, he'd taken three children, one from each of the tribes – including the Eldermistle's daughter, Eira.

Eira would have celebrated her birthday in two days' time. Frostine knew this because she shared the same birthday as the missing girl.

Something no one let her forget.

Ever since the Gelidbeast had taken the children, the rules, like the superstitions, had only multiplied.

If you wished someone Happy Birthday the day before their birthday, placed a set of new shoes on a table, got your haircut on a Tuesday, failed to pay a penny in exchange for a knife, or broke any of the seventy superstitions known as Frostlaw, you could wake the beast. And if you broke three, he would come for a child.

'The ice . . .' the Eldermistle declared, ominously, 'has begun to crack.'

There were gasps from all around.

'But it's too early!'

'We're months from Appeasement.'

Frostine frowned. It wasn't yet False Spring, when the ice from the lake began to sing and the cracks started to appear when the beast woke up from hibernation. For as long as she could remember, there had been no real summers or springs or autumns in the Frostwilds; only a winter that hadn't left for over two hundred years, thanks to the Feast of Appeasement the Frostwilders held every year at this time, which ensured that the ice cracks disappeared, and the beast returned to his slumber.

To Frostine, an eternal winter had always seemed like a small price to keep children safe.

She glanced now at the largest, oldest pine in the forest. Scratched in the centre of its vast trunk was the Frostlaw toll. According to legend, the Gelidbeast had carved the marks himself, which was why it glowed so fiery red. Every time someone broke Frostlaw, it changed, as if by magic. Right now, a fiery '2' burned in the icy bark. It was the highest the toll had been in forty years. The last time it had gone past three, those children had gone missing.

'If there's another offence, there will be a hanging. Our children's lives are at stake,' hissed the Eldermistle.

There were gasps and dark mutterings.

Noel, a man at the back with grey hair dressed in shaggy tan furs, shook his head. 'Why a hanging? If the Gelidbeast takes another child, that would make two deaths instead of one.'

The Eldermistle turned his burning eyes on Noel. The man flinched.

'Because the second death will be payment for causing the first,' breathed the Eldermistle. He said it softly but the effect was as if he'd shouted. 'An example will be set, so no one else suffers as we did.'

Nobody else dared to object. Most, in fact, seemed to agree.

'An example must be set,' muttered one.

For most it was enough just to look at the aged parents of the missing children, who sat at the front – a hollow honour. They were old now, marked by grief. Some of them could have been grandparents, but weren't.

The Gelidbeast had taken that away.

Frostine and Iclyn grew sombre as they glanced at them too.

Then, like they always did, the Frostwilders said the names of the missing. Part prayer, part promise, to ensure that they did not transgress again.

'Eira, Lumi, North,' came the soft chant.

The Eldermistle nodded, satisfied.

'A reminder that age is no excuse,' he said. 'Parents, you must be the example, but unlike the beast we will *not* kill children. Nonetheless, if Frostlaw is broken, someone will pay. So be warned, children: your parents will be held accountable for your crimes, should you break the law!'

Frostine swallowed. That was new. She looked over at Iclyn to see what her sister thought, but she wasn't there. She was admiring the crossbow of a boy from another tribe, several seats away.

'We will begin preparations for the feast tomorrow,' said the Eldermistle, dismissing them.

On the way home, Frostine checked her traps. A small fluhare had frozen in the night, its fur white with grey stripes. She took it out gently, saying her thanks to the winter sprites, as was the custom. The fur would make excellent new boots, and the meat would be a welcome stew. Even so, she touched the fur with regret, thanking the animal for its life.

Behind her, Iclyn huffed as she trudged through the waist-high snow. 'Probably have to give that up for the Feast of Appeasement,' she grumbled.

Frostine sighed, then nodded. 'You're right.'

It was hard enough trying to feed themselves in the Frostwilds, as so little grew and hunting in the frozen forest was so treacherous, without giving what little they had to the Gelidbeast. But at least in False Spring the ground was softer and more vegetation was exposed, and thus more game was around too. Now, in True Winter where so little was available, not to mention with Far being sick, it would be even harder. Most of the hunting would fall on her. Iclyn was just too young.

As if Iclyn could read Frostine's mind, she said, 'I can

200

help this time.' She grabbed the bow and the sheath of arrows slung over Frostine's shoulder. 'I'm getting better, look!'

She quickly fired an arrow into the wind as a flock of snow geese crested the sky. She was off by at least a hundred metres, and apart from a hiss, the geese barely noticed.

'You showed them all right,' snorted Frostine.

'The wind was in my eyes,' complained Iclyn.

'Sling for you.'

Iclyn pulled a face. 'The sling is for babies.'

Frostine bent down and took her hunter's sling from a small compartment she'd added to Godmor. Over the years, she'd added lots of refurbishments to her leg: there was a place for several ice picks, a knife and the sling. Godmor had always been too big, so Frostine figured she might as well make the most of the space. As they walked through the frozen forest, Frostine scanned the horizon, sling primed. Ten minutes later, there was a small thump, and another fluhare fell.

'Not for babies,' she told Iclyn with a grin. 'And now we can keep one of these for ourselves.'

Iclyn rolled her eyes. She'd seen her sister use the sling too often to be impressed. 'Bringing down a whole deer . . . now *that* would be impressive,' she said. 'That's what I want to learn.'

'You will, eventually,' Frostine told her. 'The sling is good for small game – it's easier to run away from game that might turn to chase you, if you miss.'

Iclyn snorted. 'But you can't run.'

Frostine's eyes widened. 'I can. I just don't. There's a difference. Besides, unlike some people, I never miss.'

Then to prove her point, she ran. Iclyn tore after her, pushing her into the fresh snow, where they had a snow fight, giggling like mad.

'I'll be as good as you someday, you'll see,' Icyln promised.

Frostine nodded, face serious. 'You will. You'll be as good as I am now.' Iclyn looked pleased until Frostine gave her a wolfish smile, her teeth sharp, and pointed out, 'But because I'm older, by then I'll be even better, so you'll never really catch up.'

'Yes, I will!' yelled Iclyn.

Frostine started to run once more, despite the fact that Godmor was pinching again. Some things were worth a bit of pain, like beating your little sister home.

Some of the Frostwilders had told Frostine's father that it would be impossible for a girl, born like her, to be a hunter, but Far had taught her anyway.

He'd told her, 'There's guessing that something is impossible and then there's knowing if it really is. It's amazing how often things turn out to be possible when you try them. Two hundred years ago, before the Gelidbeast changed the forest to ice, no one would've thought it was possible to survive here, in perpetual winter, but we have. You'll be the same.'

He was right.

Frostine wasn't as fast as some of the others. Perhaps with a better prosthetic, one that had actually been made for her, she might have been . . . or perhaps not. Frostine didn't like to dwell on what ifs. She preferred to be prepared. If she couldn't be fast, she could be smart instead.

But smart took practice. She learned that lesson quickly when she went after a boar and missed. She managed to escape only because Far distracted the boar with food. She realised that if she was going to survive, her options were to give up the bow and stick to smaller, safer game, or become so good that she never missed. She chose the latter, by practising every chance she got.

By the time she was thirteen, Frostine could take down a fully grown deer from a distance most hunters thought impossible. It was one of the reasons Iclyn wanted to learn how to hunt bigger game, like her sister. Frostine wanted her to get better at the sling first, as mastering one would only help her when she did eventually move on to the more powerful weapon. Alas, Iclyn didn't see it like that, and was impatient.

Later than night, she woke Far to give him his stew. He still looked feverish and worried.

'Is it true they're bringing the Feast of Appeasement forward?'

Frostine nodded. 'The Frost Toll is at two.'

Far grew pale. He tried to get up and started to cough uncontrollably. 'I have to help,' he said.

Frostine pushed him back down. 'You can help,' she said. 'By resting.'

That evening Frostine and Iclyn made new shoes by the light of the wood burner. Iclyn sighed as she scored a hole into the leather she'd help cure from the fluhare. 'I just don't get it,' she said.

'I needed a new pair because mine are starting to fall apart,' said Frostine.

Iclyn rolled her eyes. 'Not the shoes. I meant Frostlaw,

and the Feast. Everything we do every year to appease a beast we've never even seen. What if it's all for nothing?'

Frostine paused. 'What do you mean?'

'Well, according to our history, it's been two hundred years since the Gelidbeast started to plague our lands, creating the Long Winter and making us live or die by the Frost Toll,' said Iclyn. 'I just wonder sometimes, if we're all being . . . I dunno.' She frowned as she pierced a hole through the leather. '*Silly.*'

Frostine blinked. 'Silly? Three children were taken, Iclyn. Think of all those families who lost their loved ones.'

Iclyn looked sceptical. '*I am.* Just because no one found those children, doesn't mean some mythical beast took them. What if he doesn't even exist? I think someone should break Frostlaw again, get the toll to three on purpose, just to see.'

'See what?'

'If he's real!' said Iclyn.

Frostine was shocked. 'If he is real, he takes a child. That's not worth the risk,' she said, placing the new shoes on the floor. 'Time for bed now.'

And she blew out the lantern, missing the determined look that crossed her sister's face.

Someone, somewhere, was screaming.

Frostine felt on the side of her bed for Godmor, but it wasn't there. She looked all around her bed. She hopped to the kitchen, and her spine turned to glass.

Godmor was on the table, wearing one of the new shoes.

Frostlaw had been broken.

But it wasn't just that which stuttered her heart and made her feel like she might shatter. It was the trail of blood, the open door, and the sight of her sister, in the distance, being dragged off screaming by something huge and monstrous.

The Gelidbeast.

There was a faint shout from Far's room. 'What is it? What's happened?'

Frostine looked from the kitchen to the empty hallway. In that cold second, she made a decision. 'Nothing, Far. Go back to bed.'

'Are you sure everything's all right?'

Frostine put Godmor on, then fetched her hunting gear and coat. 'It will be,' she said.

Then she shut the door behind her and followed the trail of her sister's blood.

Frostine had always planned on going hunting that morning. She just hadn't thought it would be something this big.

If she didn't get her sister back from the beast, they would come for Far. Even though Iclyn had put Godmor and the new shoe on the table, thus breaking Frostlaw, it was Far, as the adult, who would be held responsible. Far who would be hanged for Iclyn's stupidity.

Frostine was furious. If she ever got Iclyn back from that creature she vowed to shake her until she wept, then hug her until her bones cracked.

Above her head, the night sky was dancing. Swirls of green and purple light lit the way. It was midnight. Not even the most seasoned of hunters were about. She hoped that she would have enough time to find the beast and her sister before the Frostwilders woke and followed the blood trail to their cabin.

She trudged on towards the frozen lake, where the Gelidbeast lived below.

From behind her came a thin cry. Frostine turned to see a spark of blue, like the glow of a paraffin lamp. It darted behind the trees as soon as she turned. Something was following her. She pulled her furry hood over her head and continued on as fast as she could.

After an hour, she reached the lake. At the centre was

a large, ragged opening surrounded by cracks. Frostine would have to go carefully – with a rope, she thought. She didn't know how far the hole went and she could plunge to her death deep below.

Another thin cry made her turn.

Behind her stood an ice sprite with frost lips, icy skin and hair like a glowing sapphire.

Frostine had never seen one before. According to stories, before the Long Winter, the sprites were pale green and brought the spring, making the rivers flow and flowers bloom. But as the world froze, they began to change. Their skin got tougher, hard enough for their thin fingers to poke holes in the ground to crack the ice and let some of the frozen shoots grow. Many believed it was thanks to the ice sprites that anything grew in the Frostwilds at all. It was why they were always thanked for every kill, for allowing any animal to survive.

Frostine looked at the sprite and felt the need to explain. 'I have to go after it. He took my sister.'

The sprite just stared, blinking pale, glowing eyes. Frostine frowned. What was the point of a magical sprite if it wasn't going to do something?

She took out an ice pick from one of the compartments in Godmor. The sprite flinched.

'I'm going to stake it in the ice, then knot my rope

208

around it and shimmy down,' Frostine explained. 'Could you help me? It might make this easier.'

The sprite just stared.

'I'll take that as a no,' sighed Frostine as she began to abseil slowly down the ice tunnel.

The sprite whispered, '*Crack*.'

'I'll be careful,' Frostine said, softening slightly.

The sprite shook its head and pointed at the cracks.

'Right,' said Frostine. Perhaps the sprites had lost it over the years. 'Well, wish me luck.' She began climbing down, her legs banging against the ice walls.

'*Crack*,' called the sprite from above.

Daft thing, thought Frostine as she continued to abseil down.

She was around two metres down when she realised her mistake. She needed more rope. She swallowed, released the rope and then tried to continue with her ice pick, in its compartment in Godmor, wishing she had the other one that was currently staked up at the top – if only the sprite could help, she could bring the pick to her! She got a metre further before the pick she was holding slipped and she began to fall, screaming, down the frozen tunnel of ice.

She saw something faintly blue dart ahead, before she hit the bottom hard, landing on her wrist. There was a

210

crunching sound. The pain made tears leak from her eyes.

A faint sound made her turn. The sprite was staring at her.

'You were right there,' Frostine snapped. 'Couldn't you have helped?'

'*Crack,*' said the sprite, staring at her.

It was dark down here, even with the faint glow of the sprite. Frostine glared at the creature, wondering if it had willed her injury. But after a while she realised it wasn't looking at her arm, but somewhere in the distance.

It pointed a finger towards what looked like a large palace, far away.

Frostine blinked. A palace? Down here?

There was blood on the ground. She began to follow the trail once more, down a long, icy passage, holding her arm gingerly to her chest. Soon she began to hear what sounded like voices far away.

Voices were a good sign.

Iclyn was still alive.

Frostine walked until she came to a set of steps that led into a grand room. At the end was a large dais, where on a golden throne sat the Gelidbeast, monstrously large and made of ice. He had horns like a stag and glowing red eyes, and long talons at the ends of his frosted paws. Iclyn was bound at his heels.

'Iclyn!' Frostine cried, sliding on to her knees in a heap and gathering her sister's body in her lap. She sagged in relief when she saw the rise and fall of Iclyn's chest. She was just asleep.

The beast looked surprised and somehow amused. 'A child? One who has entered my kingdom willingly? What luck.'

'Let my sister go!' screamed Frostine, trying and failing to release the bindings on her sister's limbs. They seemed to be made of ice.

The beast appeared to grin. There were certainly a lot of teeth. 'And why would I do that?'

Frostine reached behind her and got shakily to her feet, fixing an arrow into her bow, despite her damaged wrist. 'Because if you don't, I'll kill you.'

'You?' said the beast, with an air of astonishment.

He took a deep breath. For a moment Frostine imagined that he wasn't just scenting the air but something else as well. Then his eye fell on Godmor and raked over her hurt wrist, and he laughed.

'I have been the most feared creature in the Frostwilds for two centuries,' he said. 'It was I who turned the forest to ice. I who chased the summer and spring and autumn

212

away. I who changed the sprites. I who killed hundreds of men who sought to bring me down, some the size of bears ... and yet you, small and weak as you are, think you can kill me? I would be insulted if it wasn't so amusing.' He waited and then seemed to frown. 'I said, it was amusing.'

There was the sound of forced laughter.

Human laughter.

From the shadows three humans, their legs bound in ice, shuffled forward. They were dressed in tattered rags. Two had long beards and the third had almost-white hair.

'Meet my servants,' murmured the Gelidbeast. 'So useful, as you can see, helping to build this palace and tend to my needs. Although, unfortunately, unlike me, humans have such short lives. So I always need a fresh supply around every forty to sixty years. Lovely of this one to come at just the right time, don't you think, Eira?'

The white-haired woman nodded, dully, not meeting Frostine's eyes.

Frostine frowned. *'Eira?'* The Eldermistle's missing child?

Eira's eyes snapped to Frostine's. They burned like black coal.

Frostine blinked, and looked from the woman to the two old men as she realised who they were. 'North? Lumi?'

The men inclined their heads.

'You've been here this whole time?' said Frostine. 'Alive?'

They nodded miserably.

'You see, despite my name I am not a complete beast,' said the Gelidbeast, cocking his icy head. 'I would prefer to keep you as a servant, like the others, than to eat you.'

Frostine raised her bow once more. 'I will not be your servant!'

The beast tapped two of his long black talons together.

Hundreds of ice sprites begin to appear. Within seconds they were on Frostine, trying to take her weapons. Frostine saw the sprite that had guided her into the palace, pulling at her sling.

'You!' she hissed, snatching it back, feeling betrayed.

The sprite shook its head, then whispered, '*Crack.*'

'Poor creatures,' said the beast. 'Over the years, as they've turned slowly to ice, speech has simply left them. That's all they can say now. That one pointless word.'

As if in agreement the ice sprites all said it together: '*Crack.*'

Frostine saw red. She grasped the sprite that had tricked her, stuffed it inside the sling and launched it at the beast. There was a *thwump* sound. The sprite shook itself off the beast's massive frozen belly, shaking a finger at her.

214

'*Crack*,' hissed the sprite.

The beast chuckled. To Frostine's horror, it seemed suddenly to swell, growing even larger. Frostine took off her shoe and flung it at the beast. There was another *thwump* sound. Before her eyes the beast grew larger still. He seemed to find this very amusing.

'By all means, child, keep going!' he laughed.

Frostine hesitated. If the beast grew larger every time she tried to hurt it, did that mean she couldn't kill it?

As if he could read Frostine's mind, the Gelidbeast nodded. 'Can't kill me, I'm afraid. Not with weapons in any case. They just make me stronger.'

He clicked his talons and the ice sprites gathered.

'I think that is enough talking for tonight,' he said. 'Take the children away. Tomorrow they can begin their new lives.'

The ice sprites swarmed around Frostine again.

'Wait,' cried Frostine.

The beast sighed. 'Yes?'

In Frostine's fear, she scrambled for something, anything, to say to make him stop. Suddenly she had an idea. 'You are a creature of your word, right?'

The beast looked intrigued. 'Why do you say that?'

'For over two hundred years, you've kept that word,' said Frostine. 'If the Frostwilders prepare the feast and don't break Frostlaw, you won't take their children. Correct?'

The Gelidbeast smiled. 'You might say I am actually a very lenient sort of beast. You get two chances, but when the Frost Toll reaches three, it is my right to take a child . . . or two.'

'So,' continued Frostine, thinking quickly. 'You wouldn't come for the children unless someone had broken Frostlaw three times?'

'I couldn't.'

Frostine frowned. He said *couldn't*, not wouldn't. Was he bound by the rules just as much as they were? 'You couldn't,' she repeated. 'Why not?'

The ice sprites screeched, '*Crack.*'

Frostine wished they'd stop talking about the cracks so she could think. Then she blinked. Wait. Were they trying to tell her something?

'Unless someone breaks Frostlaw, you can't get out?' she said.

The beast nodded. 'All you humans have to do is stick to the rules and you'll be safe.'

He clicked his talons and the sprites swarmed once more, ready to take her away.

'Wait!' cried Frostine again. 'I have something to bargain.'

216

The beast chuckled. 'Why would I agree to a bargain? I have everything I need.'

Frostine shook her head. 'No, you don't. Not according to the rules.'

The beast leaned forward, intrigued. 'Go on.'

Frostine took a deep breath. 'The rules say you can take a child, but only if Frostlaw is broken three times. Correct?'

'Yes.'

'Well, you didn't take me,' Frostine pointed out. 'You took my sister when she broke Frostlaw. That is your right.'

The beast nodded, he seemed impatient now. His smile had vanished.

'I, however, did not break Frostlaw,' Frostine continued. 'You did not come for me. I came here myself.'

She looked at the beast and could have sworn that he shrank ever so slightly.

'So, if you take me . . .' she ploughed on, 'you would be breaking the rules.'

The beast blinked and then – yes – right before her eyes, he shrank again. Frostine was sure that he was now the size he'd been when she'd first arrived.

The beast did not look pleased.

'So, my bargain is that I will stay, willingly,' Frostine

said, 'if you answer one question of my choosing.'

The beast hissed and fog steamed from his flat nostrils. 'I can give you riches and food aplenty in exchange instead.'

'I don't want riches or food. I want an answer to the question I choose.'

For a long moment, the beast simply stared. 'What is your question?'

'I will tell you – but first you must agree to answer it,' she said.

'Very well – I have some terms of my own, though.'

That seemed fair. She nodded in agreement.

'What is your question?' he asked.

'How do you kill a Gelidbeast?'

Frostine saw anger flash in his eyes, then he said, 'First, I will present you with a riddle: to understand how I die, you need to know how I am born. I will give you three guesses. After that you will stay with me.'

Frostine gulped, then nodded again.

The beast looked satisfied.

Frostine stared at the beast and thought hard. Every year, the Frostwilders hunted and gathered food for the Feast of Appeasement so that the beast would return to his slumber and leave their children alone. Yet earlier, he'd told her that she could have 'food aplenty'.

Food was always so sparse in the Frostwilds, so difficult to get in their frozen world, his offer had struck Frostine as strange – why would he offer it so generously when it was so scarce? Something told her the food was important, but why?

'Would you die if we didn't bring you food?' she asked.

'Is that your first guess?'

Frostine nodded.

The beast grinned. 'No. A Gelidbeast does not require sustenance in that manner. I could live forever without one morsel of food or drink passing my lips.'

Frostine frowned. He didn't require *food*.

Did he not eat the food? He said that he didn't require sustenance in that manner ... so something else sustained him? He was unlike all other earthly creatures as far she knew. Everything lived off food. Why not a Gelidbeast?

Frostine blinked. He'd said a Gelidbeast could live forever without a morsel of food. So perhaps there wasn't a general lifespan, like with most earthly creatures ...

So how did you kill something that wasn't exactly of this world and might live forever? Frostine wondered. And what did keeping Frostlaw have to do with it?

'If no one ever broke Frostlaw, you would die,' she guessed.

The beast seemed to grin at that. 'Oh no, no, no. That

could *never* kill me. Only one more guess left.'

Frostine was confused. *Why would it* never *kill him?*

What was the reason for Frostlaw in the first place? All those superstitions the Frostwilders believed in: getting your hair cut on the wrong day, dropping a knife, walking under a ladder . . . People feared something bad would happen to you if you did them . . . and in the Frostwilds, that fear was that the Gelidbeast would come for you. She paced up and down as she thought hard.

Frostine frowned. He didn't require food. Weapons fired at him made him stronger, not weaker. They made him grow. She blinked; it was there on the edge of her mind.

He shrank when she pointed out that he wasn't following the rules. And even if no one ever broke Frostlaw, he would still live . . .

Why?

What made him live?

Frostine thought of his riddle: 'To understand how I die, you need to know how I was born.'

The answer came in a rush and she rocked back on her heels, gasping.

Fear.

Fear is what sustained him! When the Frostwilders followed the Frostlaw, their fear of what might happen to them kept him alive.

'If we stop believing in you – stop fearing you – you'd die.'

The beast laughed in surprise. 'You are almost there,' he said. 'You are clever, I must admit. Smarter than most. But still, not smart enough.' He looked for a moment like he pitied her. Then he clicked his talons and the sprites began once more to swarm around her. 'Now you stay with me.'

Frostine was shocked. 'But I guessed right! You have to stick to your word!'

'Technically, you are only half right. And I am sticking to it,' replied the beast. 'We agreed three guesses and then you stay. I said nothing about letting you go if you got it right or indeed only half right. Language, my dear, is so very important.'

Frostine closed her eyes in horror as she realised her mistake. 'Wait!'

'No, no, the waiting is over.'

'*Crack,*' said the sprites desperately.

Finally, Frostine understood.

They wanted her to make the ice crack.

'The cracks appear whenever someone breaks Frostlaw!' she cried. 'If we keep breaking Frostlaw – that's how you die!'

The beast narrowed his eyes. 'You have had your

guesses. Now it is time for you to become my servant.'

Frostine shook her head. She was right, she knew it! She needed to break Frostlaw, just like Iclyn had done: on purpose. Iclyn wasn't an idiot . . . she was a genius. She was going to be insufferable when Frostine told her. Frostine almost grinned at the thought.

But what could she do? She didn't have a ladder, or an umbrella . . .

Her eyes scanned the grand ice chamber from the frozen dais to a tall pillar where the other humans were waiting – and fell on Eira. It would be Eira's birthday in one day's time. Just like hers.

'Happy birthday, Eira!' Frostine called. One day early.

'No!' cried the Gelidbeast, who began to shrink.

The ice sprites jumped and up and down in glee as a sudden huge break appeared in the ice. '*Crack*,' they cried happily.

The Gelidbeast shrank more. It was working!

'Seize the girl!' he cried in anger.

But the ice sprites shook their heads. Perhaps his magic over them was weakening too.

Suddenly Frostine heard loud voices, and the sound of booted feet. Several Frostwilders, including her Far and Whit of the freshly cut hair, stormed into the ice palace, led by the Eldermistle and armed with crossbows.

'We saw the rope and realised you must have gone after the beast, Frostine,' said the Eldermistle. He turned to the others and shouted, 'Fire.'

'Wait!' Frostine cried as an arrow flew straight at the beast. 'No!'

'This is no time to be soft, girl!' said the Eldermistle. 'The beast should die for what it's done. You were right to follow it. It's time we ended this once and for all.'

'It won't die, though!' Frostine cried.

'We'll kill it. Shoot!'

And before Frostine could say anything, ten arrows found their way into the beast.

The Gelidbeast laughed as he began to grow, even larger than when she'd first arrived. 'Oh, I needed that, thank you,' he purred.

'What's happening?' cried the Eldermistle in confusion.

'Violence and fear makes him grow,' said Frostine desperately. 'But I know how to kill him. You have to trust me.'

'I wouldn't,' said the beast almost jovially. 'Tricky thing, this child.'

The cracks had started to disappear.

Frostine swallowed. Then she saw the knife sheathed at the side of Whit's belt.

'Whit,' she said. 'Can you give me your knife?'

Whit frowned, but handed it over. Then he held out his hand for the penny she needed to give in exchange.

'I don't have a penny,' she said.

Far quickly took one from his pocket and held it out to Whit. 'We're from the same house, it still counts,' he said.

Frostine shook her head. 'No, Far. Whit, trust me right now. Do not take that penny.'

Whit blinked, hesitating.

The Eldermistle cried, 'Take it, Whit! It is Frostlaw! Do you want the beast to grow MORE?'

'He won't,' said Frostine. 'Trust me.'

Whit hesitated. Far moved closer to Whit, about to put the penny into Whit's hand himself.

'Eira!' called Frostine. 'North! Lumi!'

The Eldermistle and Far whirled around, noticing the bound humans standing quietly near the beast. Eira shuffled to her father.

'You're alive?' the Eldermistle cried, touching his daughter's aged face, her frosted lips. Tears began to leak from his eyes.

Eira nodded, then touched her heart and pointed at Frostine.

The Eldermistle blinked. 'You want me to trust her?'

His daughter nodded.

Whit's hand stayed, not accepting the penny in

exchange for his knife. Another rule, broken.

'No!' cried the beast, who began to shrink once more.

A new crack appeared in the ice. Suddenly one of the ice columns came tumbling down.

'Every time we break Frostlaw we weaken the beast!' shouted Frostine. 'Form a ladder, sprites!'

The ice sprites sprang to do Frostine's bidding.

'Now we pass under it,' Frostine told the Frostwilders. 'Trust me!'

'Do it,' cried the Eldermistle, who at last believed.

With so many Frostwilders passing under the sprites' ladder, there was another crack. The dais split in two, crashing near Iclyn, who had begun to stir awake. Her bonds broke apart as the beast shrank to the size of a bear. He lunged after Frostine, seizing her around the middle.

'Let my sister go!' cried Iclyn, awakening fully and tearing after the beast and Frostine.

Frostine thought hard, scanning the room for ideas. She saw a small table in the corner of the icy chamber. That would work! She wiggled, shaking Godmor till it came loose. When her prosthetic fell on the ground, she shouted, 'Put Godmor and my shoe on the table in the corner, Iclyn!'

'NO!' roared the beast.

'What?' said Iclyn, her face white with fear.

225

'You were right all along. We need to break Frostlaw!"

'*No . . . way!*' Despite everything, Iclyn was now grinning.

'Iclyn!'

'Sorry, right . . .'

Iclyn raced towards the dais and placed Godmor on to it. A new shoe on a table.

A crack appeared on the beast's arms. More appeared on his legs and belly and face. Light shone from the cracks as he shrank further still.

Frostine fell to the floor. She looked up into the beast's eyes. There was nothing there any more. They didn't glow. Even his stag horns were starting to vanish.

'You're a monster . . .' she breathed. 'A figment of our imagination. Something that lives only on our fears.'

The beast blinked blank eyes.

Now the sprites began to defrost, turning from blue to pale green, chasing away the shadows.

'Keep going,' said the sprite who'd followed Frostine down the tunnel, finding its voice at last.

The Gelidbeast was now no bigger than a cat. Nothing to be afraid of.

'I don't believe any more,' Frostine whispered.

'Nor I,' said Iclyn.

'Us neither,' said the rest of the Frostwilders and the people who had been taken.

226

'Good riddance,' hissed the sprites.

There was a sound like a worn-out balloon running out of air. The Gelidbeast faded into nothing as sunlight streamed inside the palace, melting the ice. Then water began to flow for the first time in two hundred years.

Not false. A real spring, at long last.

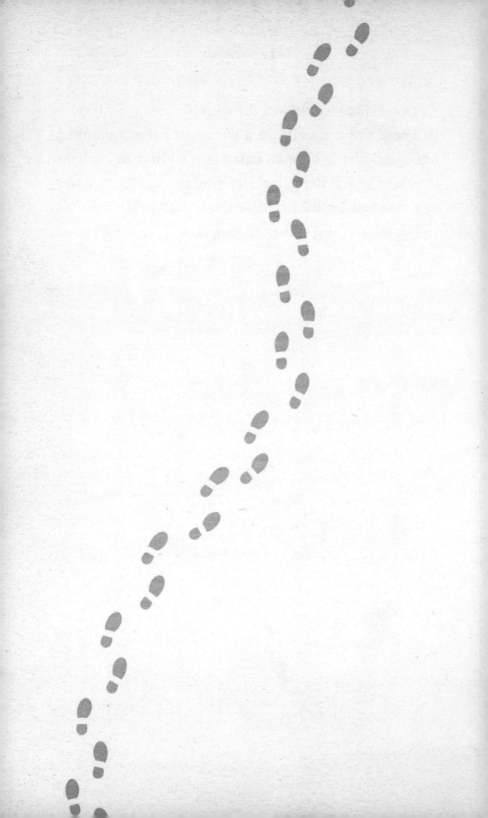

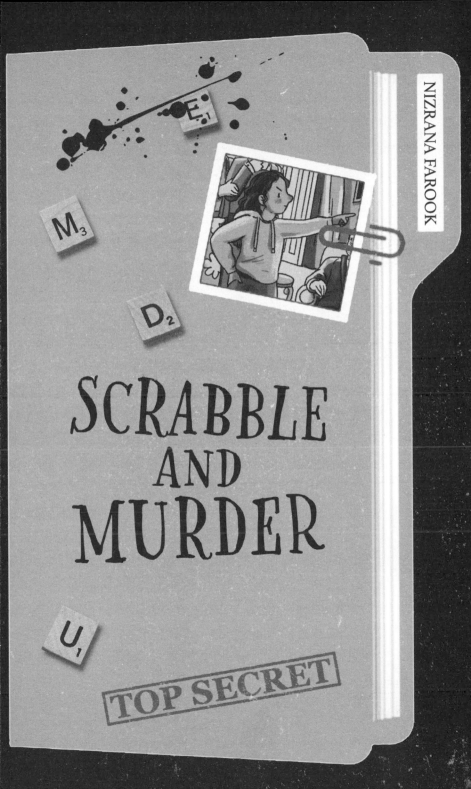

NIZRANA FAROOK

SCRABBLE
AND
MURDER

TOP SECRET

PROPERTY OF THE VERY MERRY MURDER CLUB

SCRABBLE AND MURDER

By Nizrana Farook

We were on our way to my grandmother's on the first day of the Christmas holidays when it happened. I woke up suddenly to muffled stillness and realised we weren't moving any more.

I blinked and rubbed my eyes. Cupping my hands around my face, I peered through the window at the gloom outside the car. What was going on?

'Why have we stopped?' I asked, glancing at the time on my phone. Six o'clock, but from looking out, you'd think it was the dead of night.

In the driver's seat, Mum was waving her phone in the air in concentration, trying to get a signal. Dad was missing from the passenger side. Jam – that's my five-year-old brother, Jameel – had got out of his booster and was kneeling next to me, twisting this way and that to see through the back window. Outside, snow swirled thickly around us, turning the world bluish white.

Dad opened the door and got back in, bringing a cold blast of air with him and making Jam scream. He slammed the door and the howling outside softened. There was snow on his shoulders and beard and lining the creases of his hat. He shook his head at Mum.

'It's out of the question,' he said. 'The road is impassable.'

'What does that mean?' said Jam in his high-pitched, happy voice.

'It means we'll have to stop here for the night, Jameel,' Dad explained.

'Not another stop!' I said, waking up properly at once. 'When is this journey going to *end*?' And for a whole night too. I was fed up.

'We're still about an hour from Grandma's,' said Mum. She clicked her seat belt off and it zipped back with a snap.

'There's a hotel just here.' Dad rummaged about, collecting his things. 'I've just called and spoken to the owner, and they have a room for us.'

'Yay!' said Jam, scrambling in the footwell for his shoes. 'Sounds fun!'

Mum put her hood up and jumped out. 'Come on, Saba, grab a bag.'

With a groan, I stamped out of the car, slamming the door. I picked up my case, which Mum had taken out of the boot.

'Wait for me, Saba,' shouted Jam, but I had already stalked off behind Dad.

The snow fell thickly, down my neck and into my eyes. I could barely see ahead, so I changed my mind and waited for Jam, who pushed his car door hard against the wind and came running up. Holding his grubby hand, I followed Dad, whose head was bent against the snow. Mum came up behind us.

Through the gloom and driving blizzard I could make out a massive, crumbling house set in what looked like huge grounds. We staggered on through a small parking area with a couple of big lumps, which I assumed were cars.

An old man stood at the lit doorway of the house between two white pillars, beckoning us inside. I ran in with Jam and we tumbled into bright, glorious light. The house looked ancient, but we were inside and warm and I felt that this might not be too bad after all.

The man shut the door behind us as we stamped clumps of snow off our feet. 'Well, don't just stand there! Come on then,' he barked crossly.

He went off down the hall and disappeared into a room on the right. Mum made a face at Dad, who shrugged then picked up his bag and Jam's backpack again. We followed the man.

'This is so amazing,' said Jam, as if it was the best place he'd ever seen in his life. 'Isn't it nice, Saba?'

I grunted as we went down the shabby carpet of the cavernous hall and into a bright living room. It felt almost tropical after the temperature outside. Well-worn furniture was scattered around, and bits of tinsel were draped over all the nooks and crannies. A Christmas tree stood in the corner, its lights winking on and off. There was a door at the end, leading off into a smaller room.

The old man sighed loudly from behind a wooden counter that looked like it was both a bar and a reception desk. 'Are we going to book you in today or what?' he said.

'Oh, er, yes. Thank you, Bob,' said Dad.

While Dad sorted things out with Bob, I gazed at the middle-aged couple sitting in threadbare armchairs next to the Christmas tree. They stared back with stern expressions, like people from a creepy old painting.

Across the room sat two black ladies who waved cheerfully at Mum, so she went over with Jam to talk to them. From their loud chatter I gathered that they were two backpackers called Kayla and Chenti: a mother and daughter. They were so toned and fit that I couldn't tell which was which. Who went backpacking in winter, anyway?

234

On a straight-backed chair next to the fireplace was a very neatly dressed man, stiffly reading a book. Kayla introduced him to Mum as Mr Shoto.

'Lucky for you I have a room,' said Bob from behind the counter. He opened a large book and asked Dad to write his name inside, as if we were in the Stone Age. 'Margie!' he yelled towards the door, then added by way of explanation, 'She's the missis.'

Dad filled in a line of the book with his name – Ahmed Hassan. He added his phone number and handed the pen back. 'Thank you. It's a stroke of luck that we stopped here.' He looked around the room, confused. 'Are you very full then?'

I was thinking exactly that. There was only a handful of guests for such a large place.

'*Technically,*' said Bob, tapping the side of his nose with a wrinkled finger, 'we're not supposed to have guests at all.'

'Oh? Why's that?' asked Dad.

'It's that meddling hotel inspector. "*Needs to be modernised. Health and safety concerns.*" Pah!' Bob handed Dad a rusty key that looked about a hundred years old. 'Here. Number seven. You're next to Jack and Jill over there.' He nodded towards the staring, middle-aged couple.

The staring couple were called *Jack and Jill*?

'Muuum!' I hissed. 'I don't want to sleep next door to

235

Jack and Jill. They look like serial killers.'

'What are serial killers?' said Jam loudly. 'And why are Jack and Jill serial killers?'

Mum was horrified as everyone stared at us. 'Ha ha, he's always mishearing things,' she said smiling sheepishly. 'Can't think what he means.'

Jack and Jill glared at us with what looked like pure hatred. Great. There was no way I was going to get a wink of sleep tonight.

'Well, that's that then,' said Dad with false joviality. He picked up our bags and Jam too, looking like he might fall down at any minute. 'We're going to go to our room and have an early night.'

'Oh no, you're not,' said a woman coming through the doorway. She was old too, like Bob, and equally grumpy. I guessed this was Margie. 'We're serving dinner now, it's Scrabble night.'

'Sounds lovely,' said Mum. 'But we're not hungry, just tired, so we'll say goodnight now. Ha ha,' she added, as if that would lighten the mood.

'Fine,' said Margie, throwing her hands up with a dramatic sniff. 'Never mind that we try hard to set up a nice evening of fun. There's no pleasing folk.'

'Oh,' said Mum startled. 'We're just . . . Oh, never mind, we'll come.'

No! I tried to make meaningful eyes at Mum to let her know that I did *not* agree with her last sentence, but she wasn't having any of it.

'We'll come,' she repeated firmly.

We headed out of the reception area and back to the passage, where we followed the arrows to our room.

As soon as the door swung shut, I turned on Mum. 'I don't want to play Scrabble with old people,' I moaned.

'You heard Margie,' said Mum. 'She's trying hard to spread some festive cheer. It wouldn't be right to shut ourselves away in our room.'

'Mum's right,' said Dad, dumping our cases on the floor. 'It sounds like fun.'

'I like Scrabble with old people,' said Jam.

'Exactly. It'll be great,' said Mum.

'What about dinner?' I said, changing tack. 'There won't be a halal option. Doubt they've even heard of it.'

'Nice try, but Dad already specified vegetarian to Bob.'

I huffed and gave up. There was no point arguing when Mum thought we were doing A Good Thing. That was when I noticed the room properly. There was one rickety double bed and a set of ancient bunk beds, with a small table in between and a cupboard in the corner.

'It's COLD!' I said.

'It is, isn't it?' said Dad frowning. 'It must be quite

expensive to heat such an old house.'

I took out my phone. 'We're in a remote place with serial killers next door and there's no signal!' I said with dismay. 'Why would anyone build a house where there's no phone signal?'

'Maybe, just maybe, the house existed long before mobiles,' said Mum as she tested the double bed by bouncing on the end of it. 'We'll be fine. It's a good thing anyway. It means you can put that away now.'

'We'd better freshen up and get out there,' said Dad. 'It's Scrabble night!'

Back in the living room, we were met by the smell of dinner. Bob was serving food on trays, handing it to people wherever they sat. Some of the guests were eating on their laps.

I could see the hotel inspector's point.

We sat at a small set of sofa and chairs, Mum and Jam on the two-seater and Dad and I on the individual seats. Bob came up with a tray of four plates and set it down on the coffee table without a word. A thick wad of paper was wedged under one leg of the table to balance it. An ancient TV was in the corner, playing some musical countdown show, but the volume was so low I could only watch the pictures. Christmas tunes played from a radio on the counter as Mum handed round plates of some

238

kind of veggie casserole.

There were two more people milling about now. One very thin and tall, who looked like he'd hit his head on the doorways, and the other stocky and startlingly blonde with his back to the room.

Margie came out of the kitchen in an apron. 'That's my grandson, Oliver. He's in sixth form,' she said to Dad about the tall boy. There was a note of pride in her voice. 'And Brad there is a friend of his.'

Oliver waved from the end of the room, where he was collecting Jack and Jill's trays. Brad saluted from over the counter where he was wiping a glass.

I finished my meal quickly and wondered how much longer we'd have to wait for the Scrabble. Hopefully it'd be over quickly. Through the window behind Jack and Jill the snow still continued to fall. I could see a huge build-up on the ground and flower beds.

'Can we go?' I said to Dad.

'No,' said Dad, humming along to 'Last Christmas'. 'What are we going to do there anyway? Let's just enjoy the company.'

'I like this hotel,' said Jam. Well, obviously. He liked everything.

Brad wandered by to collect our trays. He bent down near Jam, who had his head on Mum's lap. 'Hey, little buddy,' he said. 'You look beat.'

'I don't know what that is,' said Jam, and Brad laughed loudly.

'He means tired,' said Oliver as he went past.

'Snow got in the way of your vacation?' said Brad, still talking to Jam. 'That sucks, big time.'

'Are you American?' I asked him.

'Yes, kiddo,' said Brad, nodding his bleach-blonde head and grinning. '*AWESOME* that you knew that.'

I stared at him. There was something quite lame about Brad that I couldn't figure out. He wandered away back to the bar.

Some ancient song from, like, the 2000s came on, and Margie turned up the volume of the radio a little. Bob came by and squeezed in next to Jam on the sofa. He leaned in really close to Mum, as if about to share a huge secret.

'Whatever you heard about Jack and Jill,' he said, 'that's all over and done with. They're a changed man and woman.'

'What do you mean?' said Mum frowning.

'I don't know who told you,' Bob continued in a whisper, turning to Dad. 'All that serial-killer business. They weren't serial killers. Sure, they did a murder, but it was an accident. Maybe. They did the time and everything.' He waved his hands about. 'All in the past. Finished.'

'Ha ha ha ha ha,' said Dad, his face twitching. 'You're so funny, Bob.'

Bob shrugged and got up to go.

'Wait, you're serious?' hissed Mum, pulling Bob's sleeve.

'You don't have to worry,' said Bob. 'They've been out of jail a whole two weeks now.'

The music swelled. I was glad that it was drowning out our conversation because Jack and Jill were sitting with their serial-killer faces on just metres away from us.

Dad smiled weakly. 'So they've turned their lives around in two weeks? What do they hope to do now that they, er, need a new career?'

'Well, Jill wants to start one of them YouTube channels, to do up your house nicely,' said Bob. 'She learned DIY and decorating see, in prison. I got Oliver to sign me and Margie up.'

'So what are they doing here?' said Mum, eyeing Jack and Jill in terror. 'They've only just, er, left jail so they can't be in need of any time away. They must have, um, had quite a bit of that already.'

'Oh, they've been asked to lie low for a while,' said Bob breezily. 'One of them people they grassed on might be out for revenge.'

Dad's eyes were like dinner plates. 'Who's that then?' he whispered.

241

Bob shrugged. 'Someone called Babyface. Old crime partner of Jack before the Jill era. Anyway, don't worry about a thing. Enjoy Scrabble.'

He headed back to the bar, humming along to the radio.

That was it. I was out of here. I didn't care what Mum and Dad said.

'Mum! We've got to leave this place,' I hissed.

'Why?' said Jam. 'Because of Babyf—'

Mum clapped a hand over his mouth and looked at Dad. 'Where can we go, though?' she said.

Dad bit his lip. 'Nowhere in this. And we'd be safer here with everyone than in our room. Maybe Jack and Jill are reformed, like Bob said . . .'

Margie came out of the connected room with an armload of board games stacked high. She put them down on the floor by the Christmas tree. Oliver dragged a table to the middle of the room.

'Gather round, gather round,' he said.

'It's going to be team Scrabble today,' said Margie, opening up one of the boxes.

I wasn't sure if this was a Margie thing or what. I'd played Scrabble loads with my family and never heard of team Scrabble.

'Team one, Jack and Jill!' Oliver pointed at each team in turn and shouted out as if he was a game show host.

'Team two, the Hassan family! Team three, Kayla and Chenti! And finally, Team four, Mr Shoto!'

Jam cheered and clapped for everyone, especially us. Poor Mr Shoto looked like he didn't care much to be in team four, or any kind of team. He held up a finger to protest but Margie talked over him. 'Don't you worry, Mr Shoto, I'll join you.'

We all pulled our furniture a bit closer as Oliver arranged the board and letters on the table. Each team got a rack of letters and teammates could talk to each other before going up and placing their word on the board.

Soon the game was under way. Straight off Mr Shoto and Margie jumped to first place by creating a word with six letters over the pink middle square – it had an x in it too. We had a whole lot of consonants so only managed a measly three letters. Margie grinned smugly as we played our pathetic word. It soon became obvious how good she was and how competitive.

Dad whispered that the whole thing was a ruse for Margie to show off her Scrabble skills. Mum and I giggled and Jack and Jill looked at us suspiciously. They played reasonably well, certainly not as badly as us. Jam had the job of taking our letters to the board and placing them, though we had to shout out instructions as he kept getting them wrong.

When it came to Jack and Jill's turn, they shared a secret look before placing their word.

DER? I thought. That wasn't a real word.

But then Jill completed her word with three more letters and I gasped.

M U R D E R

A chill ran down my spine.

Jill leaned back, looking very pleased with herself. Kayla and Chenti didn't seem too fussed. I wondered if they knew about Jack and Jill's past.

A few rounds in, everyone had turned competitive, even Mum and Dad. Even me, though I didn't want to admit it. Jack and Jill pulled into the lead, much to Margie's annoyance. She set her teeth in a grimace and stared at the letters on the rack. Poor Mr Shoto didn't so much as get a look-in.

Margie suddenly smiled a secret smile and put her word down.

R E V E N G E

Everyone gasped. Seven letters! Margie and Mr Shoto got fifty extra points for that word on top of their normal high score.

'Fifty points! For real?' said Brad at the bar, stirring

sugar into a mug with a Rudolph print. '*Dude!*'

Margie pressed her lips together as if she was trying hard to contain her delight. Even Mr Shoto was getting excited. It looked like they had it in the bag.

We kept playing badly except for one brilliant round where we got a triple-word score. But even that wasn't enough to pull us out of the mess we were in.

Two rounds later, Jack and Jill scored a seven-letter word of their own.

'This is unbearable,' whispered Mum. 'Why are we so rubbish at this? I'm an English teacher, for heaven's sake.'

'Don't worry,' said Dad, his face a mask of concentration. 'We'll beat Jack and Jill somehow.' As if!

Oliver came round with mugs of hot chocolate for everyone. I leaned back in my chair and sipped the warm, sweet chocolatiness. I had to admit, the evening was quite fun. Sure, it was a bit tragic how competitive the grown-ups were, but even I could see that it was a pretty exciting game. Plus, it was lovely and cosy with the snow falling thickly outside while we drank hot chocolate and argued about whether GOUDA was a valid word (it wasn't). And around us, Christmas lights twinkled and carols played.

We were worrying for nothing. Jack and Jill seemed fine.

Jam had fallen asleep by the time the game ended, and even Jack looked like he was struggling to stay up. He put his Rudolph mug down and rubbed his temples. It was Jill who was concentrating on the game now. In the last round, much to Margie's annoyance, Jack and Jill won. She roughly scraped her chair back and went off in a huff, leaving the rest of us to clear up the letter tiles and pack everything away.

Mr Shoto, unlike his teammate, smiled gracefully and shook hands with everyone. 'Congratulations,' he said to Jack and Jill, and, 'You were brilliant!' to Kayla and Chenti. We got a sympathetic, 'Good game.'

There was an air of friendliness when we said goodnight and went our separate ways. Quite different to the atmosphere when we'd walked in earlier. It had stopped snowing when Bob switched off the outside light and drew the curtains shut. Oliver and Brad were washing up behind the bar when we all left around eleven. Margie still hadn't reappeared.

'Goodnight, everyone,' sang Chenti as she went off down the passage with Kayla, passing our room. 'Very early start for us tomorrow. Hope we get a bit of sleep at least!'

Jack and Jill disappeared into their room. I was pleased to see that it wasn't immediately next door but had a comforting expanse of wall in between. Mr Shoto went to the room opposite Kayla and Chenti's.

I brushed my teeth in a hurry and jumped into the

bottom bunk, trying to bury myself in the thin bedding as Dad switched off the light. I pulled the duvet over my head to block out the cold air. The room was freezing, the cold creeping into my bones. Jam was breathing deeply, sandwiched cosily between Mum and Dad. I heard the sounds of washing-up in the living room die down, and the family (plus Brad) go upstairs to the floor where they lived.

'I can't sleep,' I moaned from the depths of my inadequate bedding. 'It's too cold.'

'Put on your socks,' said Dad. 'Or your coat.'

'I *am* wearing my socks. And I can't sleep with my coat on! Can we turn up the heating?'

'You can always come and sleep with us,' Mum suggested. 'It's a bit of a crush but Jameel's like a hot-water bottle.'

Ew, no way. I was eleven, not a baby. Couldn't think of anything worse.

Someone went past in the passage outside, heavy footsteps receding slowly. The person groaned as they went. I tried to sleep, but kept burrowing among the clothes. The mattress was hard and flimsy. I could definitely feel the bed board.

Try as I might, I couldn't fall asleep. From somewhere in the house, a dull thud sounded. Like something falling on a carpet.

'That's it.' I jumped out of bed and went to the door. 'I'm going to ask Bob or Margie if they can turn up the heating.'

I opened the door and went out.

'I'll come,' said Dad sleepily, and I heard him get out of bed.

I paused outside the door and pricked up my ears. I thought I heard a shuffling on the left, near Jack and Jill's room. The noise made me curious and despite it being in the opposite direction, I padded towards it in my socks. Loud snoring came from behind Jack and Jill's door.

Terror rose in my throat as a dark shape materialised in the corridor. I tried to scream but was rooted to the spot.

The shape came closer. It was Chenti. She let out a shriek when she saw me.

'What are you doing skulking in the shadows like that?' she hissed. 'You gave me such a fright.'

'I heard a noise!' I said. 'What were you doing?'

'Nothing,' she said. 'I just wasn't sleepy.'

A crash sounded somewhere, like glass breaking.

We both looked into the darkness towards the direction of the living room. Was somebody there?

'So anyway,' I said, forgetting the glass for the moment, 'you were just chilling here in the dark? Don't you have an early start tomorr—'

'Are we going to stand here talking at this time of the night?' Chenti cut in. '*I* for one am tired and would like to sleep.' And she went back into her room and slammed the door.

I stood there in confusion. I thought she'd said she wasn't sleepy?

Turning back, I went towards the living room, passing the closed door to our room. Dad was probably looking for me. I could see a pool of light spilling out of the living room, so I headed towards it – and ran straight into Mr Shoto coming out.

'Ouch,' I said, stepping back.

Mr Shoto blushed and bowed in his formal way. 'My apologies,' he said. In spite of his politeness, he seemed flushed and anxious.

'I'm looking for Bob or Margie,' I said. 'And my dad. Have you seen them?'

'I haven't, they're not here. I will see you in the morning, Miss Hassan.' Mr Shoto stepped around me and went down the passage to his room.

The living room was super quiet. The Christmas lights were switched off, but everything else was as it had been earlier in the evening.

'Bob?' I said. 'Oliver?' Margie was probably still in a huff from losing at Scrabble.

There was a click from somewhere behind the counter but there was nobody there. Maybe someone was in the little room beyond the reception area, where Margie kept the board games.

I went in through the open door. It was much smaller and cosier, and just as tropical in temperature as the main room. It looked like a family room, much more personal and lived in. There were photographs on the walls and an ugly painting of a dying tree propped up on the mantelpiece.

I jumped out of my skin when I saw Jack sitting on the sofa. 'Sorry, I didn't –' But I couldn't continue as my mouth had seized up.

Jack was there – but he wasn't really *there*. He was sprawled on the sofa with his arms thrown out, staring straight at the gloomy painting, stone dead.

There was a knife on the carpet in front of me, just metres from my grey and pink elephant print socks. I stared at it. It was coated with a gloopy dark liquid that made me feel sick.

Dad peeped in at the door. 'There you are! I've been loo–'

He stared in horror.

250

'Saba!' he yelled at the top of his lungs, as if I had done something terrible. He pulled me away from where I was standing.

Footsteps thundered through the living room and Brad came into the snug. He yelped and stared at me and Dad. Then Oliver and Margie hurried in.

Margie picked up the knife from the floor. 'Is he dead?' she asked.

Dad groaned. 'You're not supposed to touch the knife, Margie.'

Bob came in wearing a nightgown and cap, like a nursery rhyme character in an old book. 'Margie!' he said. 'Now you've gone and done it. Killing him for winning at Scrabble!'

'You're losing your marbles, Bob,' protested Margie, turning the knife back and forth in her hands. 'It wasn't me. It was Mr Hassan that did it.'

'Me?' said Dad, staggered. 'It wasn't me. He was already dead when I came in to see my daughter.'

'You?' said Margie, looking me up and down. 'They're getting younger and younger.'

'I didn't kill him!' I said hotly. 'He was dead when *I* came in.'

'Looks like no one's going to own up then,' said Bob, as if it was a matter of spilling a bit of tea on the carpet. He scratched his head. 'Where do we put him?'

Oliver was gagging. He looked away from the body at Bob. 'Gramps, we don't put him anywhere. We should call the police. I'll try the landline.' And he went off next door to the telephone. He seemed to be the only normal person in this bonkers household.

'Police aren't going to come,' Bob grumbled. 'Not in this weather.'

'Do we leave him here till morning?' said Margie. 'I wish he wasn't lying on my aunt Jemima's throw. That's good candlewicking.'

Brad stepped forward. 'Maybe we should get the others,' he suggested.

'Now look what you've done!' said Margie, pointing to Brad's feet. 'You've only gone and got his blood on your socks. You're going to wipe it all over the house.'

'That's it!' said Bob. 'Everybody out.'

He shooed us all out to the living room as if we were pesky ants. Then he closed the door of the snug room on Jack.

'The police aren't able to come anytime soon,' said Oliver behind the counter as he put the phone down. 'PC Stanley lives close by so he might manage it, but the proper people will come in the morning – weather depending.'

'Morning will be fine,' said Margie. 'He's already dead,

252

isn't he? Not much they can do.'

Mum came into the room holding a sleepy Jam by the hand. 'What's going on?'

'There's been a murder,' I said. 'Jack's dead.'

Jam whooped. 'Yay! Just like the movies.'

'Don't be ridiculous, Saba,' Mum snapped. She turned to Dad. 'What happened?'

Chenti and Kayla came into the room now, with Jill and Mr Shoto behind them. They all looked puzzled.

'She's telling the truth,' said Dad. 'Sorry, everyone, but Jack's been murdered.'

Jill gasped.

Dad's face went red. 'Sorry, Jill. I didn't see you there. He –'

'No bother,' said Jill, looking quite resigned. 'He had a lot of enemies, did Jack. Who did it?'

Everyone shook their heads. Nobody knew. I watched Jill carefully for any sort of fakeness. She was, after all, the certified serial killer around here.

'What about the guy Jack grassed on?' said Mum. 'Could he have broken in and killed him?'

Babyface. I had been wondering that myself. There was only one way to find out.

'Bob, can you switch on all the outside lights, please?' I asked.

253

Bob shuffled to a bank of switches and turned on a few. I drew back the curtains of the living-room windows and looked out. The snow lay like a very heavy blanket under the moon, undisturbed all along this side of the house.

'I'm going to check every side,' I said. 'Nobody move!'

I ran around the house, looking out of all the windows I could find. In spite of my warning, Jam came running with me. I didn't mind, though. He wasn't a suspect. We looked through the glass strips on the front door, the fanlight on a downstairs loo, and a window in the stairway. All around the house, the snow was perfectly undisturbed.

'Just as I thought,' I said, bursting back into the living room. 'No one has entered the house in any way for an hour at least.'

'And all the empty rooms are kept locked,' said Oliver. 'Bob, Margie and I regularly check them and make sure all unoccupied room keys are behind the counter.'

'So it has to be one of us,' I said.

'Mr Hassan says it wasn't him,' said Margie.

'Of course it wasn't him!' I said. '*Bob* thought it was *you*, Margie. Also, Mr Shoto was here just before I found the body.'

'Mr Shoto?' said Bob. 'A nice gentleman like that?'

'Mr Shoto wouldn't hurt a fly!' said Kayla.

254

'Thank you, madam,' said Mr Shoto. 'That is true. I wouldn't hurt a fly.'

'Everyone's a suspect, aren't they?' said Jill.

'Even you,' said Brad. And after thinking a bit, 'Maybe *especially* you.'

'I'm the victim!' said Jill.

'Come on, people!' I said. Luckily I'd watched old detective films with Mum and I knew how things had to be handled. 'We need to stop arguing and figure this out.' I turned to Mr Shoto standing quietly by the door. 'Mr Shoto, what were you doing in here earlier?'

Mr Shoto looked completely embarrassed. 'I came in for a drink of water, but I accidentally dropped the glass,' he said. 'I cleared it up, and then I met you when I was leaving, Miss Hassan.' He looked apologetically at Bob. 'Sorry.'

So that was it. The poor man was embarrassed because he'd accidentally broken a glass. There was a chance he was lying. But then I'd actually *heard* the glass break.

'Did you look in the snug?' I asked.

'Yes,' said Mr Shoto. 'I saw Mr, er, Jack there, but he looked distracted, so I didn't speak to him.'

'Did you switch on the lights?' I asked.

'No. They were on already,' said Mr Shoto. 'Both in the living room and snug room.'

'Is this kid going to be questioning us all?' said Jill.

'Because I have nothing to say. I was fast asleep from the moment my head hit the pillow.'

'We heard,' said Chenti, rolling her eyes. 'Loud and clear.'

I looked at Chenti carefully. I was beginning to understand her actions now.

'Dad,' I said. 'For the purpose of this investigation, can you explain your movements from the time you left our room?'

Dad looked a bit put out at being investigated. 'I followed Saba – you – out of our room and went to the living room. The lights were on but nobody was there. I called out, and then left.'

'Did you go into the snug?' I asked.

'No,' said Dad. 'I didn't go into the living room either. Just stood at the doorway and looked for you. Then I went upstairs to see if you were there.'

'I can confirm Mr Hassan knocked on our door,' said Margie graciously.

'Not just Margie and Bob's room,' said Dad. 'I knocked on Oliver's and Brad's too. Brad didn't answer, but I could see that he was in the bathroom at the very end of the passage, because the light was on there.'

'And none of them had seen me,' I confirmed. 'Which isn't surprising, because I didn't go upstairs. What did you do next?'

256

'I came downstairs and looked in the living room again,' said Dad. 'Finally I decided to check the snug. I found you there with a dead man and a knife at your feet.'

'Thank you,' I said. '*Very* interesting.'

My brain was in overdrive. I'd spotted something I hadn't before. One person's actions were starting to feel quite suspect. *More* than suspect, in fact.

'Oliver,' I said, gesturing to him like a boss. 'Could we have a round of hot chocolate, please? Let's all sit down because I have something to tell you.

'I know who killed Jack.'

Everyone sat down in various seats in the room. Oliver listened from his position behind the counter as he prepared the drinks. I went and stood in front of the Christmas tree.

'I have pieced together the events of this evening,' I announced. 'And I'm going to tell you everything and unmask the murderer.'

Mum and Dad stared at me in astonishment, but Jam grinned proudly. He gave me two thumbs up, making me blush.

I cleared my throat. 'So, um, last night after dinner we started a game of Scrabble. Everything was going well but there was tension in the air. I could tell that Margie was *very* sour about losing.' I smiled apologetically at Margie's scowling face. 'But I was misled by the Scrabble. *That* was just a harmless game. The real tension was from someone setting their murder plan in motion.

'At 11 p.m., my family, Kayla and Chenti, Mr Shoto, Jack and Jill went to our rooms. Bob, Oliver and Brad were left here, washing up. Margie was upstairs, feeling sorry for herself.'

Margie huffed and crossed her arms.

'The killer had already slipped something into Jack's drink to make him feel ill,' I went on. 'And they made sure that that specific mug was directed to Jack and nobody else.'

I noted with satisfaction that Oliver had gone pale. I was on the right track.

'Soon after Bob, Oliver and Brad had gone upstairs, around 11.20 p.m., I believe Jack came to the living room to see if someone was around to ask for some help, or possibly find him some paracetamol. Maybe he'd already tried and failed to wake Jill up. I heard him go past our room on the way here. They were very heavy man-footsteps so I knew it was him and not Mr Shoto. I also heard Jack groan, and he had looked a bit ill earlier, straight after the Scrabble game too.'

258

I paused as Margie came round with the mugs of hot chocolate. I must admit it was a cosy scene in front of me, as everyone curled up with their drinks in their PJs listening to my story. One of them wouldn't be feeling quite so cosy inside.

'The killer was waiting for Jack in the living room. They greeted him sympathetically and took him to the snug room and asked him to sit down. Jack recognised his killer at this stage, but he was too weak to put up a fight. That was the killer's plan all along, and they then plunged the knife into Jack.'

There was a general gasp. Jill looked mournfully at me. Kayla put an arm around her comfortingly.

'Jack dropped on to the sofa, and the knife fell on the carpet. Over in room seven, I was in bed and heard the thud of the knife as it hit the carpet.'

There were a few nods around the room, as if they'd heard it too.

'Shortly after that, I left our room,' I said. 'Instead of going straight to the living room, I heard a sound outside Jack and Jill's room, so went down the passage that way instead. I found Chenti loitering there. She didn't want to say anything, but she was clearly infuriated. She and Kayla wanted to leave early the next day, and Jill's snoring was preventing them from getting even those few hours' sleep. No offence, Jill,' I added. 'But you sound like a tractor when asleep.'

'Fair enough,' muttered Jill.

'Chenti was going to bang on the door and tell Jill to shut up, but that would have set a bad example to me, a mere child,' I went on. 'So she got mad and stormed back into her room instead.'

Chenti shrugged at Jill apologetically. Bob nodded, urging me to go on.

'Meanwhile, Dad left room seven soon after me,' I continued, 'and headed for the living room. He didn't realise I had gone the opposite way, towards Jack and Jill's room. He peeped in the living room and called my name. The killer stayed silent in the snug, hoping that Dad would go away. Seeing no one, Dad headed up the stairs, looking for me. The killer tried to exit then, but heard Mr Shoto walk into the living room for his drink of water, so he hid somewhere in the snug room, possibly behind the sofa.'

Mr Shoto nodded to himself in agreement. The others listened with rapt expressions.

I continued with my evidence. 'In the living room, Mr Shoto thought he heard a noise from the snug. He peeped in and found Jack sitting there, but it was only a quick look. He didn't realise that Jack wasn't just distracted –

he was already *dead*. Mr Shoto then had some water, and dropped the glass. While this was going on, Chenti and I were, of course, on the other side of the building, talking outside Jill's room as I've explained, and heard the crash of the glass on the floor.'

'Well, I never!' mumbled Margie, setting her mug down.

'She's good, isn't she?' whispered Kayla to her.

I pretended not to hear this much appreciated bit of praise, and continued.

'The killer waited impatiently until Mr Shoto cleared up the broken glass. They heard Mr Shoto leave and, in a hurry to get away, snuck out of the snug. But then they heard *me* bump into Mr Shoto at the living-room door, and ducked behind the counter there,' I said, pointing to the bar where Oliver and Brad were standing.

'But how would you know this?' said Mum. Next to her the others nodded, Bob especially looking at me sternly.

'Good question! I heard a noise behind the counter when I came in. I wasn't *looking* for anyone hiding there, so wasn't to know the killer was squatting behind it. Then I went into the snug and found Jack dead.'

'It's like watching a movie,' said Jill. 'Very vivid.'

'Er, thank you.' I was flattered. She wasn't so bad for a serial killer. 'Then Dad came into the living room. He'd knocked on doors upstairs. Bob and Margie hadn't seen me, and Oliver said the same. Brad wasn't in his room, but the light was on in the bathroom at the end of the corridor so Dad assumed he was there. He came downstairs, heard a noise coming from the snug – that would have been me – and found me with the body.'

Mum nodded, as if to say everything added up. Chenti said something to Jill and patted her shoulder. Oliver still looked ashen, though Brad shook his head sceptically.

'Now *this* is where it gets interesting,' I said. 'Dad's discovery of me and the body took seconds from the moment he came downstairs. He saw me in the snug, yelled, and all hell broke loose. People came running in from all over. But the first person in was the killer. Because *he was just metres away*, hiding behind the counter of the living room.'

'Who was it then?' said Margie.

'I present to you, the killer of Jack.' I pointed. 'Brad, otherwise known as Babyface.'

'Rubbish!' said Brad, standing up.

'It's garbage, remember?' I said.

'Yes, that,' he admitted.

'How do you know it was him?' said Dad.

I smiled. 'Think about it. He wasn't in his room when

you went up to the first floor, and you thought he was in the bathroom at the end of the corridor. But you came downstairs, found me, and five seconds later he was in the room. He'd have had to pass Bob, Margie and Oliver on the way, all of whom came in well after him.'

'Drat,' said Brad under his breath.

'Did you say Brad is Babyface?' said Jill.

I nodded. 'That's how he got the idea to pretend to be Oliver's age. Everyone thinks he's younger than he is, because of his youthful looks. So he befriended Oliver, hoping to stay here and get the opportunity to kill Jack. I *knew* he didn't seem like a teenager. Just an old person trying hard to act cool.'

'It was the Google article I used for research,' said Brad glumly. 'It said that youngsters talk like that because of all the TV they watch.'

'I don't,' said Oliver. 'I should have been more suspicious. I did think it was a bit full on.'

'Exactly!' I said. 'Not gonna lie, I thought it was tragic. Brad also didn't want Jack to recognise him before he had a chance to do the deed, so pretending to be American helped with that. That and the exaggerated hair-dye job.'

'Oh, that explains something,' said Bob. 'Brad was always shy about going up to Jack. He'd keep a distance or turn his back.'

264

'That's right, *I* gave Jack the hot chocolate that made him ill,' said Oliver, looking angrily at Brad. 'Because you told me the Rudolph mug was for him and he likes a lot of sugar in his drink! It wasn't even sugar.'

'You've got blood on your hands, Babyface,' said Jill, turning to him.

'And on his socks,' said Jam, pointing.

I looked at Brad's socks. 'Good spot, Jam,' I said. 'Brad's socks have drips on them. *Drips.* He must have noticed them when we were in the snug and deliberately stepped on the carpet blood to explain it away if needed.'

Brad suddenly tried to make a run for it – where he was hoping to go in that thick snow I don't know – but Dad and Chenti jumped up and caught him. He struggled with a sulky look on his face like a kid caught doing something naughty.

Bob got up and started clapping, followed by Jam who jumped on the sofa and cheered. One by one the others stood up and clapped too.

I blushed. 'Thank you.'

It was nearly light outside and the snow still lay thick on the ground. I realised that we'd probably have to spend another day here, but it was all right really. The place wasn't bad, and with Brad being kept safe until the police got here, we were all OK.

265

I wasn't even afraid of Jill any more. I had to stop thinking of her as a serial killer now. She was *just* a killer. The distinction was important. Reformed too. She smiled at me and passed me a card printed with her YouTube DIY channel called *From Slammer to Hammer*. I was going to subscribe to it as soon as I got online.

'Well, that's it then,' said Margie, getting up and dusting off her hands. 'We have a whole day to while away now. I know! Who's up for a game of Scrabble?'

ADMIT ONE

49229442

ADMIT ONE

49229442005

THE
TICKING
FUNHOUSE

BENJAMIN DEAN

TOP SECRET

THE VERY MERRY MURDER CLUB

PROPERTY OF THE VERY MERRY MURDER CLUB

THE TICKING FUNHOUSE

By Benjamin Dean

The funhouse sat in a forgotten corner of Wonderland. It was crouched in darkness, the winter night's tentacles hugging it close. The metal of the house creaked in the whipping winds of Christmas Eve, but its groans went unheard as people hurried by. The neon bulbs around the edges of the house flickered, feeble and weak against the night, but not a single soul paid attention to its calls. It was like the house wasn't even there.

At the front, in a small booth no bigger than a cupboard, sat an old man, his face mostly hidden by an old hat that looked like it'd been chewed apart by dogs and stitched back together. His eyes flickered this way and that, watching and waiting. But nobody seemed aware of the funhouse, or of the man sitting in front of it. And that just wouldn't do.

The man stepped out of the booth and on to the metal walkway, which moaned beneath his weight. He waited for the house to quiet itself before walking to the end and hitting a large red button, hiding from sight behind a flap. It took a moment, but the house woke up, a Christmas jingle blaring out of hidden speakers. But the sound was blurred, broken notes calling out to the night. The jingle bells rattled, beckoning anybody who dared to come closer – anybody who might dare to enter the funhouse in the forgotten corner of Wonderland.

Billy Beck heard the jingle bells first and his body instinctively cringed away from them. He wouldn't ever admit it, but he'd never *really* liked Christmas. Unlike his dads, who loved Christmas as much as Billy loved summer, something about it just didn't sit right with him. Maybe it was the biting cold of December; the awfully cheesy songs and equally cheesy movies; the cake with raisins in that was apparently a tradition but was actually nothing more than an insult to taste buds everywhere. Or maybe it was because his dads insisted on decorating the house until it looked like a grotto from the first week of November until the last week of January. Either way, Christmas wasn't Billy Beck's favourite time of year, and when he heard those jingle bells, he was far from thrilled.

'Come on, it'll be fun!' Dad said, tugging on Billy's arm

and bounding towards the funhouse like a bunny that'd been sipping on coffee. Billy looked to Pa for help, but he was sprinting along beside them, grinning from ear to ear. With dawning dread, Billy knew he was outnumbered.

'How much for all three of us?' Dad said, digging into his pockets for change.

The old man at the front clapped his hands together, a grin creeping across his face. Billy found it concerning that his lips, teeth and a filthy white beard and moustache were pretty much all you could see of his face, the rest of it hidden under the ragged hat.

'It's free, for one night only.' The old man's voice was raspy, like his words were being dragged across jagged rocks as they formed at the back of his throat.

But Dad didn't seem to notice. Instead, he looked like he might faint with joy, patting Billy on the back and ushering him towards the metal stairs that led up to the walkway. A wooden door at the end summoned them closer. Smoke seeped from a crack at the bottom, and a multicoloured glow pulsed around the edges. From behind the door, the jingle bells rang out again.

'I ... think I'll give it a pass, actually,' Billy said, taking one look at the door and thinking he'd rather throw himself into the mouth of an active volcano. He ducked under the arms of Pa and took three sensible steps back

271

so Dad wouldn't be able to grab him again.

'Oh, come on – it'll be fun!' Dad pleaded.

'It's just a funhouse, Billy,' Pa tried, his eyebrows slightly raised as if issuing a challenge. But Billy wasn't going to be enticed inside by begging or dare. Instead, he shook his head and gestured towards the door, which seemed to be almost vibrating at the prospect of being opened.

'You guys go ahead. I'll wait right here.'

Dad and Pa exchanged a glance. Worry lines etched themselves around Dad's eyes, but Pa shrugged and mounted the stairs as if he'd already made up his mind that Billy would be fine waiting outside alone for five minutes. What trouble could a twelve-year-old cause in that time anyway?

'Don't move a muscle, OK? You stay right there and we'll be back before you know it.' Dad put on his serious face, his eyebrows coming down into a line. Billy didn't budge an inch. 'Did you hear me?'

'You said not to move a muscle! You're setting me up for failure already if I have to talk.'

Dad rolled his eyes, swallowing a laugh.

'Are you coming or not?' Pa called, now in front of the door and ready to go. Dad hopped up the stairs to join him. Both of them gave Billy a wave before holding hands and facing the door.

'We'll be right back,' Dad said as the door swung inward, smoke billowing out around their ankles.

They took a step towards the door, but were stopped by the old man, who called out to them from the booth. 'Merry Christmas,' he said. Billy fought a shiver as the December breeze crawled over his skin.

Dad and Pa grinned. 'Merry Christmas,' they repeated back to him. Then they stepped through the door, leaving Billy alone to watch and wait.

And wait he did. He waited for one minute and then two, which trickled into a third and then a fourth. On and on the minutes went by until ten became fifteen and fifteen became twenty. The thirtieth minute was marked by a robotic laugh, which echoed from the house itself. Maybe it was supposed to be an elf, or something just as whimsical. Instead, it crackled from the speakers with a maniacal cackle, twisting Billy's stomach.

He'd had enough of waiting. The funhouse didn't appear to be particularly large. Even if it stretched back further than Billy imagined, it couldn't take half an hour to find your way back out again. Dad and Pa wouldn't let it, knowing Billy was outside alone.

Billy stepped closer to the booth, looking up inside at the old man. His hat still covered his eyes, but his mouth was pulled up to one side in a sneer.

274

'Excuse me?' Billy uttered, his voice small and quiet. 'Are they still in there? They've been gone ages.'

The old man's lips pulled back, baring his teeth, which were crooked and stained. He shifted his head upwards, so the shadow of his hat began to rise up his face, revealing eyes that were milky white.

'Who?' he said, the rasp in his voice almost mocking.

Billy fell back a step, his heart pounding in his chest. He was suddenly aware that he was the only person at the funhouse, everybody else avoiding this forgotten corner like the plague. The wind carried laughter and the gentle tinkle of music elsewhere in Wonderland, but Billy was quite alone.

'My parents,' he whispered. 'Where are they? They must be in there somewhere.'

The old man shrugged, clearly enjoying himself. 'I don't know what you mean. There's nobody inside.' A shiver jolted through Billy, his heart now racing around every inch of his body. 'But of course you're welcome to enter the funhouse and see for yourself?'

The funhouse seemed to grow taller, looming over Billy with foreboding menace.

'I – I think I'll just wait,' Billy stuttered. But as he stepped away, the nagging thought he'd been trying to ignore slithered further into his head – he'd been waiting too long. Something was wrong, and waiting outside wouldn't solve the problem. He'd have to go and at least look inside the funhouse.

'Actually, I'd like to go in,' Billy said, trying to make his voice sound more confident than he felt. It wobbled in the middle though, giving him away.

The old man smiled and gestured to the door. 'Be my guest.'

Trying to ignore the evil grin of the old man, Billy mounted the steps before he could talk himself out of it and shuffled up to the door. It swung open as it had done before, the smoke creeping out to greet him.

'You be careful in there,' the old man called. 'Oh, and Merry Christmas.'

Billy felt his entire body go stiff as the clutch of dread wrapped itself around him. Shaking his head, and with one last look out towards Wonderland, he stepped through the open door, and the funhouse came alive.

Not a single sound from Wonderland followed Billy inside as the door swung shut behind him. Instead, a rhythmic ticking noise surrounded him, pulsing from the walls. Billy found himself in a short, narrow corridor, the glow of a thousand colours guiding the path to another door ahead. But there was something sinister about that noise, as if the tick were a cruel and mocking laugh.

'Nope,' Billy muttered, once again thinking that it'd just be better to wait outside and call the police if his parents didn't reappear. He turned and gave the door he'd walked through a push. It didn't budge an inch. Billy tried again, the shiver of fear rising up inside him like an ice-cold flame.

'Billy, Billy, Billy.'

Billy jumped, whipping around so fast that he fell backwards into the door he'd just been trying to open. Of course, it still didn't move. There was nobody else in the corridor.

'You can't leave before the fun's even started.' The voice was measured, but forcefully so, like it was holding the butt of a joke in its hand, waiting to reveal it with glee.

'Who's there?' Billy said, fear yanking the words out of his mouth with haste and throwing them into the air.

The voice didn't respond, but the edge of the door at the end of the hall began to glow a faint red, summoning him to come closer. Billy cringed back into the wall and gave the door one final try, hoping that he'd just not been strong enough the first two times. Since his dads weren't around to tell him off, he chose a curse word that would usually get him grounded for at least two weeks and stood back up.

'Here goes nothing then,' he murmured under his breath.

He stepped down the corridor, which somehow seemed to get lower and thinner the further he went, until he was pinned in from all sides, squeezing against the walls and stooping away from the ceiling. When he turned around for one final glance at the entrance, the door was impossibly small, no bigger than a stamp.

With one final push, Billy stood before the new door, hoping that this one might open. He placed his hand against the wood, trying to convince himself that opening it wouldn't just transport him further into this nightmare but actually towards an exit where Dad and Pa would be waiting.

But before he could open the door, words began to appear, etched into the wood one by one as if by magic.

As snow begins to fall,
You better think fast,
For if you start to panic,
This first door could be your last.

Billy frowned. Wasn't a funhouse nothing more than a few rooms with distorted mirrors and hamster wheels for you to run around in? Why did this sound like a challenge? Like something that could be won, or lost?

Deciding that there was no use in thinking about it

278

too much because what was the worst that could happen – like the first door, this was a question Billy refused to open – he pushed it and breathed a sigh of relief when it swung forward with ease.

The room beyond was a simple square, its walls painted with scenes of snow-capped mountains and icy landscapes. A snowman had been splashed on to another identical door on the far wall, its beady eyes seeming to fix Billy with a foreboding stare and evil grin. Billy had to remind himself that the snowman was made up of paint and couldn't actually hurt him.

Taking one step into the room, the door behind him slammed shut, followed by the metallic clicks of a thousand locks securing it in place. Well, there was another door that wasn't going to open anytime soon, but at least there was another way out of this room.

He took another step towards the snowman on the door, trying his best to ignore the constant ticking, which was only getting louder. But when he reached the middle of the room, the ticking stopped.

And then everything went dark.

Billy yelped, his senses suddenly heightened now one of them had been taken away. The room was pitch black, and it was suddenly cold. Freezing cold, as if he'd just stepped outside barefoot into a blanket of . . .

Billy thought the first flake of snow was a drop of water, dripping on to the tip of his nose. There was another drop, and then another, until it was a gentle flurry. Then the lights came back on and the room had changed. A layer of white now dusted the floor, slowly rising centimetre by centimetre as more snow fell from the ceiling, which had transformed into a stormy sky filled with menacing clouds ready to burst.

Billy was motionless as flakes of snow drifted lazily down to the floor. If he reached out and touched it, the snow felt real. Almost too real. He cupped his hands together and waited a second for it to gather in his palms. It was freezing cold, sending shivers up through his arms.

'How . . .?' Billy murmured, so captivated for a moment that he forgot to fear the funhouse.

And then the lazy snowfall started to come down faster, collecting around Billy's trainers and inching up to his ankles. His socks were already soaking wet, his toes frozen. Faster still the snow fell until it was a blizzard – a blizzard that showed no signs of stopping. And when it began to reach his knees, Billy remembered the rhyme on the door, and he started running. Or rather wading, as the snow was now past his knees and climbing towards his waist.

The snowman smirked as he approached the door, like a sentinel that would grant or refuse entry. Billy

280

ignored it and pushed, but as was becoming something of a pattern with the doors inside the funhouse, this one refused to open too.

'Please! Let me out!' Billy shouted, banging against the door as the cold of the rising snow seeped through his clothes. But shouting did no good either. If anything, the snow just seemed to rise faster.

Abandoning the door, Billy looked wildly all around him for a way out but was met with nothing except solid walls and a ceiling made of clouds. As the snow rose to his chest, he jumped up, trying to reach the sky as if that might do anything. He just had to keep his head above the snow. He couldn't let it cover him completely or he'd . . .

He stopped the thought before it could finish itself. This was nothing more than a funhouse. Nothing truly dangerous could happen in here. It surely wouldn't be allowed. But as the snow threatened to meet his ears and his hand slapped the clouds, only to find them solid and unmoving, Billy's mind raced.

You better think fast, he recited to himself in his head, unable to speak out loud now that the snow had covered his mouth. He was so absolutely freezing that his body no longer felt like his own. It now just seemed like an empty vessel, numb, his soul floating outside of it.

If you start to panic, this first door could be your last.

Billy would've snorted if he could – how was he supposed to stay calm when he was seconds away from being submerged entirely?

Don't panic. Don't panic. Don't panic.

He recited it to himself again and again, closing his eyes as the snow finally took him over, engulfing him completely. Billy felt himself being pulled down further. And further. He was surely going to be buried under this snow forever.

Don't.

Panic.

Don't.

Panic.

Don't.

Panic.

The thought became a beat, pulsing inside his own head like a heart. And then it became a ticking, like a clock. Like the ticking from the corridor. Billy kept his arms wrapped around himself, trying his hardest not to fight or panic.

The cold encasing him slipped away and Billy felt at peace for a moment, as if he were simply lost in a dream. Then he started to fall, slowly at first through the snow until he seemed to go straight through the floor and began falling through the air. He landed in a heap, all

282

limbs and yelps. But as he untangled himself and stood up, patting over his body and searching for injury, he found none. His body wasn't even cold any more. It was as if the snow had simply never happened. Except, when Billy looked up, he could see it pressed down against the ceiling, a reminder of the room he'd just been in. It was as if an invisible barrier was keeping the snow from falling down to join him.

What *was* this place? It was no ordinary funhouse, he could be certain of that.

Again, Billy found himself in a simple room, smaller than the first. A door waited to be opened, but he was getting tired of that game. The walls were an off-white, almost grey in places, and there wasn't a window in sight through which to see the safety of outside. Billy felt like he could be anywhere in the world, cooped up in a box with no way back out again.

'Why, hello again, Billy. I was concerned you weren't going to make it out of that first room, which would've been quite alarming considering we've only just begun.'

The voice rang out again, coming from nowhere in particular but somehow everywhere at once. It didn't sound human, or even robotic for that matter. If Billy were religious, he might assume it to be the voice of God. Or, worse yet, the devil.

'Who are you?' Billy asked feebly. He knew it was the wrong question to ask. His first should've been, 'How the hell do I get out of here?' but his curiosity had got the better of him.

A cold laughter skipped around the room. 'How did you like your welcome to the funhouse?' it said, ignoring the question.

'A warmer welcome would've been better,' Billy quipped before he could stop himself. He bit down on his lower lip, scolding himself, but the voice just erupted into a cackle.

'Finally, someone with some fight. This should be a lot of fun.'

'Who are you?' Billy asked once more.

'That's none of your concern. What you *should* be asking is what's coming next . . .?'

Billy took a step backwards, away from the door in case it should fling open without warning. Even though his insides quivered, he tried to stand up straight, to prove to the voice if it were watching that he wouldn't be pushed around.

'And what's coming next?' he said, forcing himself to stay calm.

'I wouldn't want to ruin the fun,' the voice replied, its words wrapped in glee.

Billy's mind raced with possibilities, which he tried to clamp down. If nearly drowning in snow was the first step of the funhouse, what else could lie in wait?

Billy almost didn't dare ask the two questions burning in his head, for fear of what the answers might be. But he had to know. 'Where are my parents?' he asked first.

'They're still here, of course. They're the whole point of all this fun.'

Well, that was something positive. At least if Billy moved forward, he'd know he was getting closer to Dad and Pa. He took a deep breath, ready to ask his last question.

'Will you let us go?'

The voice seemed to mull this over, humming to itself. 'You'll need to pass three challenges first. And you've already completed one, so you're a third of the way there. If you should pass all three – then yes, I'll let you go. But that's quite enough of that. We've got a game to play, Billy. And what lies in wait is getting rather impatient.'

Suddenly, there was a roar from behind the door. It started low, rumbling like an engine before it grew into something thunderous. The voice laughed as the door swung open by itself. A corridor of tall pine trees lay behind it, standing shoulder to shoulder and forming a path through a moonlit forest. A flurry of snow fell from a night sky, settling on to the forest floor in a thick layer, untouched by footprints.

The roar sounded again, this time from behind Billy, who spun around to find another open door with an identical corridor of trees stretching off into the dark. The roar was accompanied by a monstrous thudding getting closer.

And closer.

And closer still.

'You better get going, Billy,' the voice said. 'He's a hungry boy. But you'll have time to hear my riddle, if you'd like it.'

The invisible beast was moving quickly, speeding in Billy's direction. 'Well, if we could hurry this up, that'd be wonderful.' The voice laughed, cleared its throat, and began.

'This wooded enclosure hides something quite feral, Watch out for its jaws and take a wrong turn at your peril. To escape this maze, you must follow one simple rule, Go the right way round, until right would make you a fool.'

'Your advice is to go the right way round?' Billy spluttered, aware that the monster must almost be upon him.

'Everything you need to succeed is in the rhyme. You

286

need only pay attention to what it said.'

The terrifying sound of something huge coming towards Billy filled the air – still out of sight but drawing ever closer, a growl building in its throat.

'You'd better get moving, Billy. He can run quite fast.'

Without a second thought, Billy bolted in the opposite direction, pelting through the open door ahead of him and into the forest. The stillness of night was only interrupted by his muffled footsteps as they pounded the snow, and the roar of something sinister behind him.

Billy had always been a fairly good runner and now he hoped that was enough to escape whatever was on his tail. He ran and ran, the words of the funhouse circling his head, each one a flock of fluttering birds. *Go the right way round.* That could mean anything, but so far the path was a straight line.

And then it wasn't. Ahead, Billy saw the path split off in two opposite directions. They looked exactly the same, nothing to offer a hint about which path he should choose. Left or right? Right or left? With the thundering of a hulking beast tearing after him, he didn't have long to make a decision. So, with a prayer to the sky, he peeled off to the right.

Again, he ran straight until he had to make another choice, the same one as before. It was like he'd simply run around in a circle, the forest never changing, the trees standing guard, identical to their neighbour. His lungs burning, legs aching, he went right again, singing the rhyme in his head. And then it clicked. *Go the right way round.* Each choice was simply left or right. If he kept taking the path to the right, he'd surely find the exit. Right he dashed, then right again. The growl was gaining on him, but Billy wouldn't turn back. He had to keep running.

Suddenly, something changed. Just as before, the path ahead split in two, left and right. But this time, there was an open door at the end of each path. Through the door on the right there was a burning fireplace, crackling in front of a large, stuffed armchair. It looked warm and cosy, inviting him in. To the left, the door opened to reveal a blank room, identical to the ones he'd already found himself in before. Compared to the other room, it looked cold. And now he'd stopped, Billy realised he was freezing. If he sat in front of the fire, he'd be warm in seconds. Safe, even.

Billy was dragged from his thoughts by muffled pounding racing through the snow, and when he turned around, he finally saw it. The beast was even bigger than he'd expected, covered in fur and looming down on him, at least five times his size. It had magnificent antlers that reached up even higher, but they were covered in

288

spikes. Its snout was long and when it growled it revealed sharp teeth that dripped with saliva. When it saw Billy, it stopped and lowered its head, so it was nearly touching the snow, looking up at him with narrowed eyes. Billy knew it was about to pounce.

He had to make his choice. *Go the right way round, until right would make you a fool.* To be a fool would be to go left, into a cold room when he was already frozen. But as he took one step to the right, another thought occurred to him – to trust the funhouse, to trust the inviting warmth, would be silly. Why would something that had offered him no help so far suddenly want to offer him exactly what he needed? Surely, he'd be a fool to trust it.

Go the right way round, until right would make you a fool.

Hoping he wouldn't regret it, Billy switched direction and sprinted towards the door to the left. The beast responded by leaping after him, snapping at his back and tearing his jumper. But Billy kept running for the door, eventually falling through it. Quickly, he jumped back up and pushed the door shut with all his might. The beast charged into it, nearly throwing Billy backwards. But squeezing his eyes shut and pushing with all of his strength, Billy heard a click and realised the door had closed. He slumped down to the floor, exhausted but safe. For now at least.

'Back so soon?' The voice sounded smug and taunting. 'I thought you might be dinner for our little friend. Alas, you have successfully completed the second stage. I'm sure you must be eager to learn of your final task.'

Billy pulled himself back to his feet. This nightmare had to be over soon. One more task, then he'd find his dads and they'd all be let free. If the funhouse kept its word, anyway.

'The final task is simple. There is no snow or beast, just a choice to be made. Your final door is ready when you are.'

A door swung forward, revealing a room of lights. Their wires built a tangled wall on either side, once again forming a clear path in front of him. Billy swallowed hard, desperately wanting this game to be over. But there was no going back. He couldn't, even if he tried. So, with a deep breath, he stepped up to the door and passed through into the sea of lights.

The ticking of the funhouse was back, louder than before, echoing off into the room with each sound. The lights twinkled red and silver, green and blue, on and on and never-ending, an infinity pool of stars on either side. The end of the pathway seemed to fall away suddenly, the solid floor giving way to a black, endless void. Billy dug in his pockets and found a coin, flipping it up into the air and letting it fall into the dark. There was no sound.

290

'Don't step too close to the edge now, Billy. I'd hate to lose you when you have one last choice to make.'

As if on cue, two tangled webs of light began to move towards Billy, out of the dark in front of him. They were orbs of colour, separated from each other and floating through the black. As they crept closer, Billy realised they were each holding something in their clutches. He squinted, trying to make out what it could be. His body realised before his mind could put it all together, goosebumps rising all over his body.

'DAD! PA!' Billy yelled as the balls of light came to a stop, hovering just out of reach. Dad and Pa were encased inside separate webs, seemingly asleep. Their chests rose slowly, eyes closed and faces peaceful. But there was no way to reach them without stepping from the path into the void, and the coin had proved it had no end.

'Your choice has arrived,' the voice said. Billy could've sworn there was a grave undertone to the words now. 'Both parents, so loving and kind. Each before you now. But who will you choose?'

Billy gasped, the breath leaving his body all at once. He swayed on the spot, and for a moment, he thought he might topple forward into the void itself.

'I won't choose,' he whispered. 'I can't.'

'No choice is a choice itself. Tick tock, Billy – your time

is running out.'

As if to demonstrate its point, the tangled web of lights loosened their grip on Dad and Pa, and they dropped out of their cocoons until they dangled by a single thread, both on the verge of falling into the void below them.

'My riddle! You haven't told me the riddle!' Billy spluttered, desperately trying to buy himself more time to think.

'Of course,' the voice replied. 'As you wish.'

'In order to solve this riddle,
You must think with all your wit.
For a decision lies before you,
Not an easy one – not one bit.

To choose one without the other,
Will leave one in the funhouse forever.
But perhaps there lies another choice,
In a dark place empty but clever.

The exit lies before you,
All you have to do is think.
Take a chance to solve this mystery,
Or remain up on the brink.

Now take a step, I dare you,
Before you're much too late.
It's time to make a decision, Billy,
Or will you leave it up to fate?'

'So, Billy,' the voice finished. 'What will you choose?'

The sea of lights surrounding him seemed to pulse with energy, a million quickening heartbeats surrounding him. Each breath Billy took was short and shallow, his thoughts now raging waves, building and breaking before rolling up once more. He couldn't make sense of the riddle, no matter how hard he tried. All he could see were his parents, hanging by a thread, the void below them waiting greedily to swallow them up forever.

'I won't choose,' Billy said again, muttering it again and again under his breath like a chant.

'Then if you won't choose, our game is over,' the voice said and the lights holding Billy's dads loosened once more.

'WAIT!' Billy cried as Dad and Pa dropped lower into the void. He had seconds to make up his mind, a mere moment to make a decision.

'Yes?' the voice said.

'*Take a step, I dare you.*' Billy repeated the line out loud, his eyes darting from his parents down into the black expanse below, a night sky with no stars and no end.

'*Take a chance to solve this mystery,*' Billy murmured, his voice shaking. He knew what he must do. He didn't know if it was right or wrong, or what might happen next. But he would take a chance. He wouldn't leave it up to fate.

'I've made my decision,' Billy said.

A chilling hush swallowed the funhouse, the ticking finally silenced. Billy closed his eyes, painting a picture of his dads in his head to hold on to. Then, after a deep breath, he took a step off the ledge and fell into the mystery below.

JOANNA WILLIAMS

ICE
AND
FIRE

TOP SECRET

THE VERY MERRY MURDER CLUB

PROPERTY OF THE VERY MERRY MURDER CLUB

ICE AND FIRE

By Joanna Williams

THE FIRST DAY

Have you ever been so cold that you felt as though a viper were biting at the tips of your fingers? Or that the bones in your body had become long blocks of ice? Did you ever see, as you spoke, your own breath wreath and drift into the air like the smoke of a great dragon?

London, December 1776. The air bites so hard that the River Thames has slowed and frozen into a silvery ribbon of ice, the world beneath it stilled, suspended in time. Even the fishes have been stopped mid quiver, each mouth frozen open in a silent 'o', the once-waving reeds around them held motionless as in a painting.

But where there is ice, so there must be –

'The Frost Fair!' I shout when the horse-drawn wagons loaded with tents and banners clatter past my bedroom window. Hyde Park is to be transformed into *A Five-Day Extravaganza of Icy Entertainment and Frosty Family Fun!* Activities on offer included Oxen-roasting, Gingerbread-baking, Nine-pin Playing, the Poets' Corner and – my favourite – Ice-skating.

I'm sorry. How rude of me! Let me introduce myself. Lizzie Sancho. Twelve years old. Frost Fair fanatic. I live with my family on Charles Street, Westminster, in what Papa calls a 'modest' house next to our tea shop. My father, Ignatius Sancho, is known to many as 'an African Gentleman and Distinguished Man of Letters'. That's because he's always writing letters to his friends and, when moved to protest, to the newspapers. Renowned for his generosity, he is also – according to the sign in the shop window – 'a Purveyor of Fine Fare: Gourmet Groceries, Tempting Teas and All Manner of Exquisite Edibles'. To me, he is simply the best father anyone could wish for.

My mother Anne is the business brain of the family. Born in England to Jamaican parents, she is compassionate and practical. She juggles running the family accounts with schooling me and my four siblings in 'the business of life'. Frances is seventeen. She is quick-witted, calm-

298

headed and kind. Mary, fifteen, is an expert harpsichord player, obsessed with learning the latest dance steps. Kitty, five, is prone to giggles and impulsive hugging, and Billy, who is just two, we call 'smiler' or 'the baby'. That's us, the Sancho family, in a nutshell.

It's a sunny, sharp-edged Monday morning, the first day of the Fair. Papa has promised to take me, if he can get away from the shop. Madame Cerise is bargaining with my father for an extra week to pay her bill. The hamper she heaves on to the counter is crammed with grape-stuffed geese, clove-stuck oranges, glacé cherries and sugar-coated almonds.

'My dear Madame Cerise!' Papa mops his mahogany brow; he does that when he's flustered. 'Your outstanding bill is considerably high.'

Not as high as that extraordinary wig. How does she hold her head up?

'A man has to make a living,' he reasons. 'I must ask that you pay for your goods with no further delay.'

Madame Cerise pushes her scarlet lips into a pout and pats the white rolls of that towering wig coquettishly. Clouds of pink powder puff into the air.

'Of course, Mr Sancho. But you must call me Hélène.' She stretches out the name so that it sounds like *Airlairne*. 'Next week you shall have your money without fail.

299

We must all find ways of getting by, no?'

Judging from the expensive fuchsia silk ballooning beneath her fur-trimmed coat, Madame Cerise does not have to worry about 'getting by'. For weeks now, she has been coming into the shop with her daughter, each time in a more extravagant outfit. And each time, her unpaid bill – along with her hair – mounts higher and higher.

Meanwhile, my father supplements his living as a grocer by writing classical music. His days are long, his evenings spent staying up with Mama, heads bent together at the table by candlelight, working out the family finances. Mama does not approve of Madame Cerise at all.

Papa sighs the sigh of the weary. 'Very well. For your daughter, perhaps a little hot chocolate to warm her before you brave the cold again?' I pour a cup from the pot and offer it to the girl hovering awkwardly at the back of the shop. She is, as ever, so muffled up in blankets that you can hardly see her face. I press the cup into her hands with a smile. She takes it without a word, drains it and nods her thanks as she passes it back to me. She avoids my eye. Suffering more from embarrassment than cold, perhaps.

'Come, come, child!' says Madame Cerise, handing her the brimming basket and ushering her out of the shop. Papa closes the door behind them and opens his arms wide. 'And now, my dear,' he says, enfolding me in one of his backbreaking bear hugs. 'Mama has granted you and yours truly the afternoon off! To the Frost Fair!'

When we arrive, Hyde Park is cloaked in a fine mist made silver by the sun's light. The trees, garlanded with blue-white snow, reach their branches towards one another across the avenue where we trudge crunchingly towards the Fair.

Hundreds of people, muffled up against the cold, wander among the multicoloured tents that dot the banks of the Serpentine, now a lake of glass for skaters. I watch in awe as they fly in long gliding steps, spinning neat arabesques, carving intricate patterns and sending up powdered dust in their wake. Others inch along gingerly, clutching at their companions, wobbling their way across the ice.

The food stalls are piled high with glazed game pies, cushiony cream cakes and glistening gourmandises. The heady scent of spiced gingerbread mingles with the intoxicating aroma of dark hot chocolate. As the crowds queue for food, a young boy in torn clothes darts among them. I shiver at the sight of him. The poor boy must be freezing.

'C.S. Lenier, printer at your service, sir!' A nasal voice interrupts my thoughts. Papa is peering into the tent where souvenir tickets for the fair are sold. A broad-shouldered man in a bold yellow coat bows low, waving us in. 'A ticket, sir, to commemorate your visit?'

'A printing press!' exclaims Papa, eyeing a large wooden machine composed of intricately arranged square plates and levers. It looks like a strange multi-legged creature. Papa reaches inside his coat and hands over a penny. Lenier's eyes glint. He pockets the coin and gets to work. His long fingers position the letter tiles into a tray and apply the ink.

'Look carefully, Lizzie, at the arrangement of the letters!' says Papa. It's odd. Each letter appears as if in reverse. Mr Lenier places a blank sheet of paper in the tray and pulls the lever down hard. When he lifts it up again, there is our very own printed ticket!

On this day, 10th December 1776, Ignatius SanchO and his daughter Elizabeth SanchO did visit the FrOst Fair and partake in its delights!

Seeing the appearance of my name in print like that – it's like magic!

'You see!' Papa exclaims. 'Evidence! We were here!

302

This, my dear girl, is how books are made. Pamphlets, posters, newspapers – all thanks to the printing press.'

The rhythmic boom of a bass drum cuts in. Once, twice, three times – an announcement.

I leave Papa discussing the power of the press with Lenier and follow the mesmerising beat.

There, standing on a small stage in a corner of the park, is a tall, ebony-skinned woman. She wears a robe of rich indigo, a dark velvet cloak covering her shoulders. Her hair is coiled into a crown of thick black ropes and under one arm she carries a large, round drum from which her fingers spin patterns of sound.

'Come one, come all, and hear the Black Poetess!' she calls in a warm, resounding voice. The crowd presses in closer, buzzing with curiosity. I squeeze my way to the front for a better view. Beside me, a man sketches the Poetess's portrait, for the newspaper perhaps?

The Poetess weaves her words like a spell: a powerful song of enchantment. She sings of her home across the ocean where a salt breeze whispers through the lush green forest at the sea's edge. Where the sun drenches the earth in its crimson light before sinking below the shimmering horizon. She sings of arriving in a place where children sleep in the streets and their mothers are forced to steal food. A place where a ravenous monster terrorises the land, consuming everything in its path. Where the tiny creatures living in its shadow starve, because the crumbs it leaves them are not enough to keep them alive.

I look around me at the thin and thinly dressed children that skirt the edges of the crowd like spectres. Of course! Just like the boy I saw earlier. They are the tiny creatures that the Poetess is singing of. As though she can hear my thoughts, she holds me with her luminous black eyes.

As the Poetess finishes her song, an awed hush envelops the crowd. Then rapturous applause. Raising her hands above her head, she says, 'My thanks for your praise – but if you have heard my words, spare a thought for the cold and hungry children that walk among you.'

Murmurs arise from the audience as her meaning becomes clearer. The children in need of our help are right here, all around us. One by one, people begin to offer a scarf, a coat, some food, a drink of hot chocolate for warmth.

I scan the crowd anxiously. Where is Papa? There, on the other side of the lake, buying bread and pies for a small group of children huddled round him. I am shot through with a pang of love for him and I push my way through the crowd to help. You see, Papa was born on a slave ship. He was brought to London and suffered terribly at the hands of three sisters in Greenwich who claimed to own him. Many difficult years later he escaped and found friendship, freedom, independence and, in his words, 'On meeting my lady wife – a magnificent woman of sharp mind and stout heart – utter joy!' Because of his beginnings, my father is, and has always been, a man of great compassion.

The Poetess's song echoes in my mind. I look around in the hope of speaking with her, but she has already disappeared, swallowed up by the vast and moving throng.

THE SECOND DAY

At daybreak the next morning, I help Mama and Papa to pack up a basket of freshly baked loaves for me to deliver to the neighbourhood of St Giles, one of the city's poorest parishes.

Here the streets are dark and dangerously narrow. The wooden houses teeter towards one another so precariously that you could reach out a hand from a window on one side of the road to knock on a wall on the other. I slip and stumble over the icy cobbles as I go from house to house with the warm bread. The Poetess's words jangle in my head.

When the basket is empty, I cross Seven Dials towards

Covent Garden. Here, just a few streets away, smart piazzas flaunt grand colonnades topped with elegant carvings of animals and angels that gleam in the white winter sunlight. A different world. As I step into Neal Street, I glimpse a girl in a ragged dress staring at me from a shadowed doorway. She watches me for a moment, then turns and slips out of sight. The snowy ground where she was standing is strewn with papers. I bend down and pick one up.

Are yOu cOncerned by the recent rise in 'charitable schemes' tO help the pOOr?

DO yOu wish tO increase yOur prOperty and prOtect yOur privileges at ALL cOsts?

Then jOin the Silencers!

Next meeting: 4 p.m., December 12th Upstairs at the Jamaica COffee HOuse

The 12th – that's tomorrow! I gather up the pamphlets, shove them inside my coat and hurry home.

Back at the shop, Hélène Cerise is loading up another hamper. Her bundled-up daughter shifts impatiently from foot to foot by the door. The grim message of the papers concealed in my coat haunts my thoughts. Who are the Silencers and what are they up to?

Meanwhile, poor Papa is patting down his pockets.

'Lizzie, dearest, I seem to have lost the letter I was writing to the newspaper. Do help me to find it, please!'

I set about searching the shelves that line the walls of the shop. Often littered with Papa's personal papers and correspondence, they are surprisingly tidy and I can't see his letters anywhere.

Madame Cerise cuts in. 'I have been following your recent correspondence in the *Daily Advertiser*, Mr Sancho.' Her teeth appear dark yellow against the alabaster paint she wears on her face.

'Ah yes, a terrible business,' Papa replies, shaking his head sadly. 'Four more hanged at Newgate Prison. Just for stealing food to feed their children. I am writing to protest. And I am raising a petition!'

Madame Cerise nods sombrely; her wig tips forward at a dangerous angle. 'Quite right, Mr Sancho.' She puts up a hand to stop its fall. 'I wonder, perhaps, what your Mr Cree would make of it?'

Papa bristles. Nils Cree is a rival letter-writer with whom he locks horns regularly in the pages of the *Daily Advertiser*. Each time my father publishes a letter of protest, Nils Cree writes a letter insulting him. The two men have never met, but if they ever did, sparks would fly!

'My letter puts forward a perfectly penned argument, guaranteed to win support,' says Papa, composing himself in spite of his anger. 'Are we to let hungry people hang for stealing food? No! There must be mercy at Newgate!' He opens the drawers under the counter, one by one, rifling through old newspapers and bills. 'Where on earth can it be?'

'Do not let the troubles of others bother you so, Ignatius,' says Madame Cerise, pulling her fox skin tighter about her shoulders. 'I'll have another pound of macaroons, if I may ... I seem to be developing quite a habit ...'

Desperate to find his letters, Papa reluctantly agrees to let me visit the Fair alone to hear the Poetess again, provided I return home before dark. I march through the snow, reflecting on the long nights my parents stay up working to ensure that we can eat well, that we can be warm in winter. I think of the people suffering in Newgate Prison. Of those children flitting among the well-dressed crowds in their thin clothes. And where is the boy I saw yesterday? Still no sign of him.

I make my way to a prime position in front of the stage. When the Poetess emerges from her tent, an exuberant cheer goes up from the crowd. I wave: the Poetess catches my eye and smiles. My skin tingles. Once more, she beats a hypnotic rhythm from the drum; once more, we all listen with intent.

I am spellbound. The Poetess's songs speak straight to my heart. Songs of distant libraries towering over dusty sands, of words of wisdom written by peace-loving scribes, of poetry passed down through the ages, each generation singing their truth to the next. My soul thrills with the power of the words and the music.

But as the song ends, a ripple of unease flutters through the crowd. The woman standing next to me bumps against me violently and suddenly I am being jostled on all sides. People around me clutch at their clothes in consternation.

'My purse! – My bag! – I thought I felt something! – A pickpocket!' Confusion turns swiftly to pandemonium fuelled by anger. 'Stop! Thief!' The crowd is becoming a mob. I am pushed from one person to another as people grab at anyone they suspect of stealing from them.

'Here! Look! Caught red-handed!' A tall, bespectacled man is holding a skinny, mouse-haired boy firmly by the arm at the entrance to the Poetess's tent. It is the boy I saw on Monday! In the other hand the man brandishes a bag bursting with purses, coins, notes and watches. The crowd sends up a roar of dismay. The boy struggles to get free, pointing at the Poetess and yelping, 'She paid us! She paid us to steal your things for her! Please don't punish me! Please!'

My heart skips. Surely that cannot be true!

'It's her all right!' the man thunders. 'Everything's here, in her tent! The pickpockets are working for her!'

The Poetess stares in disbelief at the bag of valuables. A stout woman clambers on to the stage and grips her by the arm.

'Call for the Bow Street Runners!'

Children scatter in all directions as four burly men in blue greatcoats push their way through the crowd. The men bustle the Poetess roughly off the stage and into a waiting coach. Heart racing, I force my way towards her through a sea of bodies.

'Where are you taking her?' I cry.

The Poetess leans out and grasps my hand: her jet eyes gleam. 'I am innocent, sister,' she whispers.

'Off to Newgate!' bellows a bearded man, climbing into the driver's seat. One sharp snap of the reins, her fingers slip from mine and she is gone.

Newgate! My legs tremble at the memory of my father's words. But the sun is sinking fast behind the city spires and the sky bleeds rose into indigo: I must get home. First thing in the morning, I will find my way to London's most notorious prison.

THE THIRD DAY

Newgate Prison is, as I feared, a desperate and dismal place. Precious little light penetrates the gloom of its corridors, even at dawn, and its air is thick with a putrid stench that seems to ooze from the walls. The courtyard is eerily quiet. Rats, squat and sharp-eyed, scratch through the frost and filth in the darkness.

I have persuaded the warden – a small, hunched man with a heavily lined face – to let me in by promising him a hamper of Sancho's groceries. He shakes his head disapprovingly as he leads me along the corridor, muttering, 'You can't stay long. I could lose my job, I could, just letting you in.'

At an iron door he stops and jangles the large bunch of keys hanging at his skinny waist. 'Five minutes,' he grumbles, twisting the key with a snap and pushing the door open. 'And no shenanigans.'

The Poetess paces up and down the short length of the dingy cell. At the sight of me, she gasps. 'Thank you, sister! I knew you would come.'

I glance around at the filthy walls. 'I'm going to get you out of here,' I promise.

311

'No shenanigans!' calls the warden from the corridor.

'She's innocent!' I shout back. I turn back to the Poetess. 'This isn't right. I'm going to find out who has framed you and why.'

'I trust that you will, sister. You are a seer, a listener, blessed with a gift for observation.'

Her words warm me. Mama often says the same.

'I loved listening to *you*. When you sang, I felt as though I were in a dream. And yet it felt so familiar ...'

'That, my girl, is the power of Anansitori. The web of stories spun by Anansi that connects us to one another. Your mother and father, they are of African heritage, yes?'

'Yes.' My father travelled across the ocean in bondage. My mother was born free on English soil. Both are proud of their African blood. My siblings and I wear this pride like a protective blanket. It binds us to one another in a city that does not always seem to see us for who we are. Mama says it unites us with other people in the city who share our heritage. Since I was a tiny child, I have taken comfort from the small gestures of mutual acknowledgement that black and brown people give each other: a look, a smile, a gentle nod that says 'I see you'.

The Poetess looks up at the barred light of the window.

'I was a poet for my community. I have within me songs and histories, myths and mysteries that are precious to my

312

people. If I die, they will die with me. I sing to pass them on. I too was born on the west coast of Africa. Snatched from my parents in the night, stolen away from a peaceful and prosperous life in a city you heard me sing of. I was taken on a ship to England, to Bristol, where I was sold to a cruel master. I ran one night, flying through fields under cover of darkness.'

She leans against the wall, tracing a finger along a line of notches made by a former occupant. 'By day I sang for pennies and kept moving to avoid capture. Hungry, exhausted, I hid in stables and outhouses by night. After weeks of flight, I arrived in London.' Her eyes flash with hope. 'I heard tell of the Chief Justice, Lord Mansfield, and his ruling to protect us from being sent back into bondage overseas. But I see so many people pushed to the edges of their lives by poverty, here in this wealthy country: children sleeping in the streets, mothers begging for food.'

'So you sing to show us what you see?' Is this why her words move me so deeply?

'I sing to shine a light on what is all around us but sometimes remains hidden. Some, like you, will hear. Others will pass on, unchanged. But those that truly hear me will stop and ask themselves what they can do to help, as you have done. Children are often the eyes and ears of a community. The truth will come to light, I have no doubt. The question is, why is the boy lying and who is he protecting?'

The Jamaica Coffee House stands at the junction of Monmouth Street and Little Earl Street. The only way to get to the upstairs room without going through the front door is via a dilapidated staircase that runs like a rickety spine up the back of the building. Clutching the freezing handrail, I creep carefully up the icy steps. I sweep a pile of snow away from the window ledge and peer in at the window.

Seated around a vast table are ten or so women and men, their silhouettes made grotesque by their obscenely large wigs. Each wears a Venetian carnival mask, lavishly adorned with flames or feathers. Through the frosted pane, I spy a golden cat, a harlequinned jester, a beaked plague doctor; all hollow-eyed. Their silks and jewels glimmer in the wavering candlelight.

The table is piled high with turkeys and turtles, ducks and dormice, cauliflowers and courgettes, peaches and pineapples. A man in a silver mask and the feathered black hat of a highwayman stands and taps three times on his glass with a silver fork. The group stand solemnly, join hands and begin to chant, 'Feed the rich! Punish the poor!

Silence the ones who speak out! Feed the rich! Punish the poor! Silence the ones who speak out!' Over and over, louder and louder. The sound of it chills me to the bone.

On the wall behind them, I can just make out a series of drawings. Portraits covered in red crosses. I peer closer. There is an image of the Black Poetess, a scarlet X covering her face.

I reel back from the window in horror and crack my head on the handrail behind me. I scramble down the staircase and run and run until I am back in the shop. I slam the door shut and lean against it, my blood beating against my skull with every breath.

In the kitchen, by the soft light of the fire, Kitty and Billy play Ring a Ring o' Roses around the table where Mama and Papa stand side by side, packing up another basket for the people of St Giles.

THE FOURTH DAY

My night is tormented with unanswered questions. Who are the Silencers? Did they frame the Poetess? How? Who is the girl in the hood and why did she lead me to them?

When I come downstairs the next morning, my parents are sitting together at the shop counter, Mama's

315

arm around Papa's shoulder. Papa holds his head in his hands. The *Daily Advertiser* lies open in front of them.

I sit down opposite them. 'Mama, Papa, whatever is the matter?' Mama pushes the newspaper across the counter to me.

BLACK POETESS SENTENCED TO DEATH

FOLLOWING A SERIES OF FELONIOUS THEFTS AND PICK-POCKETINGS AMONG THE FROST FAIR CROWDS, THE BLACK POETESS HAS BEEN PLACED UNDER ARREST AT NEWGATE PRISON AND WILL BE HANGED AT DUSK ON 14TH DECEMBER.

My heart lurches.

On the same page, a letter:

Dear Sirs,

In light of news of the Black Poetess's arrest I must bring to your attention that certain members of the Sancho family have been seen visiting this criminal in her prison quarters.

Spies in league, no doubt!

Would you buy your groceries from a den of thieves?

Boycott Sancho's Tea Shop and Grocery Store!

Signed,

Nils Cree

316

I can't believe my eyes! Was I followed to the prison?

'Mama, Papa, I'm so sorry,' I falter. 'But the Poetess is innocent! I was trying to help her!'

'I know, Lizzie,' says my mother, covering my hand with hers. 'And we must help, but – such a dangerous place for a child! And now . . .'

'We'll be ruined . . .' my father murmurs.

Mama insists that I stay at home for the day. 'For your own safety – here, where I can keep an eye on you.' Papa, with Frances's help, spends the day rewriting his lost letters to the newspaper and resurrecting his petition. Mama manages the shop with Mary, while I run around after Kitty and Billy.

That night, I lie awake in bed with the worry of the world crouching on my chest like a goblin. How can I have caused my parents so much anguish?

I cannot believe that the Poetess has been sentenced to death! How will I find the proof I need to save her if I can't even leave the house?

My thoughts are distracted by the sound of someone throwing stones at my window. There, across the street, a small, hooded figure, muffled up in blankets. The girl from St Giles!

I signal that I have seen her and tiptoe downstairs. I open the door gently so that the bell does not tinkle an alarm and step outside. She beckons me across the road.

'I can't stay long,' she whispers. 'But I had to come. I want to help. My name's Gracie.' Her nose and cheeks are pinched pink with cold. 'I can't let an innocent person hang! It's not Jack's fault.'

'Jack?'

'My brother. The boy caught stealing at the fair. She said she'd feed us if we worked for her. She makes us put up their horrible posters, deliver their nasty pamphlets. But sweets are the only food we get. She's got Jack hooked on sugar. So we keep going back. And she said that if we ever told anyone . . .'

'Who? Not the Poetess, surely?'

Gracie frowns and shakes her head. She looks around nervously and thrusts a bag of papers into my hands. 'Here. I'm sorry. But I've said too much already. I have to go now . . .' And like the drift of smoke when water is thrown on a fire, she is gone.

I shiver and go back inside. I open the bag. It is full of portraits like the ones on the wall at the meeting, more pamphlets, and – Papa's lost letters to the newspaper! How on earth has Gracie got hold of those?

318

THE FIFTH DAY

The next morning I am exhausted: my chest is flooded with icy dread. The Poetess is to face the gallows this evening. To free her, I need to prove who has framed her and how. Now I have a bag full of evidence, but how does it all fit together?

Papa sits at the counter, furiously scribbling columns of numbers with his quill. Doing his accounts, no doubt. If people really do stop coming to the shop as that letter threatens, we will struggle to pay our bills.

I place my hand on my father's arm. I want desperately to tell him that his letters are safe and sound but I need all the parts of the puzzle to fit together first in order to protect Gracie.

'Papa, is there anything I can do?'

He pats my hand reassuringly.

'Thank you, my dearest. Your company is quite enough. Perhaps you can dictate the accounts to me – make light of a dreary task.'

I pick up the first pile of papers.

'Hélène Cerise. Ten pounds of sugared almonds, twenty pounds of Malaga raisins ...'

I watch as he writes. 'No, Daddy, not L.N. Cerise ... Hélène – It's French for Helen. You don't pronounce the

319

... Oh. My. Goodness. May I?'

I take up the quill and write:

L. N. Cerise

I stare at the letters in the name.

'I've got it! I think I may be able to save the Poetess!' I jump up and grab my cloak. 'How quickly do you think you could gather a crowd at the Frost Fair, Papa?'

'Well, with the family's help, and our brothers, sisters and friends across the city – I have already petitioned many supporters of the Poetess!'

'And we need to get in touch with Lord Mansfield!'

'Well, that's...'

'We're running out of time, Papa!'

'Very well, very well. Give me your instructions...'

At two o'clock, I step on to the Poetess's stage clutching the bag and scan the crowd Papa has gathered. Word has got round fast and people have come from all four corners of the city to be here. Fruit sellers and coach drivers, writers and actors, sweeps and sailors, poets and politicians: all manner of people young and old stand before me. Papa stands at the centre. A few rows back is Madame Cerise. I beat the drum to gain their attention.

'Ladies and gentlemen! Three days ago, you were

enchanted by the words of the Black Poetess.'

'Until she stole from us!' shouts a ruddy-cheeked actress in a feathered hat.

'Yeah! Turning our own children against us!' adds a curly-haired coachman in red livery.

'Are you sure? The children I see among you now were so hungry that they would have done anything to be able to eat. Yes, they took your purses and your money. Yes, someone paid them to do that – but it was not the Poetess!'

'Prove it!' pipes up a high-pitched voice from the back of the crowd.

'It was Madame Cerise!'

Hélène Cerise looks aghast. She thought she was coming to hear the Poetess publicly denounced. Wild with panic she begins to push her way out of the throng. Two heavy-set washerwomen bar her way and hold her by the arms. Another holds on to her wig.

I hold aloft a copy of Madame Cerise's grocery bill. 'For weeks that woman has been buying up every kind of confectionery you can imagine! Buying sugar to bribe and hold to ransom poor hungry children in need of food. It was Hélène Cerise who bribed the children to steal your purses!'

'Impossible!' hisses Cerise. 'I've never seen those children before.'

Feed the rich.
Punish the POOR
Silence the ones who speak out!

'Ah, but you have, haven't you! In fact, you paid one of them with sweets to pretend to be your daughter. You brought her into the shop to steal my father's letters. We thought he was just being scatty, as usual – sorry, Papa – but she was stealing his letters for you while you distracted him with your incessant haggling.'

'Nonsense,' Cerise snarls. 'I was in the shop when those purses were stolen!'

'*You* were in the shop,' I continue. 'But your accomplice was here at the Fair. He was the one instructing the children to pick pockets and hide the loot in the Poetess's tent, so that when the constables arrived, she would seem like the guilty party. Your accomplice knew exactly who was here and made a note of where they kept their money when they paid for their souvenir tickets! Mr Lenier!'

Whispers of interest as the crowd look around for Lenier: he is nowhere to be seen.

'But that doesn't make any sense!' an elderly shoemaker in a green frockcoat pipes up. 'You're suggesting that they planned for our possessions to be found. Why steal all that money only to give it back again?'

Quite. 'A brilliant question. I asked myself the same. But you see, the object was not to get the money. The object was to silence the Poetess – permanently.' I show the poster of the Poetess, her face overwritten with a large red X, and a shocked gasp goes up from the crowd.

'This – all of this – is the work of the Silencers!' I read from one of their ghastly pamphlets. 'It's all part of their plan to – "Feed the rich, punish the pOOr, silence the Ones whO speak Out!"'

A fearful hush settles over the crowd. People shift nervously.

'This is the Silencers' creed. They print these pamphlets and get children to deliver them up and down the city. But look at the letter "o"s – they're larger than all the other letters.'

'So what?' challenges a reedy voice.

'If you bought a ticket to the Frost Fair, please take it out and look at it closely . . .'

'She's right! Look at the "o"s!'

'It's a glitch in the press that was used to print them. Those tickets were printed on the same press as the pamphlets because C.S. Lenier – the printer – is a Silencer! Rearrange the letters of his name. An anagram of the word Silencer! It's a code. The names are a signal to other Silencers so that they can work together. L.N. Cerise! *She's* a Silencer. And of course, Nils Cree, their contact at the *Daily Advertiser*. These three have preyed on vulnerable children, sought to ruin my father, and were even prepared to send an innocent woman to her death!'

At that moment, a carriage pulls up at the entrance to the park. Mama steps down from the carriage, lifts out Gracie and Jack and holds each of them firmly by the hand. Next comes the Poetess, followed by a tall, stately looking man with a serious expression. He offers her his arm and together they walk to the stage. She graciously takes her place once more on the podium and looks out at the sea of faces staring at her.

'I must thank you, Lizzie, for working so hard to secure my freedom. And thank you to Lord Chief Justice Mansfield for agreeing to listen to what the children had to say this morning and guaranteeing their safety. Thank you, Gracie and Jack, for your extraordinary courage in coming forward.'

Lord Mansfield steps forward and bows to the Poetess. 'It is you we must thank, for opening our eyes to the reality of our own sorry situation. My niece, Dido Belle, alerted me to your cause.' He gestures towards the entrance of the park, where the carriage awaits. Inside, I can just make out the figure of a girl, her dark silhouette framed by the coach window.

'Lenier is at Newgate as we speak,' Lord Mansfield continues. 'The Silencers will be imprisoned, their possessions sold and the money used to furnish a local almshouse for the poor. A place where these children and their families can sleep safe and warm, eat well and begin to build a future.' He turns to the Poetess. 'I fear we have not made you as welcome as we should have done.'

The Poetess eyes him squarely. 'When I arrive in a place, I hope that my poetry can help people to listen with care, to see what is happening around them with open eyes, and to find new ways of being good to one another. I look, I listen, I learn. And then I move on.'

She takes my hand in hers.

'The truth is like a flame, burning brightly in the darkness to show people the way to a more just and kind life. Lizzie, you have a special gift. Keep using your voice to speak out and help others to do so too.'

The Poetess turns back to the crowd.

'Here, in this very corner of the park, everyone can speak their truth. Where there is cruelty and selfishness, let there also be kindness and courage. Where there is ice, let there also be fire.'

At this, the Poetess steps down from the stage. The crowd parts like water before her. I watch as she vanishes into the silvery mist, her black cloak billowing out behind her, and I realise that in all the time she was with us, we never asked her name.

SERENA PATEL

SILENT NIGHT

TOP SECRET

PROPERTY OF THE VERY MERRY MURDER CLUB

SILENT NIGHT

By Serena Patel

It was all an accident really. Later, when he had to explain to his mum what had happened, that's how Arjun began the story. He really hadn't meant to spy on his neighbours. He really hadn't meant to see what he saw. And he definitely hadn't meant to cause a police incident on his street. But you can't just ignore a murder when it happens right across the road from your house!

It was all his mum's fault, anyway, as far as Arjun was concerned. If she hadn't called the doctors about all the throat infections he kept getting then:

The doctor wouldn't have said he needed his tonsils out.

He wouldn't have had to have an operation during the first week of the year.

He wouldn't have had to spend a week at home to recover and prevent infection.

He would have been back at school that week and not spying on the neighbours.

And, most importantly, NOT causing a major police incident.

But as it was, he had no tonsils, all his friends were in school and he was stuck at home.

Arjun had tried entertaining himself. He'd played PS4, which was no fun when your friends weren't online because they'd all gone back to school. He tried reading but just couldn't get into anything. He had tried doing the homework the school had thoughtfully (annoyingly) sent for him. Well, truthfully he hadn't tried that hard.

Since Mum had to work it was just Arjun and Ba, his grandmother, in the house. She'd been living with them since his grandad had died two years ago. She was all right, but she didn't speak much English and liked Arjun to speak Gujarati to her. Arjun felt awkward about that because he often got his Gujarati words mixed up and so avoided any lengthy conversations.

So, to pass the time in a way that meant he could stay in his room and because he had nothing else to do, Arjun had taken to watching the daily routine of his neighbours. There was Mrs Jones next door who always went out at 9.17 a.m. on a Tuesday to catch her bus into town. On a Thursday, Mrs Jones would go for a walk with her other neighbour, Mrs Kaur, round the block four times; he'd see them go past each time chatting away happily. The neighbours on the other side of Arjun's house were the Singhs, who were always very nice about throwing Arjun's ball back over the fence. Across the road at number 10 lived Mr Borokov, a serious but kind man who often offered to help Arjun's mum when things in their house broke. He always went to the paper shop at 9.40 a.m. to get his daily newspaper, sometimes a small bottle of milk too. Next to him at number 12 lived a grumpy old man, Mr Abara, who was always scowling and didn't seem to like talking to anyone. Arjun never saw anyone visit him and he wondered if he had *any* friends or family. And so, this is how the days passed, Arjun watching the neighbours go about their daily lives while he was stuck indoors. A boring, uneventful start to the year.

Now, it was Monday again and it looked like it was going to be the same as all the other days – a whole new week of boredom. Mum had just left for work, kissing him on the head as he tried to dodge out of the way while eating his lovely warm porridge. Ba already had the pressure cooker on and the whole kitchen smelled of daal. She was folding laundry now as she did every morning while watching her soaps. Every so often she'd yell at the characters in Gujarati. Arjun took the opportunity while she was distracted and went up to his room.

Arjun's bedroom was at the front of the house overlooking their street. It was always quiet apart from the sound of the odd car door opening and shutting, or delivery drivers dropping off parcels. But this morning there was shouting – very loud, sweary shouting!

Arjun scrambled over to the window and peered between the open blind slats. It was Mr Abara and Mr Borokov from across the road. They were shaking their fists and yelling at one another over the fence that divided their front gardens. It must have been cold outside because Arjun could see their breath puffing out in angry clouds as they shouted. His eyes widened. This was the first bit of excitement he'd seen in ages!

'I warned you before, I gave you a chance to come clean, you only have yourself to blame. Wrong is wrong!' Mr Borokov shouted.

'What are you talking about? You have no right to pry in my business!' Mr Abara roared back.

'I have nothing else to say. Every action has a consequence,' Mr B replied darkly and walked away.

Arjun watched Mr Abara. He was glaring at Mr B's back and gripping the shovel he was holding so tightly, his knuckles changed colour. Arjun had never seen one of his neighbours so angry. But what was it all about?

What did Mr B know about Mr Abara and why were they both so angry about it?

Just then Mr Abara turned to face Arjun's house and saw him looking. He looked surprised and then frowned. Arjun gasped and ducked, embarrassed to have been caught gawping. He waited a second and then poked his head above the windowsill.

Mr Abara had gone and the street was quiet and still again.

A few hours later, Arjun was sitting on his bed, half-heartedly playing his PS4 when he heard a loud bang, so loud it made him jump! He stumbled across the room to the window but the street was empty. Nothing to suggest where the noise had come from. He went downstairs to see if Ba knew what it was.

'What noise?' she asked in Gujarati. 'Probably just the telly. This baddie just shot that one, see!' She pointed to the screen.

'No, it was loud,' Arjun insisted. 'It can't have come from the telly, can it?'

Ba shook her head dismissively and returned to watching her programme.

Arjun helped himself to some warm daal from the

cooker and returned to his room. As he slurped away, he heard a car pull up outside. Arjun wandered over to see who it was. But he realised quickly it wasn't a car he'd heard. It was a black van, the kind that delivery drivers sometimes use. Out stepped Mr Abara from the driver's side. He was wrapped up in a big coat, scarf and gloves. He opened his garage doors and grabbed some tools – the shovel Arjun had seen him gripping earlier, a hammer, a saw and a roll of black bags along with a plastic sheet. He threw them all into the back of the van with a loud clunk. Arjun felt a chill run down his spine. What did Mr Abara need all those things for?

Arjun had often stayed up late at his friend Mo's house, watching movies his mother would never allow. Scary films with axe killers in scary masks. He couldn't help thinking that the things Mr Abara was putting in the van would be quite useful for disposing of a body. He heard his mother's voice in his head – 'Don't be so ridiculous!' it said. 'You have such an overactive imagination, Arjun. Apply that to your schoolwork once in a while!'

Arjun sighed. Imaginary Mum's voice was right, he was getting carried away. Mr Abara was probably helping a friend or having a clear-out of old stuff. He glanced at his watch. It was 2 p.m. Still a long time till Mum would come home that night. His throat felt a little sore. Arjun lay down on his bed and let the dull ache wash over him. It wasn't long before his eyes started to close.

Arjun woke up with a start. It was pitch-black in his room – how long had he slept? The alarm clock on his bedside table glowed. It was 6 p.m. already; he'd been asleep for four hours! He padded downstairs. The house was quiet. On the kitchen table was a note from Ba saying she'd gone round to Mrs Kaur's house to watch their weekly cooking show together.

Mum was still on her double shift. There was some chicken and rice in big pots on top of the cooker; the note said to warm it carefully in the microwave. Arjun realised he was starving again so he put some in a plate and heated it up. While the microwave hummed, he went into the living room to switch on the telly when he noticed movement outside through the window. It was someone across the street.

Knowing no one could see him without the light on in the living room, Arjun crept to the window and peered through the half-closed blinds. Snow was falling lightly on the ground. Over the road he could see a shadowed figure. It was Mr Abara, and he was dragging something heavy out of his garage. It was long and bulky and wrapped in plastic. What on earth was it? Arjun looked to his left, up the street and to his right, down the street. It was quiet and deserted. He happened to look over at Mr Borokov's house. The lights were off. That was strange. They always came on at 4.30 p.m. in the winter. He had them on some sort of timer. Arjun knew that not only from watching out of the window all this time but because Mr Borokov had once spent twenty mind-blowingly boring minutes telling him and Ba all about his home security once. Ba's grip on his hand was vice-like that day as he'd tried to back away and sneak off down the street while Mr B rambled on about the difference between movement and light-sensitive sensors.

Arjun looked back at the black van, which now had a sprinkling of snow over it on Mr Abara's drive. He was trying to lift the heavy thing off the floor and into the van but he couldn't quite get it off the ground. After a bit of a struggle, he managed to push it upwards and in. Looking like he was heavily out of breath Mr Abara closed the van doors and jumped into the driver's side, and then the van pulled away, disappearing into the dark. Where would Mr Abara be going at this time of the evening with a big, heavy bundle and some tools in the back of his van? This was so suspicious. And that's when Arjun noticed something.

He grabbed his jacket and ran outside, careful to leave his front door on the latch. Being locked out right now would not be clever! Arjun looked both ways and around for anyone else on the street, before scurrying across the road, being careful not to slip. There, on Mr Abara's driveway, where the van had just been, was a wallet. He picked it up, brushed off the layer of snow and opened it. Mr Abara must have dropped it when he was wrestling whatever it was into the van.

There wasn't much in it, a crumpled ten-pound note and a couple of bank cards. Arjun decided he would just post it back through Mr Abara's door and was just about to close the wallet and do exactly that . . . when he stopped in his tracks. The name on the top bank card read 'Mr D Borokov'! What was Mr Abara doing with Mr Borokov's wallet? Arjun shivered as he thought back to the argument he'd overheard earlier between the two neighbours. *Every action has a consequence*, Mr Borokov had warned Mr Abara. But what if it was Mr Borokov who was now facing the consequences? A horrible thought went through his mind then. What if *Mr Borokov* was the thing that Mr Abara had bundled up in his van?

Arjun shakily put the wallet into his back pocket and quickly crossed back to his house, shutting the door firmly and then locking it from the inside. He glanced at the phone. Should he call the police and tell them what he'd seen? He thought about how ridiculous it sounded. So instead he called his best friend, Mo.

'Yo, what's up, man? You still stuck at home? When can you come back to school?' Mo asked.

'Yeah, man, it sucks, I should be back in school next week but listen.' Arjun took a deep shaky breath. 'I just saw the weirdest thing. Remember that film we watched with your big brother? The one with the axe killer in it?'

'Yeah. It was well scary; you know you wanted to hold my hand, man,' Mo joked.

'Mo, this is no joke, I think the real-life version of the axe killer is living opposite me!' Arjun said. 'But maybe not an axe, maybe a *shovel*.'

'What? Don't be silly, bro,' Mo laughed. 'That's just films, innit. Have you been watching those bad mystery programmes with your ba?'

'No, man, I know what I saw. My neighbour, the one across the way, he loaded a big, wrapped-up bundle, like the size of a BODY, into his van with a shovel and he drove away just now! What does that sound like to you?'

Mo paused. 'Well, OK, it does sound suss but still, those type of things don't happen here, man. We live in the dullest town in the Midlands. Like, it's an event if the bins don't get collected on the right day. NOTHING ever happens here. I'm sure it was nothing. Now, on to important things – wanna play some FIFA?'

Arjun sighed; Mo was probably right. They really did live a in a dull town and Mr Abara was probably just a grumpy old man, not a shovel killer.

They played online games till late. Ba came in and took herself off to bed after popping her head round his bedroom door to tut at his late-night gaming. And then eventually Arjun heard his mum come home around 10 p.m. from the hospital. He hid his headset under the pillow as Mum came in, kissed him goodnight and told him to get some rest. Of course, Arjun had no intention of going to sleep yet; he was beating Mo hands down on their game! Around 11 p.m. they switched off and said goodnight. Arjun crawled into bed but found he couldn't sleep. Then around 11.30 p.m. he heard the van returning across the road.

Arjun crept over to the window again and pulled out his phone, texting Mo in the dark.

He's back! Arjun typed quickly.

A second later the three dots appeared on screen as Mo was typing. The reply appeared: *Who is?*

The neighbour I told you about. With the van! Arjun texted back, his fingers trembling.

Oh, well, is he loading more dead people into his van? Mo joked.

No, but he's opening the door . . . and hang on, I can see inside!

And? Mo replied.

Arjun stared in silence for a second – it was dark, so he couldn't see very clearly, but he could tell that whatever the big, body-sized thing was that Mr Amara had lifted inside wasn't there any more.

Mo texted again: *Arj, what's going on?*

Have you fallen asleep? another message asked.

Arjun lifted his phone and typed: *It's empty.*

Well, there you go then, said Mo. *Nothing to worry about. Now since you're still up, shall we play another game?*

But where did the package go, Mo? Arjun typed quickly in frustration. *It was big, like the size of a person. You can't just dump something that big anywhere and the recycling centres wouldn't be open at this time if it was rubbish.*

The three dots appeared as Mo seemed to take ages to reply. *Mate, I think you're getting a bit carried away with this van business*, his message cautioned.

Arjun knew Mo didn't believe him but he knew what he'd seen. He called Mo's number. Mo answered.

'Bro,' he started but Arjun jumped right in. 'It's just too suspicious, Mo! He had a big argument with Mr Borokov earlier and guess what? I found Mr Borokov's wallet where the van had been parked after Mr Abara drove away!'

'What? You went over there?' Mo asked in disbelief. 'Mate! What if he'd seen you? I'm not saying that he *is* dangerous but, just in case, snooping round his house is probably not a good thing to be caught doing!'

'He was well gone when I ran over there and the wallet was just lying in the middle of his driveway. Maybe Mr B dropped it there, but the more I think about it, how can he have? His driveway is separated by the hedge from Mr Abara's,' Arjun explained.

Mo sighed. 'You're not going to let this go, are you?'

Arjun thought for a moment. 'Well, if Mr B turns up fine tomorrow then I'll just return his wallet and no harm done, right? Maybe Mr Abara is just doing a little sideline business delivering packages.'

'And what are you going to do if Mr Borokov doesn't turn up?' Mo asked.

'Then I need to get inside that van and have a proper look, find some evidence,' Arjun answered.

'Er, I'm not sure that's a great idea, Arj. Be careful, and phone me if you decide to go over there. OK?'

'OK,' Arjun agreed. He was kind of glad Mo had offered.

The next morning Arjun woke and made a plan. He knew from his week in the house watching out of the window that regular as clockwork Mr Borokov would go to the shops at 9.40 a.m. every day to get his newspaper. All Arjun had to do was watch and wait.

9.40 came and went.

And there was no sign of Mr Borokov.

Maybe he was sick? Arjun ran downstairs. Mum was already back at work and Ba was in the kitchen using the noisy spice grinder. Arjun pulled on his coat and shoes and went outside. It was a bright but freezing cold morning. The snow from last night had settled so there was a light frost covering everything. The street was quiet and no one was around.

Arjun made his way slowly across the road to Mr Borokov's house, his feet crunching as he walked. He'd just knock on the door, hand the wallet back and go home. He'd even let Mo have a good laugh at his expense! As he walked up Mr Borokov's drive, telling himself this, Arjun started to feel a bit better.

Then Mr Abara came storming out of his house.

'What do you want?' he yelled over the hedge.

Arjun stumbled backwards, scared for a second, and then thinking quickly how to answer. 'I . . . well . . . I found Mr Borokov's wallet so I just wanted to return it to him. He usually comes out for his walk to the shop in the morning but I haven't seen him today. Have you?'

342

Mr Abara frowned. 'No, I haven't. And you should mind your own business about what time people go about their own private things.' He huffed and went back inside, slamming the door behind him.

Arjun looked at Mr Borokov's house in front of him. He was here now, silly not to knock and check. Slowly, he walked up to the red front door and rang the bell. He noticed some letters hanging half in and half out of the letter box. It looked like Mr Borokov hadn't been down at all this morning.

Still no one answered the door.

Now what?

No harm in checking through the window, Arjun thought to himself. Perhaps Mr Borokov was lying hurt in his living room? He cupped his hands around his face and peered through the glass of the living-room window.

At first glance it looked perfectly normal. But then Arjun noticed a pair of binoculars on the floor, on top of an open newspaper with its dramatic headline: 'STOLEN DIAMONDS PART OF SUSPECTED SMUGGLING RING OPERATION!' Arjun looked around the room to see if there were any more clues as to where Mr Borokov might be. He saw there was a small table in front of the armchair and on it a dinner plate, the meal – potatoes, rice, meat – had been half finished. It didn't seem right;

343

Mr Borokov was the neatest person Arjun had ever met. He would never leave his dinner plate from last night out like that. But where was he?

Arjun suddenly felt a chill like he was being watched. He looked to his right at the house next door. Mr Abara was at his window staring at Arjun. Scratch that, Mr Abara was glaring at him!

Arjun backed away quickly and fled back home.

Ba was in the living room, reading a book. She looked up and tutted. 'Always running here and there.'

'I'm fine and it doesn't even hurt that much any more,' Arjun lied. He sidled towards the kitchen – a plan was starting to form in his mind. 'Anyway, I'm going to go and rest now. I'll just take some snacks up with me, you know, just in case!'

'Just in case of what?' Ba asked but she'd already turned back to her book so Arjun grabbed a bottle of water and a big bag of those cheesy puffs that melted in the mouth since he still had to be careful of his throat.

If he couldn't get across the street without Mr Abara seeing him then he was never going to get into the van to look for clues. So Arjun was going to do the one thing he'd got really good at over the last couple of weeks. He was going to conduct a stakeout.

As he plonked himself on to his bed, Arjun gathered

344

together a notepad, pen and of course his snack. He made sure the blinds were open and positioned himself in front of the window.

Suddenly the door opened and Ba appeared. Arjun hid the notepad behind him. 'No need to hide what you're doing. I see you sneaking about like some sort of spy. You might want this,' she said in Gujarati to Arjun, handing him his grandfather's pocket tool. 'Just in case.' She grinned and left the room.

Did that really just happen? Arjun shook his head in disbelief before turning back to the window. Back to the stakeout – he'd got everything he needed, now he just had to watch and wait.

It was actually much later that evening, when the sky had just gone dark, that the door of number 12 opened. It was Mr Abara again with another large, heavy-looking package wrapped in plastic.

As Arjun watched him heave one end into the van, it twisted awkwardly and the plastic fell open at one end. Arjun gasped. It was dark, for sure, but in any other light Arjun could have sworn he'd just seen a foot poking out. An actual foot. Attached to an actual body!

Mr Abara closed the van doors before going back into

his house. Arjun leaned back against the wall. He was sweating now; this was big – he couldn't let Mr Abara drive away with a body in his van.

Arjun made a decision right there and then. He had no choice. Like the heroes in those movies he'd watched from behind his cushion, he was going to have to investigate and stop this criminal.

He went to his wardrobe and pulled on a thick, black ribbed jumper, black joggers and that balaclava his mum had bought him for winter that he hated. However, it was perfect for snooping around in the dark. As an afterthought he grabbed the pocket tool Ba had given him and stuffed it in the pocket of his joggers. He checked through the window one last time to make sure Mr Abara hadn't come back out. He knew he might not have long to do this.

He grabbed his phone to call Mo. He had just five per cent battery. He found Mo's number as quickly as he could.

'What's up, man?' Mo answered.

'I'm doing it,' Arjun whispered.

'Doing what?'

'I'm going over there; I have to look inside that van!'

'Oh, man, not this again! Bro, be careful!'

'I am, he's gone inside. I've got a few minutes I reckon. Stay on the phone, yeah?'

The street was still silent. Arjun stepped outside into the frozen night, his breath forming little clouds of cold air in front of him, even through the balaclava. He looked around and then ran across the road, staying low and keeping one eye on Mr Abara's door the whole time. He reached the van and walked slowly round the side of it, being careful to keep to the shadows and blend in. His heart was thumping; he felt sure that Mr Abara would hear it and come out!

He tried the driver's door of the van. It was locked. He was going to have to go round the back. Arjun slowly inched sideways until he was at the rear of the van. He resisted the urge to run back across the road and hide under his duvet. Deep breath. This was it.

He opened the door to the back of the van. It was dark, he couldn't see properly, but it looked like there were two more rolled-up bundles lying flat next to the one Arjun had seen his neighbour put in here earlier. Two more bundles. Two more bodies? This was bad, really bad!

'What are you doing?' Mo asked on the other end of the phone.

'I think there's two more bodies. I can't tell,' Arjun explained.

'This is next level, man, just call the police and be done with it,' Mo instructed.

'Maybe you're right,' Arjun murmured. 'I just need to take one photo as evidence.' He pulled out his phone and stood back – straight into Mr Abara.

'Oh, um, sorry, Mr Abara, I was just, um, you know, walking,' he said, dropping his hand with the phone in it to his side. Thankfully the van door swung almost shut.

'Walking. Right by my van on my driveway?' Mr Abara growled. He glanced at the van door and abruptly clicked it shut, glaring at Arjun.

Arjun tried to stay calm. 'Well, um, it's really funny actually.'

'I doubt that,' Mr Abara muttered.

'Well, anyway, I'd better get back, my gran is waiting for me,' Arjun said meaningfully.

Mr Abara seemed to decide something very quickly then. 'No, you stay here.'

'Oh, that's OK!' Arjun joked. 'I really should get home!'

Inside his tummy felt like jelly. He looked desperately down at his phone. It was dead. Oh no! Mo must have got cut off. He just had to keep Mr Abara talking out here and hope that someone would drive past or his mum would return home. It was not the best plan but what else could he do? He took a deep breath and spoke more bravely than he felt.

'So, Mr Abara, I was wondering if you'd seen Mr Borokov yet? I'm a bit worried about him!'

Mr Abara's face darkened. 'No, I have not seen him, he's probably off meddling in someone else's private business.'

'You fell out with him, right?' Arjun asked.

'How do you know?'

'I overheard you yesterday morning,' Arjun admitted.

'Yes, well, that was nothing. Now, if you don't mind, I have somewhere to be.' He moved to the driver's door.

Arjun panicked; he couldn't just let the van go. Then he remembered the pocket tool Ba had given him: it had a corkscrew on the end. He pulled it out of his pocket while Mr Abara climbed in and plunged it into the nearest tyre of the van. A low whistling sound escaped as the air leaked out. The van visibly lowered on that side.

Mr Abara leaned his head out of the window. 'What was that?'

Arjun shrugged innocently.

Mr Abara growled and jumped out of the van to examine the tyre. Arjun stepped back.

'You did this?' Mr Abara asked, moving towards Arjun.

'I, um ...' Arjun scrambled for something to say but he didn't need to. Suddenly the sound of sirens filled the air.

'You called the police?' Mr Abara bellowed angrily.

'Why would you do that?'

Two police cars screeched to a halt, blocking Mr Abara's driveway. Officers leaped out and shouted, 'Step away from the vehicle with your hands in the air where I can see them. Now!'

'He has three dead bodies in his van!' Arjun yelled.

Mr Abara looked surprised. 'What? No, there are no dead bodies in there, where would you get such an idea?' He laughed nervously, looking from boy to police officer.

'Are you OK, son?' the officer asked Arjun. 'We received a call from a friend of yours saying you were in danger.'

Arjun smiled to himself; that would be Mo. He must have called the police when the phone went dead. 'I'm fine. But you need to check that van. I think he has bodies in there and I think I saw him get rid of another yesterday, our neighbour, Mr Borokov. I heard them arguing yesterday and then later I saw him dragging something large and heavy into the van. He killed Mr Borokov!' Arjun shouted, pointing at Mr Abara.

Mr Abara laughed. 'Look, I know how that sounds but honestly, this boy has a vivid imagination. I am moving some items for a friend, no dead bodies, I assure you! Actually, it's I who should be reporting a crime, he punctured my tyre!'

The officer looked unconvinced. 'We'd better take a

351

look inside, I think.'

The flashing blue and red reflected off the side of the van and Arjun closed his eyes tight and braced himself for what was going to be revealed.

Two of the police officers stepped forward and opened the van doors and jumped up inside. There was some rustling and clanging and then one of them emerged holding something.

'Is this what you thought you saw?' she asked Arjun.

Arjun opened one eye cautiously. The officer was holding up something – or *someone* in her arms.

'Is that Mr Borokov?' he asked quietly.

The officer smiled. 'Nope. I don't think so, unless your neighbour is made of moulded plastic.'

Arjun opened both eyes, shocked. 'Wait, what?'

'It's a mannequin, you know, like what they model clothes on in shops!' the officer grinned. 'There's a couple of them in here – that's your dead bodies.'

Arjun's face felt very hot all of a sudden. 'Oh, I . . .'

'I told you!' Mr Abara shouted triumphantly, shaking his fist.

'Not so fast, sir,' the officer interrupted. 'We're going to need to ask you a few questions about this.'

'About what?' Mr Abara asked, looking worried.

'This,' said the other officer, tipping a headless

mannequin upside down, as a wave of some very sparkly things poured out.

'Diamonds!' Arjun gasped, picking one up. 'Are those real?'

'Well, I'm no expert but I would say yes,' the officer said. 'I think what you've stumbled upon here is not murder but smuggling, and a lot of it!'

'But what about Mr Borokov? He's still missing. I haven't seen him since yesterday,' Arjun explained.

The officer looked sternly at Mr Abara. 'Do you know anything about this? Things will go much more smoothly for you if you just tell us now.'

Mr Abara gulped. 'Well, he's not dead. He's in my kitchen, tied up, the interfering old so and so. I didn't hurt him. You'll see. If he hadn't been so nosy, like this boy, I wouldn't have had to do it. I work for a factory that makes these mannequins. They seemed like the perfect cover for my sideline in smuggling. I didn't think for a minute my neighbour would be the one to suspect anything. He saw me a few days ago receiving the diamonds at a meet-up round the corner and had been following me ever since. He watched me load my van the next day and put two and two together. He always was too clever for his own good. He confronted me and told me he wanted me to hand myself in, can you imagine? I had to keep him quiet.' He looks at me. 'I saw your granny looking out the window earlier too. I thought I might have to keep her quiet as well but I never suspected you. You're just a kid!' he spat.

Things happened quickly then. Ba came out of the house just as Mr Abara was read his rights and arrested by one of the police officers. She nodded proudly at Arjun. He smiled back. And then Mum pulled up in her car.

'Arjun Dosanjh, what is going on here? I hope you haven't been bothering the neighbours! And you're supposed to be resting your throat, you do want to go back to school next week don't you?' she muttered as she walked up to him.

'You'll never believe it, Mum,' Arjun said, smiling sheepishly and handing her a large, sparkling diamond as the snow started to fall again around them. 'But I can explain!'

E.L. NORRY

NO PISTE FOR THE WICKED

TOP SECRET

THE VERY MERRY MURDER CLUB

PROPERTY OF THE VERY MERRY MURDER CLUB

NO PISTE FOR THE WICKED

By E.L. Norry

I'd only been at Grosvenor High a month and already we were on a school trip abroad. As new schools went, this was pretty sick.

As the coach pulled into the hotel car park, I tried to keep my cool, but man, it was hard. A massive hotel with wooden window-frames loomed in front of us. I hurriedly stuffed *Death on the Nile* into my bag before Ishan woke up. Reading old whodunnits might not seem cool for a thirteen-year-old boy, but they were the only books on the shelf in the last children's home I was in and they were totally addictive. I related hard to Hercule Poirot: being considered different and always underestimated.

I swapped the baking heat of Egypt for the icy freshness of snowy mountaintops. Stepping off the coach, I squinted because the snow was so bright. The sky was

357

light blue and stretched for miles. I gazed up at a gradual slope – the beginners' one – so Ms Scarlett had said. To one side was a wooden hut labelled *San Simone Ski School Hire* and the ski lift could just be seen past that.

The whole place had this mad calm feeling and I vowed to not mess this opportunity up. New school, new foster home; maybe I could finally ditch my ABR (always be ready) bag and have a proper fresh start.

Ishan nearly stood on my heels as he clambered off the coach, rubbing his eyes.

'I wanted to go to France,' he grunted, looking around. 'So did Mrs Miller but that new teacher picked this resort.'

'Italy looks kinda amazing.'

Shrugging, he pulled out his clicky stretchy pop-tube thing that had driven me mad half the trip. 'I hate pasta.'

Teachers think that being a foster kid I'm a waste of space, so I know what they're playing at – partnering me with Ishan, the kid with the fidget cubes and tics. It happens at every school I've gone to; they reckon by bunging us 'special kids' together we won't bug anyone else.

Ms Scarlett pushed diamante-encrusted sunglasses on to her head, making little circles at the corners of her eyes.

'Eight B. I *already* have a migraine, so please . . .

don't add insult to injury, all right?' She consulted her clipboard. 'Come and collect your bags.'

Mrs Miller checked the coach for stragglers while Mr Duncan helped unload the rucksacks from the luggage compartment. After we'd got our bags, we followed the teachers to the hotel.

Some girls made the V-sign behind Ms Scarlett's back. Someone whispered, 'From working at that posh, private school – reckons she's better than us!' They dissolved into comments so high-pitched that my ears ached.

As we walked, Ishan's bag hung open and his wallet poked out. Anyone could rob that – not that I would – but I'd been blamed for less.

'Spurs suck.'

'What?' He turned and peered at me. 'Why are you talking about Spurs?'

'You support them, right? Their logo's on your wallet – which is about to fall out of your bag.'

He frowned before zipping up his bag and catching up with the others.

Ms Scarlett confidently led the way through reception, calling 'Ciao' to everyone. I stared at the wall-mounted TV's weather report – more heavy snow was forecast, and

I hoped we'd get to have a massive snowball fight.

The rest of us turned down a long corridor while Ms Scarlett stopped at the reception desk to speak to some stubbled guy chewing a toothpick. I heard lots of laughter and Ms Scarlett saying, 'Oh! And I thought you were going back to France this ski season?'

In the dining room a woman in white overalls set tables and straightened wooden benches and glanced up as we noisily filed in. Some kids muttered 'Hi' but suddenly her smile vanished. She'd seen something, or someone, she didn't like – too many teens in one place probably. She narrowed her eyes and barged through the swing doors, which I guessed led to the kitchen.

'All right! Find a seat and don't take all day,' Ms Scarlett barked.

'She makes me think of a triangle,' Ishan said, rolling his feet in and out.

Ms Scarlett *was* sharp-looking: thin nose, long, painted fingernails, always wearing a slash of dark lipstick which contrasted with her short black bob.

I decided to humour him; if I didn't these four days would drag. 'Yeah, she's probably from Bermuda!'

Ishan barked a laugh but quickly shut up when Mr Duncan raised his eyebrows. But if he had a sense of humour then maybe being paired with him wouldn't be so bad.

As Ms Scarlett and Mr Duncan droned on with instructions, Mrs Miller hovered behind them, twisting her hands together. She was our class TA; she let me move around during lessons, and I got extra time on tests too. But the other day, after I came out of a PHSE session, she was sniffing and rubbing her eyes. She said it was hayfever, but people don't get hayfever in October.

'Did you hear that?' Ishan poked my knee with his pop tube. 'We're sharing a room.'

'Holly!' Ms Scarlett said. 'The girls are on the third floor. Keep the noise to a minimum and lights are off at nine thirty.'

A collective groan went up and someone muttered, 'We're not babies!'

'Don't act like babies then!' Ms Scarlett snapped back.

'Waaah!' I joked, behind my hand. Ishan grinned.

'Shush!' Mr Duncan roared. 'After four hours skiing every day, you'll be thankful for an early night.'

'You'll be exhausted and achy,' Ms Scarlett added. 'Believe me, I've skied here for the last six years. Now, Ishan and Luca, Mr Duncan will show you your room.'

We followed Mr Duncan up four flights of stairs, his big butt wobbling in brown cords.

361

I whispered, 'Dunkin' doughnuts – what a mover.'

We *were* pretty lucky. The others also shared, but Ishan and I got special treatment. I was becoming less bothered that they'd paired us.

Our room had bunk beds against the wall and a chest of drawers opposite. A big window looked out on to the snowy slopes, and the edge of the wooden hut that looked like it was full of skis and equipment.

'Unpack and then come to the dining room.' Mr Duncan pulled the door partially closed.

Ishan looked at me and then at the bunk bed. He snorted, clearing his throat.

'Where do you wanna sleep?' I asked.

He fiddled with the straps on his backpack. 'I don't care.'

'Cool. I'll take the top then.' I grunted, hurled my rucksack on the top bunk and took a running jump up, dangling my legs over the edge.

He leaned against the bunk bed. 'Is it true you got kicked out of your last school for punching a teacher?' His brown eyes blinked rapidly.

I hopped down from the bunk smoothly, imagining that a skateboard was under my feet and that I could just glide away if I wanted to.

'Nah. The rumours aren't true. What actually happened

was ... I punched a computer.'

I went to the window and stared out. 'I smashed the screen and when the teacher tried to grab me, I swung for him but missed.'

I pressed my face up against the glass to get a better look. Two people were locking up the ski hut, but being four flights up, they looked tiny. While Ishan popped his pop tube, I did that thing where you pretend you can squish far away objects between your fingers. A sparkle of sunlight caught something and I recognised Ms Scarlett's sunglasses. She was probably helping to sort out the equipment for tomorrow, our first day of skiing. Whoever she was with was dressed head-to-toe in yellow. They put a hand on her arm but she shook it off. The way she waved her arms around made her seem cross – even from this distance – but the question was, about what? Hmm. What would Hercule Poirot make of that?

Dinner had been laid out for us. The teachers sat on the top table and Mrs Miller gazed around with a droopy expression, looking like she'd rather be somewhere else.

'What's up with Mrs Miller?' I asked Ishan.

Ishan glanced at the top table. 'She's upset about some teaching thing. Heard her tell someone "the Scarlett woman" wouldn't give her a reference.'

Halfway through stew and dumplings, a red-haired girl slammed down her tray and took the empty space next to me on the bench. I shifted up, sneaking a look at her.

'I can't listen to them any more!' She grabbed a napkin from the pile in the middle of the table and started angrily tearing little strips off it.

'What's up, Hols?' Ishan sighed.

'Oh, they're just all going on about how brilliant they are at skiing and all the places they've been . . .'

Holly and I didn't have any classes together, but last week she joined me in detention, her first one. She cried all the way through, trying to explain she only forgot her PE kit because of problems at home.

She grinned at me in a way that made me suspect she'd just been dared to come over to the Losers' table for a laugh.

'And you're the new boy, Luca.'

I kept my eyes on my plate. 'You don't say.' It was a novelty being the new kid – until it wasn't.

'What's your deal then?' She pushed mushy green veg around her plate.

'What's yours?' I barked; I hated people up in my business.

'Mine? Not much. Mum's depressed so she's gone to

some spa – there wasn't anywhere else for me to go.'

She was just happily spilling her guts?

She stared at me, still smiling. Maybe she hadn't come over as a joke. Maybe I could turn the defensive dial down a notch.

'Where's your dad then?' I asked.

'Where's yours?' she spat.

'Prison.' That shut her up; always a definite closer, that reply. It never bothered me – *I* hadn't been dumb enough to try and rob a Tesco Metro.

'My dad moved out a year ago,' she said softly. 'He went off with someone and broke Mum's heart. My grandma's in a home.' Holly popped a shapeless nugget into her mouth.

'What's that food?' Ishan peered at her plate.

'Vegan nuggets.' She shrugged. 'They're OK. Ms Scarlett is vegan too – has a crazy dairy allergy. She says the food here is loads better than it used to be.'

Ms Scarlett appeared at our table, a frown on her face. 'Holly? There's a seating plan for a reason. Go and sit back over there.' She pointed across the room and Holly's mouth dropped open.

'*What?* Oh, miss!' She squeezed her eyes closed, struggling to chew and swallow her mouthful, before coughing and exclaiming, sounding kind of strangled,

'What a gorgeous bracelet!'

Ms Scarlett turned her wrist over. A silver and mother-of-pearl bangle sparkled as the clasp caught the light. 'Thanks. It *is* very special.'

Holly gazed at it like she wanted to eat it. 'Where did you get it?' She sounded breathless, literally hypnotised.

'A gift . . . from an ex.' Ms Scarlett gave a throaty laugh and whispered, 'He wanted it back when we split, but then he always *was* rather deluded!'

Holly coughed and a tiny piece of vegan nugget sprayed on to the table. *Eww.*

'Nice deflection,' Ms Scarlett said, narrowing her eyes. 'But flattery won't get you anywhere. *Move.*'

Holly grumbled and picked up her tray. I felt sorry for her; the others were laughing, and when she got back to her table they made a big show of ignoring her. I knew what that felt like.

'Can you pass the juice?' Ishan asked.

I grabbed the jug. 'It's finished. I'll get some more.'

The woman setting tables earlier was stirring salt into a metal pot on the cooker.

'Yas?' She turned to me, frowning. 'What – why you here? Kitchen not for children.'

366

'Sorry!' I held up the jug, smiling. 'We've ... um, we've run out?' I mimed taking a drink.

'Oh, OK. Drink.' She opened a large metal fridge.

On the walls hung framed, dated photographs of chefs posing outside the hotel. It was funny noticing many of the same faces, changed only by haircuts or weight and age, over the years.

'Is this you?' I pointed to a smiling chef waving a wooden spoon at another chef eating a giant éclair.

She shook her head. 'Before my time; that my mother. She work as cook here, many years.' Her eyes teared up before she sniffed and a hard look crossed her face. 'Some customers ... never happy, everyone make mistakes. My mother had to pay ... and she no work here any more.'

I didn't know what to say to this. She slammed down a jug of juice. 'Here your juice.'

'Oh. OK, thanks.' As I headed out, the stubbly guy Ms Scarlett had been talking to earlier barged past me, nearly jabbing me in the cheek with the toothpick he was chewing.

The next morning it took us ages to get ready. Salopettes are basically a padded onesie – I could barely move wearing so many layers. Ishan got stressy because he couldn't get comfortable, but I made him laugh enough to forget the weird labels and seams, though we were late for breakfast.

Holly was heading out as Ishan and I went to grab croissants.

I asked, 'Your mates still being weird?'

She nodded. 'They keep talking about this one instructor. They watched him out of the window last night when I was trying to sleep.' She yawned. 'He was lifting sandbags, carrying stuff back and forth, and all I heard was *blah blah* muscles, *blah blah* fit . . . so embarrassing. I had to get earplugs.'

'You lot!' Mr Duncan shouted. 'Make your way to reception, please. You're with the beginners and Ms Scarlett has agreed to take that group.'

'I – I just need the loo,' Holly muttered, rushing off.

Outside was cold, crisp and the sky bright blue. I was hyped; I'd watched some YouTube videos, so that I wouldn't look a complete fool, but knew it'd be different to skateboarding.

'Andiamo!' Baptise, our ski instructor, hollered as we queued to collect our skis, poles and goggles from outside his hut. 'No messing!'

'Where's Ms Scarlett?' Ishan asked. 'She said I could have special goggles 'cause these will feel too bulgy.'

'*Bulgy?* Hmm.' He frowned and checked his clipboard. 'She's . . . gone . . . with the advanced group now. Mr Duncan is by the lift – he take beginners with me, Miller is back at hotel with some sick girl. You go now!'

The sick girl had to be Holly – I felt sorry for her, missing the first day.

The ski lift looked like a fairground ride. As it came up behind us, Mr Duncan said, 'Put your poles in one hand and squeeze up!'

Ishan and I laughed nervously as the chair lift jerked behind us and Mr Duncan, lifting us into the air.

Ishan chattered to Mr Duncan, but I couldn't stop staring at the mountains that stretched for miles. Total freedom. For once I felt very lucky indeed.

Mr Duncan fumbled to answer his mobile. Less than halfway up the slope, a group was crowded round a big sack, or lump, of something. The ski lift jerked to a stop. Something like oil stood out starkly against the blindingly bright snow. The oil actually looked red . . . blood? Was that a . . . body?

I nudged Ishan but he was fiddling with the strap on

his goggles, which were all fogged up. We hung with our legs dangling and feet going numb.

'Sorry, lads, but . . .' Mr Duncan cleared his throat, putting his phone away. 'There'll be no skiing today. We're heading back down.'

'What's happened?' I asked.

He couldn't meet my gaze. My Poirot senses started tingling – something bad then.

'Er . . . someone maybe . . . skied out of hours, unsupervised. An accident. That's all we know.'

On our descent, I tried to notice any other disturbances leading up to the lump and the blood. Was that two sets of footprints? I couldn't be sure; the ground was very disturbed.

In the hotel reception, Mrs Miller waited, biting her nails, while Baptise made the girls laugh, including Holly, who must have been feeling loads better.

Hadn't they all heard about the accident?

'What's so funny?' Ishan asked.

Baptise grinned while chewing a toothpick, not an easy thing to pull off. 'Little buddy, don't worry about it!'

'I'm not worried.' Ishan frowned. 'And I've never met you, so can't be your buddy, though you and Ms

Scarlett must be – I saw your photos on the hall of fame noticeboard.'

Baptise coughed and spat out the toothpick.

'Ishan!' Holly laughed, but not in a mean way. '"Don't worry about it" is just a figure of speech!'

Ishan shrugged.

Baptise disappeared into the room behind the reception desk, and Mr Duncan and Mrs Miller murmured together while ushering us into the dining room. They looked freaked out while trying to *not* appear freaked out: I should know, I'd seen expressions like that my whole life. You don't get to move around different foster families and residential homes without picking up an understanding about human nature.

I started to feel like Hercule Poirot; something was going on and maybe I should be the one to get to the bottom of it. What had happened and where was Ms Scarlett?

Dinner was louder than the night before, everyone disappointed with not skiing. The teachers kept going in and out, and the reception phone rang a lot.

Eventually, after clearing her throat, Mrs Miller said, 'We need to reveal some unexpected and frankly distressing news. It appears that yesterday evening, feeling unwell, Ms Scarlett went for a walk. But she must have . . .' She drifted off, staring helplessly at Mr Duncan.

372

Must have what? Fallen?

Mr Duncan put his hand on Mrs Miller's shoulder. 'Ms Scarlett may have lost her footing or fallen. A terrible accident.'

I spun round in my seat. 'I bet she's dead.'

'What?' Holly elbowed me in the ribs.

'It's obvious,' I hissed. 'She's nowhere to be found. The teachers are practically crying. If she was injured, even badly, they'd be happier and we'd have heard, or seen, an ambulance or airlift.'

'Oh.' Ishan's eyes widened. 'Maybe,' he murmured, picking the skin around his thumbnail.

The cook came out of the kitchen red-faced and peered around the door. Seeing Baptise at the back of the room, she beckoned him over.

❄

We got sent to our rooms early, though I heard helicopters late into the night and noticed torch beams below us out of the window, though it was way too dark to see anything.

'You awake?'

I bolted upright, my heart banging. Ishan had pulled himself up to peer at me. His hair stood on end. 'There was a fresh dump last night,' he said urgently.

Eww. 'You're disgusting!'

Aiming his torch too close to my face, he gave me a WTH look. 'A fresh dump means a new load of snow!' He started clicking his torch on and off. 'None of us can leave.'

I let his words settle. 'You mean, we're trapped?'

He gulped, nodding. 'I think so.'

'And . . .' my brain slowed down to process what he'd said, 'if the snow had come earlier then . . . her body might not have got discovered at all.' A thought popped into my head, Hercule-style. 'Maybe that was the plan all along!'

'*Plan?*' Ishan looked concerned.

I sat upright and gripped the covers. 'Maybe someone *hoped* the body would be covered by fresh snow . . . Maybe there wasn't an accident,' I said firmly. 'Think about it. Ms Scarlett was a good skier who'd been coming here for years. Remember? We should find out what happened.'

What would Hercule do?

'What if . . .' I licked my lips, hoping Ishan wouldn't think I was unhinged. 'What if someone killed her?'

Ishan gulped then muttered, 'That's stupid.'

'Is it?' People died every day: murder, accidents, old age. Just because people didn't talk about it, doesn't mean it didn't happen. It was just that real-life criminals made silly mistakes, like my dad. They were never as smart or cool as the ones Hercule dealt with.

Ishan didn't stop snorting and blinking for five minutes.

374

I felt bad, and probably shouldn't have mentioned the killing stuff out loud.

'I should look for clues.' This could be an opportunity to prove that I wasn't a massive loser or 'troubled foster kid'. And besides, I was sick of bad people getting away with no punishment. The amount of dodgy foster carers and teachers I'd had . . .

Yawning, Ishan rubbed his eyes. 'Clues?'

'She was arguing with someone outside the ski-hire hut yesterday, maybe we will find something if we checked around there?'

'We?'

I sighed. 'We're not allowed to go off on our own, are we? Got anything better to do?'

'Uh, yeah . . . maybe . . . like, not getting killed if there's a psycho on the loose.' He nibbled his thumbnail until it started bleeding.

'But there's safety in numbers, right? You're safer with me than staying in a room without a lock on the fourth floor . . .'

His pop tube started going furiously.

Outside it was just getting light. The snow was thick and the air silent. We crunched our way slowly to the ski-hire hut. Everything felt very different without schoolkids yelling and joking.

Channelling Hercule I whispered, 'First, we need a list of suspects. Who had a grudge against Ms Scarlett?'

Ishan bundled his face deeper into his scarf. 'We know Mrs Miller didn't like her.'

'Hmm. Good thinking. Could be a motive, what you said about the job thing.'

The snow around the hut had many criss-crossing footprints around it, but even so the prints of large ski boots could be made out, leading in a different direction, and a partially covered deep groove went all the way from the door halfway up the slope. It looked like something, or some*one*, had been dragged along the ground . . .

Creeping quietly back inside, I racked my brains for where else we could search for clues. Ishan headed for the stairs, but the ski jackets hanging in reception caught my eye.

'I'll be up in minute,' I said.

Ms Scarlett's jacket hung on the last peg. I rummaged through her pockets and inside one on a tattered receipt was a scribbled phone number with 'Call me' and a kiss at the end. I pocketed it and decided to call the number whenever I got a chance.

The next morning, we queued in silence for the ski lift, which was taking us to a different slope. Baptise was sick, and both Mr Duncan and Mrs Miller seemed tired and on edge. The school had insisted we try some skiing, since it had all been paid for. Apparently, 'acting normal' was the best thing to do. I disagreed, but it wasn't my decision.

Once off the ski lift, a small French woman showed us some basic moves. I was in the same group as Holly and Ishan.

Holly fiddled with the zip on her pocket as her glove snagged. A flash of silver caught my eye.

'What's that?' I leaned over and yanked at her open pocket. A silver and mother-of-pearl bracelet! 'That's Ms Scarlett's!'

'Shh!' Holly hissed, looking round. The French instructor was taking a small group down the baby slope. Holly snatched it off me and jammed the bracelet back into her pocket. 'I never meant to –' She bit the inside of her cheek.

'To what?' I said bluntly.

Ishan appeared next to me. 'Kill anyone?' he chimed in.

377

'Where did you get it?' I narrowed my eyes, waiting for Holly to flinch, but she didn't.

'Miss was alive when I saw her last.' Holly started quietly crying. 'I *swear!*' she blurted. 'Mrs Miller gave me some earplugs and I heard Ms Scarlett say she needed some air because she felt sick. Then . . . I followed her. It was really icy and I nearly slipped. She heard me and caught my wrist, stopping me from slipping over. But her bracelet snapped off, and I don't know . . . suddenly it was in my hand and I just . . . ran.'

'Er . . . and you didn't tell anyone this?'

'The bracelet belongs to us! It's . . . my grandma's!' Holly sniffed. 'Mum wore it for years, but then Dad took it. Seeing Ms Scarlett wearing it meant only one thing.' She dissolved into more tears. 'Ms Scarlett was the woman my dad left us for! When she – Ms Scarlett – broke it off six months ago, Dad begged Mum to take him back, but she wouldn't.'

Ishan whistled. 'That sounds like a . . . what did you call it, Luca?'

'Motive. Yep, I'd say that was a solid motive for wanting someone out of the way.'

Holly's nose was running. 'But I only just found out who she is!'

I narrowed my eyes, staring fiercely into hers. 'All the

378

more reason for a spur of the moment "accident".'

'I had nothing to do with it! I just ran 'cause I was worried I'd get in trouble. She yelled after me, but when I turned back round, she'd gone and someone else was walking towards her.'

'Who?' I asked.

'Did you notice anything unusual about them?' Ishan added.

Holly shook her head. 'Not really . . . their jacket was big and padded, and they wore a hat.'

Ishan and I tried to sneak on to the girls' floor below ours, but we bumped into Mrs Miller who gave us a right earful. So after dinner, I persuaded Ishan to break into the ski-hire hut with me.

When I stayed with my dad for a weekend once, he taught me how to pick locks. I guess he felt bad that he'd missed out on showing me any regular-type activities? Anyway, picking locks wasn't complicated.

Ishan shone his torch over piles of blankets, ski poles and ski jackets. We rooted around but didn't find much. At the back of the hut a satchel was slung over a chair. I tipped it upside down and shook the contents on to the floor. Receipts fell out and a photograph.

Picking them up, I turned them over. Messages and dates were written on the back and I recognised the name of the restaurant from something I'd seen before ... Hercule P would be proud.

'Well, well.'

'Well, what?' Ishan glanced up.

'We've got the culprit,' I announced grinning.

Ishan squished his mini-peapod-popper. 'Oh, I know,' he replied.

The weather report said the snow was easing off, and although we'd only skied for one day, a coach was on its way to collect us. After parents had complained and phone calls home, the school had done a complete turnaround.

We hauled our bags downstairs to dump them in reception. I rang the bell on the desk and Baptise sprinted out from behind the counter. 'Not a toy! Don't ping ping ping it!'

'Sorry, Baptise,' Mr Duncan said, glaring at me. 'Luca, stop messing about. Get yourself into the dining room – we need to eat before the coach arrives.'

Mrs Miller walked through to the dining room chatting with Baptise as the group followed them.

Everyone collected packed lunches from the table at the back of the room.

'I need to tell everyone something.' I cleared my throat. 'Listen up!'

'Luca!' Mr Duncan and Mrs Miller threw me warning glances. 'Get off that chair before we have another accident!'

'Not until I tell you who killed Ms Scarlett,' I replied.

The room fell silent, except for Holly giving a little squeak. Mrs Miller stumbled backwards and grabbed on to a chair. Mr Duncan had gone the colour of beetroot. Everyone was waiting for it to kick off, but nothing would kick off because what I was about to say was one hundred per cent correct. Ishan and I had corroborated and come to exactly the same conclusions.

'Ms Scarlett didn't have an accident. She'd been coming to this resort for six years. Her first year here she had private one-to-one tuition with Baptise and they fell in love. Item number one. Here!'

I brandished the photograph that I'd found in the hut – of Ms Scarlett and Baptise in a deep embrace. The date, six years ago, was scrawled across the back and signed 'All my love, always' in Ms Scarlett's handwriting.

Baptise laughed. 'Ha ha!' Heads whipped around to stare at him. 'Yas, good joke you silly boys make, eh?' But

381

he'd snapped the toothpick between his teeth and was typing furiously into his mobile.

'They met up every ski season. But last year Ms Scarlett joined the teaching staff at a prestigious girls' school. She called off their relationship, worried how it might reflect on her new career if anyone ever found out. That same year she got the long-standing cook sacked after she got food poisoning – making another enemy. Cook and Baptise conspired. So, Cook gave Ms Scarlett dairy – knowing she was allergic, and Baptise knew that cold fresh air made her feel better and she'd want to go outside.'

The kitchen swing doors burst open and Cook rushed out, twisting her hands together and sobbing. 'I no kill her! I no kill anybody!'

Stunned, everyone swivelled towards her as she pointed at Baptise as she sobbed. 'I only agree to make her a little sick, he promised he only want –'

Baptise was edging towards the kitchen swing doors. On my nod, Holly stuck her foot out and, as he moved backwards, he tripped over it. Sprawled on the floor, Mr Duncan ran over to him and straddled him.

'You're not going anywhere!' he puffed. No one would be able to get out from under that.

So now the accusation wasn't just the word of a foster

382

kid. We had conclusive proof!

Ishan piped up, 'He has more – listen!'

'Coming here this year, Ms Scarlett was surprised to see Baptise; he'd told her he was heading back to France. He slipped his number into her pocket, asking to meet at the ski hut. He pleaded for another chance, but she refused. She wasn't feeling well and went for a walk, but Baptise followed her. And as for the rest . . . well . . . he'd need to explain that.'

Now all eyes were on me. I knew exactly how Hercule must have felt – for the first time in my life people were staring at me, *for the right reasons*, as if what I was saying was important – and I liked it.

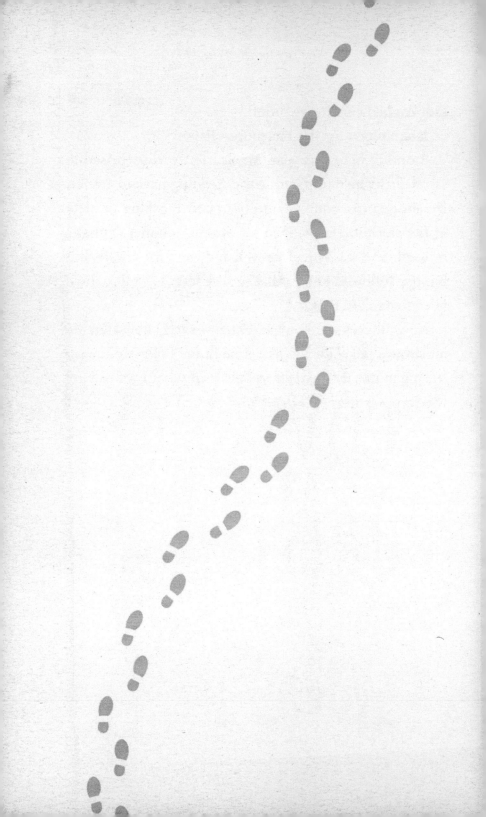

SHARNA JACKSON

THE
COVE(N)
AT
CHRISTMAS

TOP SECRET

THE VERY MERRY MURDER CLUB

PROPERTY OF THE VERY MERRY MURDER CLUB

THE COVE(N) AT CHRISTMAS

By Sharna Jackson

'Parties are pointless,' I sighed, staring down at the surging sea. It was dark now, so they'd be here soon. I pressed my face against the glass, watching the roaring, wintery waves as they crashed and frothed against the jagged, moonlit rocks below. Salty spray slapped against the foggy pane. Startled, I stepped back.

A storm was coming to The Cove.

I tightened my patchwork quilt cape-like around my shoulders and turned to Mum. She stood at the kitchen island in our large, still sparsely furnished room. Surrounded by piled plates and the smell of her food, she wiped her hands on her apron. She grimaced at her list of dishes to make, then her nimble brown fingers returned to wrapping streaky bacon around small, pale sausages.

'They're not pointless and it's not a party,' Mum said, without looking up. 'Not really. It's just a get-to-know-you gathering of four women – and a girl – at the most wonderful time of the year.'

'Is it, though?' I replied.

'Is it what?'

'A wonderful time?'

'Of course!' said Mum. 'Look around! Look where we are, what we have now. It's pretty special – and really, who doesn't love Christmas, hmmm?'

'Me.'

'Yeah, right,' said Mum, with sarcasm and a smile. 'Since when?'

'Since now. I *am* trying, Mum, but *I'm* not living the dream or appreciating the opportunity of a lifetime.' I looked back at the swelling water. 'I feel trapped – between the sea, these *nice* people and those gates.' I shuddered. 'I just want to go home,' I added softly, under my breath.

Mum washed her hands, then pressed her palms against the wooden worktop.

'It's two short years, Malorie – and we've only been here a week. Let's try to enjoy it a little bit, hmmm?' she said. 'Think of the positives – we would *never* be able to afford or experience a house like this. If it wasn't for the blessed Phoebe Morgan Scholarship – if Phoebe hadn't

388

gone to Costa Rica, I would *never* have been able to get this close to the ecosystem and –'

'– you care more about dolphins than your daughter, don't you?'

Mum sighed. 'Behave! Listen, I *know* this is a huge change – and being thirteen is tough enough already – but embrace it . . . at least try. Let's get through tonight, then have this conversation properly, in the morning, over a decent breakfast. In the meantime though, know that I hear you and I care. OK?'

I nodded. 'All right, Mum.'

Mum smiled. 'We have a plan then.' She clasped her hands together and bit her lip while surveying her work. 'So, to recap: mince pies are done, the mulled wine is bubbling, the mini turkey and cranberry rolls are in the fridge, the pigs in blankets need to be popped in the oven. I'm giving up on the rest – that's enough food for five, right?' Mum leaned forward on her elbows. 'Gah, I just want to make a good impression. They're all so lovely, and this little get-together is a tradition here.'

'Yeah?'

'Apparently, yeah. Beatrice told me they do it every year. They call it "The Coven at Christmas", which made me laugh. Get it? Cove, coven, women –'

'Witches?'

'Exactly. And look – you'd fit right in, what with that cloak you've got on,' she said, pointing at my quilt.

I looked down and smiled. 'Yeah, I guess.'

The oven's alarm beeped and Mum turned to check the time. 'Five to seven *already*?' Her eyes darted around the room and she flapped her hands. 'Mally, favour? This place still looks so bare – put a few extra decorations out, please? The box is in the attic. And throw another log on the fire.'

'Do I have to?'

She didn't reply, so I knew I did. I put my blanket on the sofa, gently placed a piece of wood on the flames and stepped across the slate floor. I ran up the stairs. On the landing, I glanced through a round window that faced the three other houses in the community. It had started to rain. Rising smoke from their chimneys danced in the direction of the wind.

Of the four houses at The Cove, ours was the largest and the closest to the cliffs. Peggy and Mark Seaver lived behind us with their three children, but I hadn't seen or met them yet. When Beatrice told Mum they were very rich and that house was just their holiday home, I felt a pang of jealousy. The Seavers had somewhere else to go, but I didn't. I was stuck here. For two years.

I sighed and looked over at Diana Dunbar's quaint

house on the right. She, like Mum, studied dolphin behaviour here at The Cove, so they should become friends. It made sense and I hoped they would be. Diane came over when we first moved in with some seriously delicious homemade fudge biscuits that I'd eat again in a second. She'd stared at me as I ate them, smiling the entire time.

Further back from the others, closer to the gate, was Beatrice's house. Beatrice Strand-Hythe and her husband Philip were apparently both retired, but from what I wasn't sure. She seemed very busy to me.

When we arrived, she waved us in at the gate with a huge smile. By the time we unloaded our first box from the van, she was at our door with flowers, chocolates and wine. Then she was suddenly in the house, running her fingers along the surfaces and shaking her head.

Mum was right, I suppose. They *were* welcoming and they did *seem* nice.

Too nice, maybe.

I said that to Mum yesterday and her response was, *Hmmm, being suspicious of everyone, all the time, is unhealthy, Mal.* She said I had to cheer up. Maybe she was right. I looked back at their houses, promising to make more of an effort later. First, it was time to decorate.

I flicked on the attic light, the hanging bulb illuminating

the perilously stacked half-opened boxes of books and research papers. Mum's not the tidiest; the attic was a clear reflection of that. I tutted and shook my head, then walked cautiously to the middle, where the roof peaked. I stood straight and scanned the space through its dense cobwebs. A brown box marked 'Christmas Things' in deep red marker sat in the far-left corner. I crouched over and cautiously approached it, reaching for the beams above to steady myself.

The box was sealed and covered in a thick layer of dust. I wiped it down, coughed slightly, then tore it open. I peered in, angling the box towards the bulb. There was red-and-green-flecked tinsel on the top, which I wrapped around my neck. Beneath the tinsel was an old pen and layers of gold baubles that I didn't really recognise but would have to do. I scooped up a selection and stuffed them into my hoodie's pouch. My hands returned to the box for one last look, and as I swept the remaining baubles aside, a sharp sensation ran along my thumb. I winced in pain and quickly jerked it away. A drop of blood bloomed from the thin slice in my skin. Annoyed, I sucked on it, and returned to the box to find the culprit.

The corner of a white slip of paper peeked out between the baubles. I pulled it free and peered at it, turning it over in my hands. A plane ticket to Costa Rica, dated this day but last year, issued to Phoebe Morgan.

Phoebe Morgan?

If she was *there*, in Costa Rica, why was her ticket *here*? I thought for a moment. Maybe she'd used a mobile ticket instead? Or she'd forgotten this one and had another printed at the airport. That's something Mum would do. I shrugged and pushed the ticket into my back pocket. Curious, I delved back into the box, which I now knew didn't belong to us.

Underneath the baubles, lying flat, was an envelope, with 'To the new tenants' neatly handwritten on the front. Since that was technically me, I opened it.

There was a photograph of a smiling, friendly-looking, grey-haired woman on the front of the card. She knelt between a Christmas tree and a roaring log fire, a duplicate of the one downstairs. 'Phoebe,' I muttered, sure it was her. She wore green corduroy trousers and a knitted red jumper with a large gold brooch – two intertwined dolphins with studded sapphires for eyes pinned to it. I looked inside.

Dearest tenant,

If you've found this, you're here – hopefully enjoying your scholarship and your new house. Congratulations! If it was rushed, I'm sorry. I was in a hurry. Protect the dolphins for me! I shall miss them.

If this card remains unopened and is still in the box, well, I knew she would kill me at Christmas. I just knew it.

Season's Greetings,

x P.M. x

The temperature immediately rose in the room and my hands felt red-hot.

'I knew she would kill me at Christmas?' I whispered. Shakily, I sat down to steady myself, my head pounding, my heart racing.

Phoebe was dead?

Mouth suddenly dry, I breathed rapidly, inhaling the dust and cobwebs around me, questions filling my mind. Was this true, or a sick joke? What happened? Why? Did it happen here? Was this house haunted now? Who the heck was 'she'? Were we safe here?

Were we next?

A sharp knock at the front door startled me. I jumped, terrified. My flailing arms hit the hot, hanging bulb. The light swung back and forth, casting eerie shadows and shedding light rhythmically across my face and the room.

395

'Mally?' Mum shouted from below. 'You coming down, hmmm?'

I froze on the spot in the stifling hot room. Voices in my head whispered advice. One urged me to rush downstairs and throw my body against the front door before Mum could open it – I had to save her. A quiet one said, 'Call the police, you idiot!' The loudest voice simply said, '*This is why you are suspicious of everyone. Find out more.*'

'Mally!' Mum shouted. It was followed by a tut, and the sound of the front door opening. A cold draft rushed up the stairs and through the room, calming me. Slightly.

'Hi!' Mum said warmly to her first guest and possible murderer. 'You must be Peggy?' I could hear the smile in Mum's voice. 'Terrible weather, isn't it? Oh, *that's* nice – let me take your coat.' Her voice got louder. 'My daughter's just coming, she'll be down in a moment. Won't she?' she said, pointedly in my direction. I croaked out a barely audible, meaningless reply that I knew she definitely didn't hear.

I couldn't stay in the attic all evening. I couldn't leave my mother with The Coven. I gripped Phoebe's card in my hand and stared at her face. She smiled back at me, safe and warm, friendly and festive. Whatever happened, she didn't deserve to die – no one did. Whatever happened, I had to know the truth. I took a deep breath and returned to the box. I gathered the gold baubles and threw them on the floor. Underneath, lay two stacks of unsigned Christmas cards, all with Phoebe's face on them.

The second set of sharp knocks at the door, six hard, quick raps meant it was time to act. I blinked rapidly and moved towards the ladder. 'I'll get it, Mum!' I shouted, pretending to be cheerful when I felt anything but. I plodded down the stairs, mind elsewhere, ears ringing, baubles jangling in my pouch with each step, towards the front door. Mum played carols from her phone as she sat at the end of the kitchen island with a woman I presumed was Peggy. Peggy flicked her long, bright blonde hair as she laughed at something Mum said, stamping her high heels against the kitchen floor. Mum smiled in return. I wondered what was so funny because I wasn't amused. Mum looked up at me and grinned, one that fell into an open mouth as she silently took in my outfit. I opened the door, letting the cold and my fears in.

'Merry Christmas!' two voices sang in unison. Diane and Beatrice huddled together under an umbrella. Beatrice leaned her head on her shoulder and pursed her lips.

'Well, Malorie, dear girl,' she said. 'Your outfit is certainly . . . interesting. Isn't it, Di?' Diane smiled softly and rolled her eyes gently. 'What, between those cobwebs in your hair and that tinsel around your neck, why, I can't tell if you're celebrating Christmas or Halloween!'

Beatrice snorted. 'Either way, I highly commend your effort, very good.' She stepped away from the umbrella and into the house. 'Janet! Peggy!' she said, taking off her brown wool coat, and thrusting it in my direction. She fluffed her long, wavy grey hair. 'Cor, it smells ravishing in here, I'm starved.'

I hung Beatrice's coat, while Diane took down her umbrella. 'I think you look fine,' she said. She reached into the tote bag she was carrying and pulled out a small silver tin. 'I've got a little gift for you, open it!'

Homemade fudge cookies I couldn't consider eating now, as I didn't trust her any more.

'Thanks,' I said. 'That's really kind.'

Diane grabbed my arm. 'I knew you liked them.' She smiled, slipped her coat off her shoulders and placed it on the peg. I gripped the tin with trembling fingers and watched Mum and the maybe-murderers, the congregating Coven, sip mulled wine from warmed mugs. Mum glanced over at me from the corner of her eye and gently shook her head.

I paced toward the sink and put the tin directly next to it, thinking I could 'accidently' knock the biscuits in there later, and conveniently ruin them. I turned on the tap and reached over for a glass, my back to the room. Mum's slippered footsteps shuffled behind me, then she

398

was beside me, shoulder to shoulder. She leaned over me. 'Mally,' she said with a stern voice and a tight smile. 'What are you doing, hmmm?' She reached up and pulled a cobweb out of my curls.

'Getting the decorations.' I gulped at my water, hands shaking around the glass. 'I didn't realise how dusty it was in there. I found these, though.' I put my glass by the sink and rooted into my hoodie's pouch. The gold baubles I had carried kangaroo-like spilled out and scattered noisily on to the blue-grey floor, startling our guests. One rolled towards the kitchen island, towards Peggy's red-shoed feet. Beatrice and Diane shuffled off their stools to gather the others.

'Oh, stop, stop! No need to do that!' Mum protested. 'You're guests!' she said, stepping away towards them while the women crouched on the floor. I grabbed Mum's arm and pulled her close to me.

'Mum!' I whispered. 'Phoebe definitely went to Costa Rica, right?'

Mum stared at me, confused. 'Yes, Mal – you *know* this. Why are you –'

High heels rhythmically struck the slate floor, then Peggy was beside us. She held a bauble up delicately in her perfectly manicured hand.

'These are nice, aren't they? They look familiar –

399

where'd you get them?' She rolled her eyes and leaned forward to touch my arm. 'My housekeeper could do with some tips, her decorations this year have been –' She stuck out her tongue in place of a word. She handed the bauble to me. 'I'm Peggy by the way, love.'

I swallowed, then nodded. 'Malorie,' I said. 'Nice to meet you. And yeah, I just found these in the attic. I think they belonged to the old owner of the house, they're not ours.'

'Ooh, they're *Phoebe's*?' said a widely smiling Peggy. 'That totally makes sense. She always had lovely things, did Phoebs. I wanted everything she had!'

'You did?' I croaked, then coughed. My heart raced. Maybe it was Peggy? Maybe she wanted Phoebe's possessions?

'Oh yeah!' said Peggy, running her hands through her hair. 'But, y'know, since Mark got promoted to partner, we can afford most things now.' She reached out to touch my arm again; this time, I recoiled slightly. 'You know, I am *so* lucky,' she sighed.

Lightning flashed behind us and thunder rumbled through the house. Wind rattled the windows as the rain lashed against it. The storm had arrived.

'I – I think Phoebe's lucky too,' I said stammering, leaning against the sink, gripping the hard edge behind me. 'Being

400

in Costa Rica. The weather is probably better than this.'

Mum murmured her agreement. 'It *is* the dry season there.'

'It is,' said Diane, staring out of the window, holding a mince pie. 'Perfect weather.'

'Is it? I've no idea,' laughed Peggy with a shrug. 'But I'd definitely swap *this* weather for a hot beach.'

Beatrice sipped from her mug. 'Now, now – don't be negative. What's wrong with good old-fashioned character-building English weather? The water's good for you! Phoebe loved the water.' Beatrice leaned over to grab a turkey roll. She bit into it and grimaced. 'Spicy,' she muttered. She put the roll down and dusted her hands. 'I think it's lovely in The Cove. Especially here. Sorry, Peggy, but *this* is the best house in The Cove. Janet and Malorie here are the lucky ones, I say. Very lucky.'

Were we? Being plunged into the midst of a possible murder didn't feel lucky. I looked at Beatrice. Maybe it was her? Maybe she wanted the house? It *was* the best one, she was right about that.

Beatrice swivelled on her stool. 'Actually, *do* tell us all the source of your luck, the whole story of how you came to The Cove.' She first looked over at Diane, who bit into her mince pie, then at Peggy, who nodded and gulped her drink. 'I mean, it all happened so quickly, didn't it?

One moment, Phoebe was . . . here and then poof! Gone. Her furniture moved and the locks changed! Then all this scholarship stuff.' Beatrice scratched her neck. 'All so sudden. Brilliant, obviously, for you all, but very sudden. I never knew she had *that* arranged.'

'No one in at the university did either,' added Diane, perking up. 'It was a lovely surprise.' She smiled at Mum.

'It was!' said Mum. She put on her oven gloves and removed the pigs in blankets from the oven. Peggy hovered over them as she put them on a plate. 'So I saw an advert from Phoebe and her charitable trust in our newsletter.'

'A trust,' said Beatrice, nodding. 'Of course.'

'My dream opportunity – right, Mally?' said Mum.

'Yeah,' I said, wishing she knew her dream was rapidly becoming a nightmare.

'My ultimate life and career goal was to live and work on the Cornish coast. Phoebe's ad said she wanted someone to carry on her work –'

'*Her* work?' said Diane, folding her arms, sitting tall in her seat. 'Really.'

'– on the mating and feeding habits of the pods, particularly the rare Risso's dolphin. I haven't seen any yet,' said Mum giddily. 'Just common and bottlenose dolphins so far.'

402

'Yeah,' sighed Diane. 'Same.'

Mum turned to Diane. 'Ah, but we will. I'm sure of it. We should collaborate! Share findings – you can have access to all of mine. Gosh, imagine – we could write papers together and go to conferences around the world!'

Diane beamed. 'Yes, that would be great!'

'Ooh, and maybe we could meet up with Phoebe in Costa Rica. Members of The Coven together – past and present.'

Diane nodded and smiled but said nothing. I narrowed my eyes, waiting for her to talk. Maybe it was Diane? Maybe they rowed over their research?

'Well, that sounds rather marvellous,' said Beatrice through a mouthful of mince pie.

'I don't get any of it,' said Peggy. 'All this clever science stuff.' She thrust her empty mug towards Mum for a refill. 'It's a bit boring, sorry – but dolphins are very cute. I'll give you that.' She leaned on her elbows. 'Never mention this to Mark, ever, but he's got a dolphin tattoo y'know?' She giggled. Beatrice rolled her eyes.

'Really?' laughed Mum, reaching over to fill Peggy's cup.

'Yeah! Around his belly button of all places.' She gulped a mouthful. 'Blame the nineties, good times.'

If the message in her card was the truth, Phoebe hadn't had any good times – any time for a year now. I bit my tongue, but I needed to speak up. I started slowly.

'Thinking of good times, recent ones.' I took a deep breath. 'Did you have your party here last year too? Does Phoebe like Christmas?'

'We did and, gosh, she did love Christmas, old Phoebe,' laughed Beatrice. 'If she could have celebrated it every day, she would have. Certainly, without a doubt.'

Diane nodded. 'She played carols all the time. Even in summer.'

'Did she?' laughed Peggy. 'That's weird.'

'Ah, it's charming,' said Mum. 'Quirky. Can't wait to meet her!'

'Hmmm,' said Beatrice. 'Yes, she always loved Christmas. Especially when we were girls –'

'– and even more as an adult,' said Diane, smiling and shaking her head. 'She liked all the *stuff* – the tree, the food, the decorations –'

'– she even made her own cards,' snorted Beatrice. '*Who* does that?'

Phoebe did. I squeezed my eyes shut and saw her face, smiling up at me from the card. I shook her image away.

'What? Why are you shaking your head?' asked Beatrice, sitting up straight. 'Ah, I've heard from your mum that apparently you don't like Christmas.' She smiled. 'That must be why.'

404

'No,' I said. I opened my eyes and shifted my feet. 'It's not that. It's just . . . interesting to me,' I said, putting my damp hands in my pouch and nervously gripping them together.

'What's interesting?' asked Beatrice. 'Out with it.'

'Well,' I took a deep breath. 'I just wonder why Phoebe would decide go to Costa Rica then. At Christmas?' I looked down. 'It doesn't make sense to me.'

The room fell silent. The carols ended with a sudden stop. The rain fell harder, splashing on the tiled roof, running down the gutters and back to the sea.

'I – well. I – I mean . . .' stammered Beatrice, shifting in her seat. 'Some people crave change, don't they?'

'New starts,' added Diane.

'Of course,' I said. 'I just wonder what was so wrong with . . . the old. With keeping things the same.'

Diane looked up at me, I'm certain her eyes narrowed slightly. Next to her, Peggy shrugged.

'I thought it was just about those dolphins,' said Peggy, slightly confused, swaying on her seat. She thrust her mug in the air. 'Always the dolphins. Getting herself as close to them as possible. Right?'

'Yes, well, that too, of course,' said Beatrice. She put her hand over Peggy's and leaned close to her. 'I think you need a glass of water, young Peggy,' she whispered.

'Pfft, I don't!' said Peggy, snatching her hand away. As she did, her grip on the mug slipped and it flipped into the air before smashing into shards on the floor. The mulled wine spilled blood-like from its broken brown bits and flowed towards the window.

'Ooh, I'm sorry, let me help clean that up,' said Peggy, without moving from her seat, staring down at the spill.

'No, no,' I said. 'Don't worry, I'll do it.' I unfurled a wad of kitchen paper from the roll and crouched down to mop up the mess. The wine turned the white paper an ominous red.

Is this what happened to you here, Phoebe?

I cautiously looked up at the group, wondering if anyone was looking down. Diane was. She stared at me; her eyes once blue, now black. I quickly looked at the floor and concentrated on cleaning up what was left of the cup. I felt her coal eyes burning holes into my back, as I walked to the bin. Mum placed another log on the fire, but the room was already hot. I had to get away from the heat, away from Diane's eyes.

'Excuse me,' I said, walking past the women, head down, but the hairs on my neck standing up. I ran straight to my bedroom. In the dark, I grabbed my laptop from my bed and moved to the bathroom, the only room in the house with a lock. I immediately opened the small window and leaned out, gulping in the salty storm and cold sea air. Then I slumped to the floor and held my heads in my hands. Downstairs was suffocating, but I couldn't leave Mum there with them for too long. They were dangerous and I didn't trust any of them.

Not Diane, with her stares and her strange reaction to Phoebe's research.

Nor Beatrice, with her obsessive love for this house and keenness to know what happened here.

Or Peggy either. I was less sure of her reasons to be involved. For now.

I briefly closed my eyes.

Yes, the 'she' Phoebe had fearfully written about in her card had to be Beatrice or Diane.

But which one?

I opened my laptop, wincing at its bright light. I searched for Phoebe, starting with images. Deep into Google, past page three, were photographs of Phoebe, here outside this house, one of a young Phoebe with her parents, wearing her dolphin brooch. Another, with her and a small girl. There were images of Phoebe and Diane at the shore, and together in a lab, smiling widely. There weren't any photographs of Phoebe in Costa Rica, though.

Of course, there weren't. The dead didn't take selfies.

I opened a new tab and searched for news on Phoebe,

looking for something, anything, scrolling past all the other Phoebe Morgans in the world, hopefully happy and if not, at least alive. There were links to her research, but not much about *her*, apart from a short article on a website called the Cornishwoman Online. I squinted at my screen. The article was called *Meet the Locals*.

I skimmed the words for anything of note between the journalist's quick-fire questions and Phoebe's frustratingly short answers.

What's your most prized possession? asked Alyson Payne.

Phoebe answered: *My brooch, a Morgan family heirloom, which has been in my family for many years.*

That was no surprise.

What's your pet peeve?

Jealousy. Can't stand it! I used to have silly fights about petty things with my best friend Bea when we were little girls. We've moved past all of that, though!

Bea? Beatrice? She did say she'd known Phoebe since she was a girl, but had they moved past petty things?

What are you most proud of?

My research. I work long, hard hours, alone on the coast by The Cove, but it's all worth it.

I read that twice. Alone? The photos of Phoebe working with Diane proved that wasn't true. I revisited the other tab to make sure I was right. I was.

408

What's your favourite song?

I love Christmas songs; my favourite is I Saw Three Ships. It's not the most popular one, but I listen to it all the time, and look out over The Cove.

I leaned against the door. 'Diane . . . or Beatrice. Beatrice or Diane . . . Not Peggy . . . no real reason.' I took a deep breath. I didn't know what to do next. I couldn't just confront them. Not yet.

On the other side of the door, Peggy shouted, 'Hello,' and thumped the door twice.

Scrambling in shock, my laptop slid and clattered on the floor. I grabbed it, clambered quickly to my feet, and slowly opened the door.

Peggy's eyes were pink, and she smiled at me. She looked down at my laptop, tucked under my arm.

'You're *just* like my kids, you are – always on your doo-dahs, all the time. Even in the bathroom,' Peggy tutted gently.

'Yeah,' I said. 'I get the best Wi-Fi in here,' I lied.

'Really?' said Peggy. 'See, that's why I like being that little bit closer to the gates.' She leaned into me, as if to share a secret. 'No offence, but *I'm* not obsessed with this house like Beatrice the Queen of The Cove is. Pfft. I don't *care.*' She threw her hands in the air. 'I don't care about any of it!'

Beatrice. I swallowed, gulping down words I could

409

have shared to fill the brief silence. I didn't need to worry.

'So, can I use the bathroom now or not?' said Peggy with a laugh.

'Oh yeah – of course,' I said, squeezing past her. I looked up at the attic, imagining Phoebe up there, smiling, combing through her boxes for ornaments for her Christmas tree, before I ran down the stairs, dropping my laptop on the sofa.

Over in the kitchen, Mum roared at a joke Diane made. She nudged Diane in the ribs playfully and Beatrice chuckled and chortled along with them. Mum looked up at me and grinned.

'Join us, join us!' she said. 'These ladies are so fun.'

'Are they?' I said, clenching and unclenching my fist.

'Yeah!' said Mum. 'I'm having a great time!' She sighed, slumped forward, and covered her eyes with her palms. 'Ah, I am so relieved.'

'About what?' said Diane, smiling down at her.

'Ah, you know, about fitting in around here,' said Mum. 'You've made us feel very welcome.'

My chest rose and fell. 'For now,' I said under my breath.

'What was that?' said Beatrice, cocking her head in my direction.

'For now,' I said louder.

Peggy sauntered down the stairs. 'Right.' She clapped

410

her hands, breaking the rising tension. 'What did Can we put some proper music on now, please? I thought this was a party?' She twisted her hips. 'Malorie, you're young – play us something new. Something fun.'

'All right,' I said quietly. I walked to Mum's phone and held it in my hand. I thought for a moment, back to the events of the evening so far. I knew then exactly what I had to play. I had the perfect song.

This one was dedicated to Phoebe.

The music came through the speakers, a jangly, jaunty song, punctuated with Christmas bells.

'What's this?' asked Peggy, swaying cautiously, unconvincingly to the music.

'My favourite Christmas song,' I replied.

'I thought you didn't like Christmas,' said Beatrice.

'I don't,' I replied.

The lyrics began.

I saw three ships come sailing in,
On Christmas Day, on Christmas Day
I saw three ships come sailing in
On Christmas Day in the morning

Beatrice's face immediately fell, and she slowly took deep breaths through her nose, her shoulders rising with each one. She gripped the edge of the kitchen island with pale white knuckles and looked up at Diane, who nodded with wide, wild eyes.

Together they got up from their stools.

I was now certain they'd killed Phoebe. Together.

Diane raised an eyebrow at me, but quickly smiled sweetly at Mum.

'Well, this was lovely, Janet,' she said. 'But we have to be going. Come on, Peggy.'

Mum looked up at Diane, then at Beatrice, confused. 'Really? Already? But we're having such a great time! And there's still so much food!'

'Lovely leftovers for you,' said Beatrice. 'It's important to keep visits short and sweet.' She stared at me. 'Plus, it's your first Christmas at The Cove and . . .' Her hard eyes bored into me. 'And . . . who knows how long you'll . . . stay. So we'll leave you to enjoy it, while you can.'

I squeezed Mum's phone tightly in my hand and turned the music up slightly.

'You two are so *boring*,' said Peggy, sticking out her tongue slightly and blowing a light raspberry. 'But fine, fine. I'd better get back to Mark anyway. He gets funny if we're apart too long.'

Mum looked at me and shared a disappointed shrug. 'Well, OK,' she said with a sigh. 'Mally, help them with their coats?'

I inched slowly towards them with Mum by my side, as they stood with their backs to us, Diane and Beatrice talking together in low whispers. They hurriedly put on their coats. Diane grabbed her umbrella and opened the door. The rain was lighter now and the storm had begun to clear. 'Many thanks,' she said, pulling Beatrice's elbow.

'Yes, thanks for having us!' said Peggy, turning around to give me an enthusiastic hug. Don't go with them, Peggy! I said to myself as we embraced. You're not safe with them! As Peggy removed her arms from my neck to pat me on the shoulder, I tried to step away from her, but her camel-coloured coat was caught on my hoodie.

'Ooh!' she laughed. 'We're stuck together forever now! What will Mark do?'

'Peggy,' Beatrice said quietly but sternly behind her. 'Hurry up. You're letting their heat out.'

Peggy pulled at her coat, and as we separated, something flashed in our porch's light. I leaned in to look closer. Two blue sapphires, the blue sapphires of Phoebe's gold intertwined dolphin brooch. Stumbling backwards, I stared at the brooch Phoebe never wanted to take off, that she would never have given away, and then up at Peggy. I searched for answers, for reasons, in her eyes. I found nothing in them. She grinned at me instead.

413

You too, Peggy? You're involved too?

'That's so lovely,' said Mum, reaching out to touch the brooch. Diane craned her neck into the doorway to see what Mum was admiring. When she saw what it was, her hand flew to her mouth and she rubbed her lips and chin, trying to hide her reaction. But I saw her. She put her hand firmly on Peggy's shoulder and pulled her back.

'Peggy, it's time to leave,' she said.

'Night!' said Peggy brightly. 'See you soon?' she said, raising an eyebrow in my direction and blowing a kiss.

'Definitely!' said Mum, smiling and waving. 'Night!' She shut the door and leaned against it. 'Well, *that* was a successful evening, wasn't it, hmmm?' She walked to the kitchen with a smile and picked up a mince pie.

I still held her phone in my hand. I unlocked it, then pressed nine three times. The music faded.

'We're not safe here.'

'Mally, don't start. I said we'd talk tomorrow –'

I lifted the phone to my ear. 'Police, please?'

'Mally!' Mum shouted, reaching to slap her phone from my hand. I twisted my body away from her.

'The Cove. Come quickly. The old owner of our house, Phoebe Morgan, hasn't gone to Costa Rica. She's dead.' I looked at Mum, who gasped and shook her head. 'Her plane ticket from last year is here and I found a card where

414

she said she's in danger.' I cradled the phone between my ear and shoulder and pulled both the ticket and the card from my back pocket.

I handed them to Mum. I watched her while she read, her eyes growing wide when she reached Phoebe's last line. 'Yes, and one of her most treasured possessions, something she would never take off, is now with one of the neighbours.' I snatched the card from Mum's hands and jabbed at Phoebe's image on the front. 'The neighbours did it together, for different reasons, jealousy mostly, I think. They know that I know and we're scared. Please come, quickly.'

The call ended and the music restarted. I pushed Mum's phone into her palm. She wobbled on her feet and leaned on the kitchen counter. 'Mally,' she whispered, her face con torted. 'Mally . . . are you serious? What is this? What have you *done*? Is this a joke?'

'No. It's a murder, Mum.'

I ran towards the front door, locked it, then flew up the staircase.

'Where are you going!' shouted Mum. 'Stay down here! I . . .'

'I have to do something urgently,' I shouted back.

On the landing, I looked through the round window. The Coven were huddled together on Peggy's pink-gravelled driveway. Diane had her head in her hands, while Beatrice jabbed her finger close to Peggy's face and towards the brooch. Peggy simply shrugged and laughed as she leaned against her porch.

I stepped quickly across the attic, to the box marked 'Christmas Things'. Phoebe's face smiled back at me.

'I did it, Phoebe. I figured it out,' I said. I reached into the box, grabbed three cards and her pen. I stepped back down the ladder and glanced out of the window.

The Coven were gone.

In the kitchen, I laid out the three cards.

'Mally, where did you get those, I can't...' Mum's voice faded as I tried to concentrate. I tapped the pen against the worktop. I leaned forward with Mum hovering and looking over my shoulder.

'Read these and you'll understand,' I said.

In the card on the right, I wrote: *Dear Diane, I hope you'll get all the credit you crave and deserve this Christmas. Love Malorie and Phoebe.*

In the card in the middle, I wrote: *Dear Beatrice, I'm sure you'll get to spend time in the biggest and best house this Christmas – not mine of course! Prison. Love Malorie and Phoebe.*

In the card on the left, I wrote: *Dear Peggy, Thanks for opening my eyes to all the things money can't buy, but will cost*

416

you the world. Merry Christmas. Love Malorie and Phoebe.

The sound of sirens rang across The Cove as I forced the last card into its envelope. Then bright blue lights flickered and flashed over the house, and across the sea.

THE VERY MERRY MURDER CLUB